The Rachel Experiment

The Rachel Experiment

A From Sunset Park, With Love Romance

Lisa Lin

The Rachel Experiment

Tule Publishing First Printing, May 2023

The Tule Publishing, Inc.

First Publication by Tule Publishing 2023

Cover design by Ashley Santoro

ISBN: 978-1-959988-26-7

Praise for Lisa Lin

"An absolute delight of a rom-com, Rachel's awkward interactions will have you laughing out loud as you root for her and Luke to get together. It's about time there are more Asian-American heroines!"

—Lyn Liao Butler, author of *The Tiger Mom's Tale* and *Red Thread of Fate*

"Lisa Lin's *The Rachel Experiment* is a delightful read with an abundance of laugh-out-loud moments. Lin writes relatable characters who are determined to grow beyond their comfort zones and who help each other do so. You'll immediately root for Rachel and Luke, but you'll also love Rachel's supportive friends, the delicious food, and the tender family moments. Brimming with Lin's signature humor, *The Rachel Experiment* is a hopeful and heartwarming romance."

—Lauren Kung Jessen, author of *Lunar Love*

"Don't miss this grumpy-sunshine opposites attract, tropetastic rom-com you'll wanna curl up with!"

—Priscilla Oliveras, *USA Today* bestselling author of *West Side Love Story* and *Island Affair*

"Giving a fresh start to former sweethearts, debut author Lin handles complicated family culture and romantic tension by writing passionate, strong-willed protagonists and triumphantly delivers a satisfying second-chance romance."

—Library Journal Review

"*The Year of Cecily* is full of heart and humor with just as much familial drama as witty banter. This is the rom com you've been looking for."

—Sally Kilpatrick, *USA Today* bestselling author

"A delightful debut about finding the courage to go outside your comfort zone and follow your heart. This second chance romance is sweet, breezy, and sure to satisfy. Make it your New Year's resolution to add Lisa Lin to your auto-buy list!

—Lenora Bell, author of *One Fine Duke*

"*The Year of Cecily* is an absolute delight. You won't be able to put this book down. I devoured it."

—Jayci Lee, author of *Booked on a Feeling*

Dedication

For the other 2/3 of the L-Squad, Liana De la Rosa and Elizabeth Bright. Awesome and talented writing friends who have talked me off too many ledges to count and supported me on this crazy path to publication so I could make it to where I am today. But most of all for always being happier and more excited for me than I am for me. Thank you!

Chapter One

THE MEETING HAD been going so well. Generally speaking, as a financial analyst with Kirkland Young and Sloane, one of the nation's biggest wealth management firms, Rachel Bai's days consisted of collecting data and researching, making recommendations, and presenting her findings at meetings. However, most of her time was spent working alone, which was her preference. And frankly it was probably better for all involved. Today was not her lucky day.

"Well, thanks for meeting with me," Tricia Watkins said with a grateful smile. The new liaison from the New York City Fire Pension fund, one of her major clients, Tricia had suggested they grab a quick lunch to get to know each other. So now they were seated at Townsend Bistro where she was eating a delicious Cajun salmon salad at Trish's recommendation and drinking mineral water. Expensive brand-name mineral water. Rachel had agreed reluctantly because she was always afraid she'd do or say something socially awkward to make it all go to hell. Today was no exception.

"I should be the one thanking you. You're the one who paid, after all," Rachel pointed out reasonably. Then she paused. "So, thank you."

"My pleasure," Tricia assured her. Tricia was exactly the type of person who intimidated her and made her nervous. Her lunch companion carried herself like she was born to wear her tailored blazer, blouse, pencil skirt, and high pumps, while Rachel was wearing flats and an off-the-rack generic suit from Ann Taylor. Tricia was the epitome of calm, polished, and poised. Someone who was confident and wouldn't be thrown by a simple conversation over lunch because of course she'd know what to do and what to say. Unlike Rachel.

"I'm looking forward to getting to know you better as we continue working together. Here's hoping for a long and productive relationship," the other woman continued.

Rachel frowned as a boulder settled in the pit of her stomach. More lunches? More interactions? More opportunities to show how inept she was at this sort of thing? "Hopefully we'll both be too busy for all that." Seeing the look on Tricia's face, Rachel scrambled to backtrack. "I mean, assuming the projections and investments work out, more work and more money for all of us. The important thing is the firefighters are happy. Win-win, right?" she added desperately.

"Definitely." Tricia got up from the table though her smile had cooled several degrees and was wary now.

Rachel groaned inwardly. She had screwed up again. Even though she hadn't meant to. "Anyway, I will get this paperwork to you as soon as possible." She was much more comfortable when things were on a business footing. At least she knew what to do. Most of the time.

"That sounds great. But you're right about the increased workload if all this takes off. I barely see my husband and kids these days. What work-life balance, right?" Tricia said with a laugh.

"I wouldn't know," Rachel said with a shrug. "I spend most of my days at the office. No husband or kids, so I don't have that problem. Though there are times I wonder why I bother renting an apartment when I'm hardly ever there. Maybe I could consider giving it up," she mused. "It would save money, and there may be some tax benefits. What do you think?" she asked Tricia. "Though it would be awkward to find a place to store my clothes and shower and wash up if I did just live at the office full-time. Maybe I can find a nearby gym?"

The look in Tricia's eyes told her she had way overshot the mark in trying to relate. Crap.

"Anyway, it's time I got back to work. Thanks again for lunch." Rachel pushed up her glasses and stuck out her hand. Then saw Tricia hesitate. Surely she hadn't gotten this part of it wrong. To her relief, Tricia returned the handshake. After a brief goodbye, the two went their separate ways.

With a sigh, Rachel shook her head and started the ten-block trek back to her office. She should be used to it by now, this inability to carry on a decent conversation over a simple meal. Somehow, from birth she seemed to be missing that particular gene that everyone else had inherited. While most people seemed to have an intuitive sense of how to act in these situations, she had the uncanny ability to never know the right thing to say, and whatever she did say always ended up making things a thousand times worse and more awkward.

Despite her best efforts, she'd never possessed the easy ability to connect with people and it always made her feel like the odd man out. She wished she could be like everyone else. Someone who could make friends easily, act normal. Be normal.

But, as a person who dealt with numbers and reality, Rachel knew that such wishes were useless. For better or worse, she was who she was. And the fact that she was a weirdo didn't prevent her from being good at her job. She always believed in focusing and maximizing on her strengths. Maybe someday she could work on making new friends and find someone who didn't mind her weird and awkward ways. She thought back to New Year's. She and Cecily Chang had made headway into a friendship of sorts. So perhaps she wasn't a total lost cause after all.

But for now, work called. In that arena she excelled. Rachel clung on to that thread of hope all the way back to the office.

LATER THAT AFTERNOON, Rachel knocked on her manager's door with no small amount of trepidation. Out of the blue, she'd gotten an email to drop by her manager Jake's office at four thirty—a demand not a request. That was all the two-line message said, so Rachel had no idea what to expect. She could be getting a promotion, fired, or asked to head up the recruitment/hiring committee. There was no way to know.

She hoped she wasn't getting fired. Had Trish called and lodged some sort of complaint?

Jake Clyburn gestured for her to enter and take a seat. But he kept her hanging by taking another five minutes to finish writing his email or whatever it was he was doing.

"Hey, Rachel, thanks for coming by."

"Sure." It wasn't like she really had a choice in the matter.

He steepled his hands on the desk and gave her a direct look. "I'm just going to cut to the chase. How do you feel about California?"

"California, sir?"

"Yes, the Golden State, home of Hollywood, beaches, palm trees, wine country?"

"I'm familiar. I'm just not sure what you're asking. I have no particular feelings about California. I visited a friend there recently; it was nice." At least she knew now this had nothing to do with her disastrous lunch today. Thank God.

"Well you're about to. We're sending you to San Francisco."

"Excuse me?" What the hell?

"There's an opening in our San Francisco office," Jake explained. "We want you there to head up a new team."

"I'm flattered, sir, but there wasn't anyone who already

lives there available for the job?"

"You did hear me say you'd be heading up the team, right?"

"Yes, but I'm still confused."

"We think you have a lot of potential, so we're giving you this chance to step up and take on a more managerial role. I know you've wanted a chance to move up the ladder for a while now, and this is it. This is a great opportunity."

Rachel's palms began to sweat. It was true, she had been hoping for a promotion but didn't think it would happen this soon. "I'm going to need some time to pack, find a place to live. When would I start?"

Jake smiled. "Don't worry about that. I'll have the office manager in the San Francisco office get in touch with you and they can help you organize the logistics from their end. They can help you find a new apartment, et cetera. But we want you there within the next sixty days."

Well, that wasn't a lot of time. And she'd probably been picked because she was still single. Transplanting her across the country was a less daunting endeavor than someone who had a family and had to juggle school, daycare, and their spouse's career as well.

What the hell. She could use a change of pace and California might be interesting. If nothing else, it would give her an excuse to get away from her sister Claudia's wedding madness for the next two months while she prepared to move. Talk about a silver lining.

"How long will I be there?"

"We anticipate six to nine months, with a possible extension. It all depends on how things go. If the team is successful and becomes permanent, we may relocate you there for good."

"I see."

"Will that be a problem?"

"No, sir." At least she wouldn't be alone in a city full of strangers. She could reach out to Cecily and let her know she was coming back to San Francisco. She could get insider info on which neighborhoods would be best to live in, and closest to the office, where the best restaurants were. The essential stuff. She and Cecily were friends, right? It wouldn't be weird for her to reach out and ask. When she visited San Francisco a few months back, Cecily had offered to let her stay at her place. Surely, she wasn't misreading the signs there.

Just then, Jake cleared his throat. "There is one other thing I wanted to bring up though."

"Of course, sir."

"I know you've been with Kirkwood Young and Sloane for almost ten years now, and your work has always been exemplary."

"I assume that's why you picked me, and why I'm being set up for a promotion."

"Yes, of course. Your evaluations have always been top-notch. However, there was one thing that stood out."

"What's that?" What could she possibly be doing wrong after all these years? Jake was right—her evaluations had always been high, and she'd always taken the constructive criticism to heart and strived to constantly improve.

"It's just that you tend to work alone, and your new position will involve much more teamwork."

"I understand, and that shouldn't be a problem."

"In addition, you'll be meeting with potential clients, taking more meetings, and going to events where you'll be expected to network and develop relationships with local elected officials and business leaders."

Now this was a problem. Normally, her job consisted of her sitting behind a computer for most of the day and that suited her fine. Having to interact more with co-workers and clients would be putting her out of her comfort zone, to put it mildly. As evidenced by today's lunch. And the idea of meeting local officials and developing relationships there was enough to give her an ulcer.

Seeing the look in her eyes, Jake nodded, but there was a sympathetic gleam in his eyes. "I know networking and people skills aren't your strengths, but I'm confident you can work on them and get where you need to be. In fact, you're going to need to. Because by the end of this trial period, if you don't perform as expected, we may need to re-evaluate."

Rachel gave a hard swallow. "Would I be allowed to come back to the New York office?"

Jake gave a slow shake of his head. "Unfortunately, because you'll be gone so long, we'll have to find a replacement for you. There should still be a lateral analyst position in San Francisco, but that's no guarantee. We'd have to find another branch office to send you to."

Rachel had never been good at subtext, but even she

could read between the lines. Either she proved herself and earned the promotion, or she'd be out on her ass. Or relegated to the Omaha office. Neither of which were acceptable options.

Jake then looked at his watch. "I think I've taken up enough of your time, and I have another meeting." Taking that as her cue, Rachel stood. Jake extended his hand, and she shook it, gingerly.

"Congratulations, and good luck." Though his smile was encouraging, Rachel couldn't help but detect a note of doubt in Jake's voice. Meaning he too wasn't one hundred percent sure if she'd be up to the challenge.

In a slight daze, Rachel nodded, murmured her thanks, and made her way back to her office. Part of her was excited and thrilled at this opportunity. But Rachel also realized she was facing a daunting challenge not unlike climbing Mt. Everest. With no proper equipment or prior training.

No matter what, she was determined to succeed and make this work. She'd figure out a way. Somehow.

Chapter Two

After spending two hours in a bridal shop with her sister Claudia and their mother, Rachel decided the road to hell wasn't paved with good intentions. It was paved with silk, lace, chiffon, and tulle. And the blame for the fact she could even name all those fabrics was something she laid squarely on Claudia's shoulders. Her little sister refused to make up her mind.

"I don't know," Claudia said, biting her lip. "The bodice is nice, but I don't think there's enough detailing. Where's the wow factor?"

"The neckline is too low." Their mother Rose frowned.

"Maybe you're right. We need to keep looking."

"I saw a satin dress back there that would be perfect." Without another word, the two of them left to investigate.

If they were going to ignore her and not even ask for her input, why was she here? Rachel heaved a sigh and began trying to answer work emails on her phone. She still hadn't told her family about the promotion and move to California. She was saving that for dinner tonight. They should be happy for her, shouldn't they? This would be the sort of thing most Asian parents would crow about. Under the guise of complaining that they never saw their child anymore because they were so busy working. Though that didn't explain the nervousness in the pit of her stomach at the prospect of dropping this news on the three of them later that night.

Fifteen minutes later, her mother and sister came back.

"Rachel, put your phone away. We're supposed to be here for Claudia. That is so rude." Rose gave a disapproving tsk.

"I've been sitting here for two hours. What do you want from me?"

Claudia rolled her eyes and smoothed the skirts of the gown their mother picked out.

"As usual, Ma nailed it. I'll have to lose ten pounds to fit into it properly, but it's perfect. What do you think?"

Rachel pushed her glasses up the bridge of her nose. The dress had a full skirt and a lace bodice with beading. The back had satin ribbons that tied together like a corset. Claudia literally looked like a fairy-tale princess.

"It looks nice. They all looked nice. You'll look great in whatever you decide on."

Claudia and Rose shared a look and Claudia shook her head. "I don't know why I brought you. You're no help."

It was on the tip of her tongue to ask why they'd dragged her out of bed at eight in the morning on a Saturday for this if that's how everyone felt. But under it was hurt. It was one thing to feel excluded, it was another to know you weren't actually wanted.

"While we're here, can we revisit the bridesmaid dresses?"

Her sister frowned and lifted her chin to a stubborn angle. Never a good sign. "What's wrong with the dresses?"

"I have concerns about the color."

"What's wrong with the color? It's a nice buttercup yellow. It's bright, it's spring, it's happy."

In fact, it was so bright, Rachel was surprised it didn't glow in the dark.

"It's going to make us look jaundiced." She'd looked it up on Google, which confirmed her suspicions that yellow didn't tend to be flattering on Asian skin tones.

"Rachel, your sister is already under a lot of pressure. Stop making things worse," Rose scolded.

With an inner sigh, Rachel gave up. If Claudia wanted a bunch of sallow-looking bridesmaids who resembled rubber duckies on her wedding day, that's what she would get. She'd just have to grin and bear it like a dutiful sister.

She made a mental note to take the dress to Goodwill the day after the wedding. At least she'd be able to get a tax deduction out of it.

"We still have to go over the seating chart this afternoon," Rose fussed. She looked over at Rachel. "You're not bringing anyone to the wedding, right?"

Before Rachel could respond, Claudia cut in. "Of course not. I already gave her plus-one spot to my college roommate Stephanie."

For some reason, that put her back up. "How did you know I wouldn't be bringing anyone?"

Distracted by the dress, Claudia gave a wave. "Please. Your life consists of waking up, going to the office, coming back home, and going to bed. You have no life outside work and barely any friends. You don't go out, get invited to anything. No way you found someone to bring. It's no big deal."

The fact her sister said it in such a matter-of-fact tone, no malice, made it a double punch. That she was such a foregone conclusion, and such a social loser that her sister already gave her slot away. It would have been better if Claudia had actually been trying to lash out.

Her sister's summing up of her life made her feel like crap. Not least because there was a kernel of truth to it.

Seeing the look on her face, Claudia's brow furrowed. "Hey, I didn't hurt your feelings, did I? I'm sorry if I did."

"Of course not," she replied woodenly. "You're just telling the truth, right?"

"It's not all bad," her sister said, trying to extend an olive branch. "You're the most successful of all of us. So, your hermit lifestyle pays off. Everything has a silver lining."

Her sister's beaming face, full of goodwill, deflated Rachel like a balloon. Now she felt like a bitch for making her sister feel bad for making her feel bad.

How dare she ruin everyone's day?

"Rachel will find someone," Rose insisted. "It's only a matter of time. There's someone out there for everyone." She gave her oldest daughter a slightly pitying look.

It made her want to take a vow of spinsterhood right then and there, just to spite them. And take vows after finding a convent to join. God knew she wasn't having trouble with the vow of chastity at the moment.

All Rachel knew was that she hoped Claudia was having a good time, and that her mother was getting all the wedding business out of her system, because it surely wasn't in the cards for her.

IT WAS THE moment of truth. Rachel felt like a doctor about to tell a patient a fatal diagnosis.

But part of her was also excited to tell them her great news. It was no wedding, but a serious accomplishment that would surely earn her some well-deserved praise. Delivered Asian-style of course. After the morning she'd had dress shopping, she was desperate to end the day on a high note.

Her family, however, had other plans.

"I don't know why you have to move so far away," her father said with a disapproving scowl.

"San Francisco is only a six-hour flight," she pointed out. "Read a book, take a nap, watch an inflight movie, the trip will pass in no time."

By the look on her father's face, she could tell that was the exact wrong thing to say.

"You should ask your company to find you a different job, so you can stay here."

"You can't possibly be serious, Ba," she protested.

"Why not? San Francisco is too far away. What if something happened? We wouldn't be able to get to you.

You'll be surrounded by strangers. It's not safe."

"Don't be ridiculous."

"Rachel," Rose warned. "Listen to your father."

Of course. Her mother had always played the dutiful wife, deferring to her husband in all things, like a proper Asian wife and mother. It was maddening sometimes. In her entire life, she couldn't remember her mother ever challenging her father about anything or arguing. It was always, "Go ask your father." "You know what your father said."

"No can do. I'm going; it's final."

"You were always so stubborn," her father grumbled.

"Besides, I won't be alone. Cecily lives there too."

Smooth as silk, her mother stepped in. "See, there you go. I'll give Judith a call, so Cecily knows, and she can check in on you. We'll all rest better at night knowing you're not alone. Now, was that so hard?"

She instantly regretted dropping Cecily's name. And they'd just become friends not that long ago. She wouldn't be surprised if Cecily decided to never speak to her again over this. Who liked to be volunteered without their consent?

"Never mind that." Claudia pouted. "This puts me in such a bind."

"You?" Rachel said, surprised.

"Yes. This screws up all my wedding planning. You being so far away makes it so much harder."

"I'm sorry my career has so inconvenienced you."

Oblivious to the sarcasm, Claudia pressed on. "You

better still be able to make my wedding. I can't lose you. Having four bridesmaids is unlucky!" She pointed an accusing finger at her.

Rachel waited a few seconds so she could form a proper response. "Don't worry. If I have to, I'll quit my job to make sure I don't miss the wedding. I'll hitchhike if I need to. The wedding is all that matters." Here she was, with amazing news she was happy about, and her family was crapping all over it. And her sister was making it about her, as always. Just once she'd like to have a moment where her parents could finally say, "Good job, Rachel. We're proud of you." But it seemed that moment would never arrive.

"Rachel, that's enough." Her mother's voice was filled with warning and the look in her eyes drilled home the point. *Tread lightly. Don't you test me.*

"Are you making fun of me?" Claudia demanded, her face starting to look like thunderclouds.

"Me? Never."

"You know how hard Claudia's been working on this wedding. Why are you provoking her?" Rose scolded.

Why was she always the one in the wrong? Did getting married mean you get a pass to be overbearing, dramatic, and completely insufferable?

"I just thought you could be happy for me." For once.

Claudia scowled. "Jobs come and go. You can always find a new job. A person only gets married once. It's the most important day of my life! How can you possibly think the two can ever compare?"

"The divorce rate is over fifty percent in this country,"

she couldn't help pointing out. "So the idea that people only get married once is demonstrably false." Claudia was really leaning into this fairy-tale thing, and it made no sense. Yes, it was about love and a lifelong commitment, et cetera, et cetera, but in her world, marriage was a more practical matter, a transaction with legal and financial implications. It wasn't all just about playing princess, which seemed to be all her sister cared about. It was about what happened the next day and the day after that.

"Are you saying I'm going to get divorced? I can't believe you're trying to curse my wedding." Claudia looked close to tears.

Oh, for fuck's sake.

"Rachel, apologize to your sister," her father ordered.

Being all the way across the country was looking better and better.

"I'm sorry," she parroted dutifully.

"Are you giving up your apartment?" Her father asked after a tense few minutes of silence.

"Of course. It would hardly make sense for me to pay rent on two apartments."

"I don't know. You said the job means you'll be meeting with more people and working with a team right?"

"Yes..." Where was her dad headed with this?

Ray threw her a skeptical look. "I think you should keep the lease on your apartment here. A promotion is great, but it doesn't sound like it's the best use of your talents. You've always worked better alone. You may end up coming back to New York. Why go through another apartment search?"

Claudia nodded. "Yeah, this sounds like a recipe for disaster. You try hard but people just aren't your thing, sis. Remember I tried to set you up with Danny Tran? He ran away screaming after thirty minutes. And when you accidentally insulted my client by wondering if her dress was the most flattering color for her."

"So none of you think I can do this?" Rachel asked, flabbergasted. It was one thing for her to recognize that her people skills sucked and to doubt herself, but for her whole family to have no faith in her was another thing entirely. It stung.

And as for the incidents Claudia mentioned, those were only mostly her fault. Danny Tran had asked her what her hobby was, and she'd told him the truth. "I'm a podcast fan. Especially the true crime murder ones. The more bloody and gory, the better." She'd only asked about the dress color because she'd always heard that neon green was a hard color to pull off. She'd meant no harm.

"We're only being honest and realistic. Of course we want you to do well in San Francisco," her mother said. "It's just that the prospects don't look good. We are well aware of who you are, flaws and all. You have your strengths, like your father said. You just need to focus on them. No need to beat yourself up. No one's perfect after all." Then Rose looked to the rest of the table. "Anyone else want the rest of the dumplings, or should I pack them up for you girls to take home?"

"Ohh, give them to me," Claudia said. When Rachel

gave her the evil eye, her sister just shrugged. "If you're determined to go ahead with this whole California thing, you need to start packing and getting rid of stuff. Why fill your freezer with more food that you can't take with you?"

"I still have a few weeks," Rachel grumbled.

"It wouldn't hurt you to lose a few pounds so you can make a good impression on your new boss and co-workers," Rose commented. "Some new work clothes wouldn't hurt you either."

And that was the end of that. So much for her sharing some good news and basking in some family praise and approval.

SINCE HER PARENTS were determined to call Judith Chang and get them involved, Rachel decided it was better for Cecily to hear directly from her first. As soon as she got home, and got comfortable, she plopped on the couch. She glanced at her watch. The time zone should work out and be okay. It was barely dinner time out west.

Hey. So I have some news that I thought you should hear from me first.

...That sounds ominous. Is everything okay? Do you need bail money?

No, no bail money.

That was an odd conclusion for Cecily to jump to. It made no sense to ask someone all the way from California to post bail for her in New York. Maybe it was a lawyer thing.

Then what's up?

My company is promoting me and transferring me to their San Francisco office. I'll be moving there within the next two months.

Cecily sent back two praise hand emojis.

This is great! Guess the city made an impression on you when you visited last spring.

At least someone was happy for her.

Thanks.

Do you need help finding an apartment here? I have some contacts I can reach out to.

Someone from the office will be helping me out with that, but thanks.

Well if there's anything I can do, let me know. Wait. So you'll be here in August, right?

Yes.

Wait a second. Let me check something.

Rachel's brow knit in confusion. What was there to check? But ten minutes later, Cecily was back.

Sorry about that. So anyway, Adrienne's birthday is on the 20th. She's having a party, you should come. I just checked with her, and she said she'd love to see you again. The more the merrier.

Oh. Thank you.

Keep an eye out for the E-vite. It'll be nice to see you again. And a good opportunity for you to meet some new people, make some new friends. Hell, maybe even some good business contacts.

Rachel gave a derisive snort. A birthday party for a friend she knew slightly, and a room full of strangers? Cecily was definitely throwing her into the deep end of the pool with this one. But what the hell, why not embrace the challenge.

I appreciate you asking and Adrienne issuing the invite.

Sure. A cross-country move is tough. Anything I can do to ease the transition, I'm happy to do. Us New York girls need to stick together right?

Absolutely.

Gotta go. Jeffrey just walked in the door with dinner. I'm going to tell him you're moving here. I'm sure he'll be excited too. Keep me posted, and don't hesitate to reach out if you need anything. Bye!

Rachel let out a deep breath. What a marked difference from her family's reaction. Though logic would dictate that her family's reaction should carry more weight because they had known her longer and better. Cecily was a friend, but a relatively new friend, and they were still getting to know each other better. Her parents' and Claudia's skepticism was probably more accurate.

That being said, the things said at dinner were still running through her head and they still rankled. But instead of wallowing, Rachel was determined to use it as fuel.

Yes, she wasn't the best at relating to people, but that didn't mean she couldn't work on it and improve. As a financial analyst a huge part of her job was compiling data and research. So why not approach this problem the same way? She did a quick search on Amazon and ordered a bunch of Kindle books, including Dale Carnegie's *How to Win Friends and Influence People*, Lee Iacocca's autobiography, Peter Andrei's *How Highly Effective People Speak*, *Whatever It Takes* by Brandon Bornancin, and Jemma Roedel's *She Thinks Like a Boss*. Brené Brown's *Dare to Lead* was going at the top of her TBR list.

Thinking back on her lunch with Tricia Watkins, Rachel also Googled 'How to make small talk' and 'Appropriate conversation topics at lunch.' And while she was at it, she was going to Google how to make new friends in a new city. Cecily and Adrienne were a good start, but clearly she needed all the help she could get.

She bookmarked the best search results and checked to make sure all the books she'd bought downloaded correctly. Going for broke, Rachel decided right then and there she was going to take the plunge and order new furniture and decorations for her new place in San Francisco instead of renting. She was committing and going all in here. Rachel made a note about putting up her apartment on Craigslist the next day. That way, failure wasn't an option.

She was going to prove to her family that they had underestimated her. She was going to nail this promotion and kick all sorts of ass. They'd see.

Chapter Three

"HEY, YOU GOT a second?" Luke Trudeau walked into his co-worker's office next door, a man on a mission. He'd just finished meeting with a new client and had some time before his deposition later that afternoon. And to think, when he was a kid, he wanted to be a great defense attorney like Matlock, solving cases, helping the innocent. Instead, most of his days were spent reading behind a desk. Though he loved his work. And he was still doing defense work, just in a different sort of way.

Bea Nolan didn't even bother looking up from her computer screen.

He walked in, sat in the chair across from her desk, and made himself at home.

"I'm not talking to you right now."

He raised a brow. "Fine. Be that way." But curiosity got the better of him and almost immediately he caved. "What did I do?"

Bea glanced up from her computer and gave him a look. "A dance-a-thon for your niece? Really?"

"I just left the forms in the break room like everyone else. You're free to ignore them. But it's for a good cause—Sasha's school's raising money for the local Ronald

McDonald House. And the class who raises the most money gets a pizza party. But no pressure. Like I said, totally voluntary."

His friend just looked at him in total silence. Then with a sigh and roll of her eyes, she capitulated. "Fine, I'll grab one and fill it out when I leave tonight."

"I thank you, and Sasha and the Ronald McDonald House thank you."

"Just saying, you shook us all down back in February when she was selling Girl Scout cookies. Isn't the point of this for Sasha to do things on her own?"

"A good leader always knows when to delegate. Besides, it teaches initiative and entrepreneurship. And I just left the forms in the break room. No one was twisting arms to sell cookies." Luke smiled at the memory. This was his third year helping Sasha sell cookies and as usual, he'd made a killing. All for a good cause, of course.

Bea snorted. "As if anyone can resist the damn Samoas and Thin Mints. They're like crack." Then she frowned. "What did you come in here for, anyway? We got off topic."

He cleared his throat then looked around. Bea gave him a puzzled look. "You okay?"

"Yeah, everything's fine."

She gave a sigh and threw down the pen she was holding. "Okay, out with it. What now? Do you have another niece or nephew selling something? Candy bars? Magazine subscriptions?"

Well it was now or never. He closed the door and sat

back down. Bea looked at him and raised a brow. "Must be serious."

"This is just between us."

"Oh, this ought to be good."

He took a deep breath and just blurted it out. "I'm thinking of opening my own practice."

Bea said nothing for a few seconds, blinked, her mouth a surprised O. "Wow."

"Yeah I know, it's a big step."

"Hell yeah. And of all the people here in the office I wouldn't have pegged you as the one who'd want to strike out on their own."

He frowned. "What do you mean?"

"You're doing well here. I always got the 'If it ain't broke, don't fix it' vibe from you. You have a good thing going at Bradford Long and Price. I didn't expect you to want to take on the extra work of a solo practice. I saw you sticking around, trucking along here at the firm. I mean, you're clearly on the partner track, so I thought you'd just ride that escalator up to the Promised Land."

"I'm not lazy," he said, slightly affronted. Was that how everyone saw him? As someone who just coasted through life? Who never bothered to try and took the easy way out?

"And I didn't say you were," Bea shot back with a roll of her eyes.

"Then what are you saying?"

"That I'm surprised you want to go down this path. That's it."

"So you think I should forget about this whole idea."

"I'm not saying that either. You're a grown-ass man, or you're supposed to be. It's a free country—do whatever the hell you want."

"I'm worried it's a bad risk," he admitted.

"Well, it is a risk. Starting your own small business always is. Though that being said…"

"Yes?" he asked, a tad impatient.

Bea gave him a considering look. "Since the firm is going through a merger this may be the perfect time for you to strike out on your own. Things are in flux, so why not take advantage?" It had come as a surprise to everyone when the news came down. Bradford Long and Price was in the process of merging with Harmon Burke, another major respected big firm in the city.

"I hadn't even thought of that, but you're right," he confessed.

His friend rolled her eyes. "Trust you to pick the perfect time to do something like this without even realizing it." Then she frowned.

"But?"

"If you want to do this, I suggest you do your homework." She saw his grimace and let out a triumphant, "Ah ha! You see? That's exactly what I'm talking about."

"Fine. Go on."

"I'm saying find out for sure what you're getting into before you start on this plan. How much money can you afford? Make sure you don't lose your shirt."

Luke shifted his feet as the gears started to shift in his head. "That is an excellent idea. I should do some research so I know what I'm getting into."

"Exactly. Good luck, whatever you decide to do. For what it's worth, I'll miss you around here.

"Aww, Bea. You care." He put his hand to his heart.

Bea shook her head but there was a smile on her face. "Go away—I have work to do. But if I can help with this new venture, let me know."

"Yes, ma'am," he said with his most winning smile and a confidence he was most definitely not feeling.

He went back to his office, shut the door, and sat down behind his desk with a sigh.

Bea expressing doubts had put a complete damper on his enthusiasm for the whole endeavor. He and Bea had started at the firm together, and he'd always considered her a friend and ally—someone who wouldn't bullshit him and who would give it to him straight. And if Bea didn't think he had what it would take, should he even pursue the idea?

Okay she'd sounded skeptical of the risks of starting any small business at all; it wasn't that she thought he himself didn't have what it takes, Luke reminded himself. But Bea still made a good point. He needed to do his homework, cross all the t's and dot the i's. How hard could it be? Maybe he'd need a little help but that wasn't a big deal. He could totally do this if he wanted.

Though how the hell was he going to find someone to help him do all the financial planning?

LOOKING AROUND HER new apartment, Rachel felt a deep sense of inner satisfaction. Her plan had gone off without a hitch. Meaning the moving trucks had arrived and dropped off her things when it was supposed to, and the new furniture she'd ordered had also arrived on time. The whole place was still a mess of boxes, but for now the essentials were taken care of. Her bed was set up, and she'd grabbed some towels and toiletries, so she had a place to sleep and could take a shower tonight. She wasn't looking forward to unpacking, but it'd get done. She'd already called her parents to let them know that she'd made it to San Francisco alive, despite their dire predictions.

In a tank top and yoga pants, Rachel wondered what her next step should be. Her new job started Monday so maybe it was time to get some last-minute practice in. The past few weeks, she'd made progress plowing through the stack of books she'd ordered and the ton of online research she'd done. She hadn't met many of her new neighbors yet, but so far, they seemed like New Yorkers. They kept to themselves, minded their own business, and expected you to do the same, which was just fine with her. But on Monday, she was going to be meeting a whole new set of people who may not mind their own business. And ask her semi-personal questions. "How do you like it here so far?" (Too soon to tell.) "Where did you move here from?" (New York. Brooklyn if you wanted to be more precise.) "Any husband and kids?" (No and hell no).

Perhaps what she should do is try to get cleaned up and find a place to grab a drink and some food to eat. Maybe a neighborhood bar or pub sort of situation. She could grab a seat at the bar and use the bartender as practice. Bartenders were trained experts in listening and pretending they actually cared about what you had to say. Who better to try to hone her small talk with?

Thirty minutes later, Rachel—now dressed in a peasant blouse with jeans and sensible espadrilles—walked around her neighborhood, trying to find that perfect bar/pub. Eventually, she found the Wild Saguaro, which appeared to be a semi-seedy honky-tonk sort of place. Not what she had in mind, but her rumbling stomach told her not to be picky. Worst-case scenario, she could grab some nachos.

Rachel took a deep fortifying breath, opened the door, and walked inside. She was immediately hit with a wall of noise and music. She fought her way through the crowd to the bar. It took a few minutes to get the bartender's attention, and a few more before she got the shot of Jose Cuervo she'd asked for. She tilted her head and tossed the tequila back in one fell swoop. The bartender looked slammed, so much for conversation practice, and who knows when she'd get the nachos she'd ordered. But she'd come too far to turn back now. Maybe tonight wasn't meant for self-improvement. Plus she was still jetlagged as hell.

"That was impressive," an amused voice said beside her. Surprised, Rachel whipped around to locate the source. She found herself looking at a tall man with wavy dark hair, piercing blue eyes, a strong jaw, and chiseled features. He wore a dress shirt, suit pants, and what looked to Rachel to be very expensive wingtips. The epitome of *GQ* model material. He looked as out of place as she felt, but he seemed at ease. And Mr. *GQ* was talking to her. This did not compute.

"Who are you and why are you talking to me?" she asked.

Mr. *GQ* raised a brow. "Is that how you respond to anyone who tries to talk to you?"

Rachel waited a beat, considered. "If they're a stranger? Pretty much, yes."

"Fair enough. I'm Luke. It's nice to meet you." So Mr. *GQ* had a name. He stuck out a hand and Rachel shook it reluctantly. It was also getting hot in the bar, which was another minus to the whole situation. She was out of her comfort zone; the least the non-comfort zone could do was make the atmosphere cooler and more bearable.

"I'm Rachel."

"So, Rachel, what are you doing here?"

"I'm here because I got promoted."

"Well congratulations. So you're celebrating? By yourself?" Luke asked, looking baffled.

"It's a long story." She sighed.

"Sounds like an interesting one. I'd like to hear it."

It was time for her to call bullshit. "Is this some game you're playing? Wander into a bar and try to pick up a woman you think will fall for a clichéd line like that?" This whole evening was not making sense. She was tired and starting to get seriously hangry, and she didn't like it one little bit. Men who looked like him didn't talk to women like her, especially ones from California. They dated emaciated models and actresses.

Luke gave a small laugh. "I promise you it's not a line. This is seriously the most fun I've had in months."

"Maybe your definition of fun needs work."

"Indulge me for a minute won't you?"

"Okay, I suppose," Rachel replied. She paused as her head scrambled for something to say. "Well I know what I'm doing here, but why are you here? You're not dressed for a place like this."

He shrugged. "I suppose I got a little homesick."

Rachel took a look around. "A place with taxidermy all over the walls, American flags everywhere, and cowboy boot lamps reminds you of home?"

"Oh yes, ma'am" he said with a grin.

Rachel frowned. "I'm not old enough to be called ma'am. Don't do that." You had to be at least forty or forty-five to qualify, right? Or at least have reproduced.

"Nope, sorry. It's a force of habit. Comes from being born and raised in Texas." Now that she was paying attention, she did hear a slight twang in his voice.

"You're from Texas? How did you end up here in California?"

"Have another drink with me and I'll tell you all about it." Was he trying to flirt with her? Was this what was going on here? Or was the Jose Cuervo going to her head? At least the nachos had arrived.

Rachel took another look around the room. "Sure, why not? Maybe we can find a place to sit. That bear mounted on the wall over there is starting to creep me out. Besides, it doesn't look stable or securely attached. I don't want it to fall on me, can't afford the medical bills." She gave a shrug.

Luke laughed, which just served to confuse her further. She hadn't meant to be funny, she'd only been telling the truth.

WHEN LUKE WALKED into the Wild Saguaro that night, he had no idea this was how his evening was going to go. He'd just finished a client meeting and wanted to have a beer or two, listen to a few songs on the jukebox, then head back to his apartment. Instead, he was talking to the most attractive and interesting woman he'd met in years. Rachel was unlike anyone he'd ever met before. No one he knew was so unfiltered and he was here for it.

Rachel blinked owlishly as she grabbed her second tequila shot and chased it with a nacho. "Well, what now?"

"I see a table on the other side of the bar. Let's go before someone else grabs it." Rachel got on her toes and swiveled her neck around. Luke extended a hand to help guide her (Southern gentleman code demanded nothing less) but Rachel just marched toward the table like a woman on a mission, food and drink in hand. He could do nothing but chuckle and shake his head.

They got settled at a high top and silently studied each other as Luke nursed his beer and Rachel tossed back another tequila.

"You should probably have more food," Luke advised, amused. "Are you sure the nachos will be enough?"

"You're probably right." She sighed. She grabbed a nearby menu. "Maybe I should order something else." In short order, Luke grabbed a waitress's attention and ordered more food for the both of them.

"So tell me about this promotion," he asked, turning his attention back to his dining/drinking companion for the evening. Who had him wondering what those eyes looked like without the quirky glasses and how that lush mouth would taste under his.

"Well I just moved here for the job. I'm excited and nervous."

"Why nervous?"

"Because I suck with people," she said bluntly. "I'm moving to a more managerial position as a senior financial consultant, and that means more meetings, networking, and leading a team. I have basically no social skills and barely know how to talk to people. To the extent I didn't even get a plus-one to my sister's wedding. I put my foot in my mouth nine times out of ten, though I don't mean to. My family already thinks I'm going to fail. But I'm determined to figure it out and make it work. There is no way I'm going back to New York. I'm willing to learn. I have books and I'm doing research."

"Research?" he asked, intrigued.

"This was an experiment, to try to put all the things I read and learned into practice. I was going to try practicing small talk with the bartender, but that obviously was a bust." She frowned. "I should have factored in that it was a weekend and the bar would be busy. Miscalculation on my part. I'll have to try to find a better time to come back."

Luke blinked. That wasn't the answer he'd been expecting. "If tenacity counts for anything, I think you've got this in the bag."

"Thank you," Rachel said as she looked around as if absorbing the atmosphere.

As they ate, Luke began to think back to his conversation with Bea, and how he needed help with the financial aspect of his plan. And fate seemed to have dropped the perfect solution into his lap. The way he saw it, this was the universe answering his prayers by bringing an interesting woman into his life who could help him solve his problem. Maybe it was time to turn on the charm and get her to agree to a nice professional lunch sometime next week where he could broach the topic properly. And offer her proper compensation of course.

Something out of the corner of her eye caught her attention.

"What's that?" she asked, as though she'd seen an alien.

He turned his head too and a grin spread over his face. "A mechanical bull."

"In a bar? Seriously? That's a thing?"

"You've never seen one before?"

"I'm from New York," she said, as if that explained everything.

"Wanna try it?"

She narrowed her eyes. "I don't want to ride a bull.

Aren't you supposed to be telling me your life story?"

"Are you afraid to ride the bull?"

"How hard can it be? All you have to do is try not to fall and yell 'Yee Haw' a few times."

"That's offensive," he said as seriously as he could, while his lips twitched.

She made a go-ahead motion with her hands. "Start talking."

"Are you sure you don't want to try the mechanical bull? You'll have fun, I promise."

"No."

"How about if I pay you a hundred dollars?" Now it was a matter of principle, he was going to do whatever it took to get her on that bull. The more resistant she seemed, the more he wanted to convince her that she should have some fun and give this a chance. This was a honky-tonk after all. If you couldn't let your hair down here, where could you?

Immediately her interest was piqued. "Let me see the cash first."

He reached for his wallet, pulled out five twenty-dollar bills, and placed them on the table. She scooped them up before he could blink.

"Deal." With a decisive nod, Rachel hopped off the barstool, and made her way to the pit where the mechanical bull was. Luke hurried to keep up.

There was no way he was going to miss this.

"Let me observe some other people do this first. I need to get the lay of the land," Rachel muttered as they made their way to the mechanical bull.

"How about I let five people go ahead of you before you go in the ring?" he offered generously.

"I was thinking ten. Five is nowhere enough time for observation," she protested.

He was about to ask what she needed to observe when the machine started up again and cut off all conversation. While everyone was laughing and cheering on the petite blonde who was trying her luck on the bull, Rachel was taking it in with laser-like intent and focus. Her brows were furrowed in concentration, and Luke would swear he could hear the gears in her head spinning. He was starting to find it kinda hot.

When Ms. Petite Blonde inevitably fell off the bull and was dusting herself off, he saw Rachel's lips purse.

"What are you thinking?"

"That she's about eight to ten inches shorter than me, so that probably affects the mass and center of gravity on that thing. Maybe I need to try to hunch down to cut down on how much I sway, more stability that way."

Luke blinked in surprise. "Are you trying to math your way out of this?" Most people he knew would just climb on and have fun. He'd never seen anyone try to figure it out.

"Math and science," Rachel corrected. "This is a simple matter of physics and calculus. Maybe some geometry, trying to figure out optimal angles. Which was never my strong suit, but what are you going to do? At least I'm not doing proofs to show why two triangles are congruent. This is actually more fun and interesting."

"Interesting is one way to put it," he murmured, intrigued all over again.

"I can do this," Rachel muttered to herself, rolling her shoulders.

Half an hour later, he was mesmerized. And laughing so hard his abs were getting sore. True to her word, Rachel had gotten on the mechanical bull and gave it a good-faith effort. She'd lasted eight seconds before she got thrown off. With a mighty scowl, she got up, dusted herself off, and made her way back over to him.

He whistled and gave her a well-deserved round of applause. "Hands down the best hundred dollars I ever spent."

"I can't believe I only lasted eight seconds," she complained.

"Hey, don't be so hard on yourself," Luke said, his lips twitching. "Those things aren't as easy as they seem."

"So much for math and science. I was defeated by a mechanical bull."

"You gave it your best shot—that's all that counts. I honestly didn't think you'd do it," he confessed. Truly he was impressed. For a city girl, she had done well.

"A hundred dollars was on the line." Then she gave a groan. "I think I'm going to be feeling this tomorrow."

"Lots of water and aspirin," he suggested.

"I blame the tequila. I can't believe I did that," she mumbled. "Such a bad combo."

He gave a slight chuckle. "But you've also been eating so that should dampen the effects. Tequila gets a bad rap."

Then he frowned. “Seriously, are you okay?”

She gave a wave. “I’m fine. Just catching my breath.”

“We can just sit here and talk,” he offered. The more time he spent with her the more fascinated he became.

“Really?”

“Sure. Unless you have somewhere else you’d rather be. I’m enjoying this.”

He saw the wheels turning in her head. “Why the hell not. Guess it’s a night of unprecedented events.” She gave a shake of her head and a sigh.

Luke couldn’t resist a somber nod. “Getting thrown off a mechanical bull isn’t an everyday event,” he agreed.

“This whole day has been weird,” she said. “Me being here at all is weird. These things don’t happen to me.”

“I’d argue that’s false, because they have happened to you,” he pointed out. Reasonably, he thought.

She pursed her lips. “Are you a lawyer?”

“Guilty,” he admitted. “What gave it away?”

“Damn lawyers.” She sighed.

“Hey, we aren’t all bad.”

Rachel gave another wave of her hands. “We’re getting off topic here.”

“Of course. So why don’t you think these things don’t happen to you?”

“Because I’m boring!”

At that he gave a hearty laugh. “I can assure you, Rachel, the last thing you are is boring.”

She lit up at that compliment. “That may be the first time anyone’s said that to me.” Then she frowned again.

"No, that's not true. Or I wouldn't be here. Because I made a friend. We are friends now, aren't we?"

"Exactly."

She blinked then thankfully grabbed some water instead of reaching for more tequila. "Maybe I should just embrace the crazy and go with it."

"That's the spirit."

"I mean, why not, right? Tomorrow I go back to my normal life. This is the perfect opportunity. No harm, no foul."

"What happens at the Wild Saguaro stays in the Wild Saguaro," Luke murmured in agreement. Unless he was very much mistaken, the tequila was starting to go to her head.

Rachel took a deep breath. "So, do you wanna have sex with me?"

He nearly choked. "What?"

"I'm serious. I can't think of anything crazier than sleeping with someone I just met. So how about it?"

"I think this is the tequila talking," he said quickly.

"I'm perfectly sober. But if you're not interested, just say so."

The hell of it was, he was interested. More than interested. And he was a man after all. Turning down an offer of sex went against every instinct wired into the Y-chromosome. But still he had to know.

"Why me? You could ask anyone else here for a one-night stand, but you asked me."

Rachel looked at him as if the answer were obvious.

"Well, look at you." She waved a hand up and down to encompass him.

"So you think I'm reasonably attractive and that's your sole criteria?"

"Come on. Like I'm the first person who's told you you look like you belong on a magazine cover."

"I'm not sure how I feel about being wanted only for my body," he quipped. "I have feelings, you know."

"Forget it," Rachel muttered, getting up.

Before he could think twice, he shot out a hand to stop her. "I'm just trying to figure out how serious you are about this. Are you sure this is what you really want?"

"Why would I be making an idiot of myself otherwise?" she growled.

"And you're sure you're sober?" She had only had three drinks and it'd been over an hour or so, and she'd eaten. But still.

"I'm fine. Would it make you feel better if I took a breathalyzer or something?"

"Just checking," he murmured. The fact that she was still clear-headed enough to respond quickly was a good sign. She wasn't slurring her words, and her eyes weren't dilated.

He looked at her for a long, charged moment.

In the end, there was really no decision to be made at all.

"Your apartment or mine?"

Chapter Four

WELL CLEARLY THERE was no going back now. This was actually happening. In the list of insane, out-of-character things she'd ever decided to do, this had to top the list. But the way Rachel saw it, tonight was an unprecedented night. Who would have ever thought she'd end up at a bar, talk to a heart-stoppingly attractive man, accept a dare from said heart-stoppingly attractive man to ride a mechanical bull, get thrown off the bull, then proposition him for a night of unbridled hot sweaty sex?

Perhaps unbridled hot sweaty sex was giving in to flights of fancy. In Rachel's experience, sex was a pleasant and enjoyable enough activity but never anything out-of-body or transcendental. A couple of decent orgasms should suffice. And given the man's looks he appeared more than capable of delivering.

But to answer his question… "How about yours? I don't have condoms or anything at my place. I'm assuming you do."

"I don't know if I should be flattered or insulted by that assumption," he said with a raised brow.

"Are we doing this or not?" If he was going to back out, he should at least have the decency not to string her along.

He gave her a searching look then gave a slow grin. "Oh we are absolutely doing this." Ever the Southern gentleman he claimed to be, he guided her out of the bar, and ordered them a taxi. Ten minutes later, they were up in his apartment.

Without a word, he led her to the bedroom. He moved to turn on the lights, and she blurted out, "Don't!"

Luke gave her a confused look. "What?"

"I think it'd be better if we left the lights off," she explained hastily. The truth was, she was afraid he'd be disappointed in what he saw. Better to try to maintain an air of mystery.

"Why?" he asked as he began to unbutton his shirt. Good God the man had impressive pecs and chiseled abs. Rachel wasn't ashamed to admit she'd started salivating a little.

Oh what the hell, she might as well admit it. "I just don't want to disappoint any expectations you might have."

"And what expectations might those be?" And now the belt was coming off, slowly through each loop. Was he a stripper in a past life?

"I don't know! I'm sure you've slept with countless women and I don't know how I'm going to compare," she mumbled.

"I'm not going to give you a number, but I assure you, the only woman I'm thinking about is the one I'm looking at right now." His tone had softened to a caress and Rachel felt warm and flushed all over.

"You need to relax," he continued. "This was your decision, after all. But if you've changed your mind, just say so. I'm more than happy to call you an Uber or taxi home. If you have any doubts, now's the time to say so."

The fact that he was totally leaving the ball in her court did make something click in Rachel's brain. He was letting her know she was the one in control tonight. Which meant he was definitely the right man to have this once-in-a-lifetime crazy experience with.

"I want to stay." Her tone was low but resolute.

"In that case," he said, "why don't we get this party started?" He walked over to her and gave her a kiss as he ran his hands up and down her body. Rachel's hands trembled slightly as she tried to unbutton and unzip her jeans. Luke pulled away and gave her an amused smile.

"Relax," he crooned.

"I'm trying," she insisted.

"I have an idea," he said. "Do you trust me?" He looked deep in her eyes as he waited for an answer.

Without a word she gave a nod.

"Good. I think you need help unwinding, and I have the perfect solution." He led her to the bed and laid her on it gently. The next thing Rachel knew, he was stretched out beside her and started kissing her again.

Damn, the man was a good kisser. For a few heady minutes, Rachel allowed herself to get lost in the sensations as he kissed and stroked, lighting fires all over her body. Before she realized it, her jeans were off and she felt exposed all over again.

"Relax," he murmured again. Then he began trailing

kisses up and down her thigh, and soon enough she forgot to be nervous and just began to enjoy herself. Instead of being intimidated by all the no doubt gorgeous and experienced women he'd had sex with, she began to be grateful for all the practice he'd had at this because this was amazing. Unaware of what she was doing, her hips began moving as Luke kept moving up her legs closer and closer to where she wanted, no, needed him to be, but kept backing off at the last minute.

Rachel raised her head from the pillow and looked down at him. "Stop teasing me," she growled.

"Just wanted to be sure you were suitably at ease," he said with a wicked grin.

"Trust me, I am," she assured him, almost desperately. If he kept this up much longer, she didn't know what she was going to do. It was the most delicious sort of torture, but she didn't know how much she could take. Every nerve ending in her body was on full alert.

"In that case, I think this needs to go." With agonizing slowness, Luke drew down her panties, and she felt every second of the fabric sliding down her skin before he tossed them over his shoulder.

With a hum of approval, Luke took his index fingers and explored her now slick and slippery folds. "Very nice," he murmured. Just when Rachel thought she was about to explode, he finally got down to business. Thank God. And that was when she made another discovery.

The man was an amazing kisser, but his mouth was talented at oh so many things. Not to mention his tongue.

Over and over he swirled and licked and drove her into a frenzied ball of need. This man was still practically a stranger to her, but somehow he knew exactly what to do to drive her wild. Incredible. But he still wasn't quite where she needed him. Unable to take it anymore, unaware of what she was doing, she grabbed a hold of his hair and brought him right to the apex of her thighs. "Please," she begged, her voice a needy whisper.

"Since you asked so nicely, happy to oblige." His voice now hoarse with need too, Luke's eyes glinted in the moonlight, and she could only marvel that she was in this moment with him. Without another word, Luke lavished her clit with the attention it so desperately needed.

"Oh yes," she breathed. Before long, Rachel was thrashing and holding on to the duvet for dear life. Luke gave her one more illicit lick and suck and she was gone. The orgasm building in her let loose and she let out a small cry as the waves of pleasure crashed over her.

But the man wasn't done yet. Luke barely let her catch her breath and come back to arth before he reached over to the nightstand and grabbed a condom.

"I knew it," she muttered.

He just gave her a look as he put it on. "I can't wait anymore. I want to be inside you. Now. Is that okay?"

Rachel gave a nod and let her legs open wide. Taking the wordless invitation, Luke positioned himself at her entrance and, giving her one more kiss, pushed in.

She couldn't help giving a small wince. It had been a while since she'd done this, and she felt stretched to the max. He immediately stopped.

"Are you okay?"

"I'm fine," she encouraged. Truly she was. She just needed a moment to adjust.

As if he had read her mind, Luke lifted her up and helped her remove her shirt and bra. She hadn't realized was still wearing those. But before she could even begin to think straight, Luke was giving all his attention to her breasts, kissing and teasing her nipples, which had hardened to little pebbles.

"You are way too good at this," Rachel mumbled, dazed. The rest of the world ceased to exist. The only thing she could focus on was all the sensations that were happening in her body and the man responsible for them. Her limbs felt heavy as she rode the tidal wave of bliss.

"Oh, I haven't even gotten started yet," Luke said as he redoubled his efforts. When he began to move again, there was no more pain, only exquisite pleasure. But best of all, it looked like he was also as excited and needy as she was, if the intense focused gleam in his eyes was any indication. His strokes, which were deliciously steady and hitting all the right parts inside her, became more erratic. To her surprise, another orgasm began welling up. She'd never been able to get there without aid, but before she knew it, she was moving with him in perfect synchronicity, and he gave one more push that drove her over the edge. Her eyes snapped shut as she rode the waves. A few seconds later, Luke gave a hoarse shout as he came too.

FOR ONE OF the few times he could remember, Luke was speechless. This wasn't his first one-night stand, but this was the first one that left him feeling like *this*. By definition, one-night stands were about scratching the physical itch only—no more, no less. No risk of feelings getting involved, just in and out. Literally and figuratively. And everyone left happy and satisfied. But somehow this was different. He didn't know why but he felt no urge to usher Rachel on her way. Not only had the sex been great, but part of him wanted to keep talking to her to see what she would say next. Never in his life had he met anyone so interesting and unique—he never knew and couldn't guess what she'd say next, and he loved that.

Love? Where the hell had that come from? Surely that was just his sex-crazed brain having a temporary malfunction.

Trying to get back some equilibrium, he looked over at Rachel. She was sprawled out next to him, also trying to catch her breath. He couldn't help but be smug at the sight of her—mussed and clearly well satisfied. All because of him.

"Well?" he asked. He really couldn't wait to see what she had to say.

And true to form, she didn't disappoint. "Considering you're from Texas, a state not known to embrace comprehensive sex ed, you are remarkably well versed on the subject. I am impressed."

The last thing Luke expected to do at a moment like this was laugh, but that was exactly what he did. A deep belly laugh.

Rachel turned over to face him and scowled. "What? It's not funny! I was trying to give you a compliment." Then her voice turned shy. "It was incredible. I had no idea it could be like that. Thank you."

"It was my pleasure, literally," he said. Though part of him wanted to ask if the other men she'd ever slept with didn't know what the hell they were doing. He didn't want to think about that though. First, he got up to remove the condom, which gave him time to gather his thoughts and compose himself.

Rachel leaned back and looked up at the ceiling. Once again, he could see that her brain was working again. Clearly, he hadn't done as good a job as he'd thought. She pushed herself into a sitting position. "I need my glasses," she announced. Then proceeded to walk toward the bedroom door. He didn't mind admitting his eyes were tracking her every move.

As if she could sense it, she flushed and grabbed a shirt and slipped it on.

"It's not like I haven't already seen everything there is to see," he pointed out. "No need to be shy."

"I'll be right back," she mumbled as she made her way to the living room.

With a shrug, Luke just flopped back on the bed. Maybe she needed to check her email, or let her roommate know where she was for the night. Five minutes later, she walked back in, a determined look on her face.

"Everything okay?" he asked, his brow raised. Without a word, she made her way over to him, and pushed him back down.

Well, if this meant she was up for Round Two he sure as hell wasn't going to object. But that wasn't exactly what Rachel had in mind. Which she made clear as she leaned over and kissed his chest and made her way down. His legs were spread open and she was kneeling between them.

Then she stopped and looked up. "Do you mind?" she asked, her voice a bit hesitant.

"Are you out of your mind? Hell no," he said, not sure if he wanted to laugh or groan out loud as she started to palm him. For the next few minutes she continued to kiss and tease as he grew rock hard.

"You're torturing me," he growled.

"Turnabout is fair play," she pointed out. Then she stopped again. Now she wasn't just torturing him. This was downright cruel.

"If I remember correctly, I think this next part will work better if we adjust positions."

"Remember correctly?"

"Granted I only looked it up a few minutes ago, but still."

Wait. "You were just outside Googling how to perform oral sex?" This woman really was too much.

"Well, obviously. I wanted to do it properly. It's the least I can do," Rachel explained. "Do you mind?"

"Not at all. And for what it's worth you already get an

A for effort."

"I've always believed why settle for an A when you can get an A plus. Just sit up with your legs over the side of the bed will you?"

Obeying instantly, Luke did as he was told. Rachel got off the bed and resumed her position, on her knees between his legs.

"Now where were we?" she mused. "Oh right." Then she got to work. She opened her mouth and he watched, fascinated, as his length disappeared into it. Then Rachel began to lick suck and stroke and he was lost. Luke wasn't sure but he thought his eyes rolled to the back of his head.

And she said she'd needed to do research to do this? Clearly she was already a pro. While it was obvious Rachel was taking her current task seriously, if the look in her eye was any indication, she was relaxing and enjoying herself too. He couldn't help himself and gave another groan.

Rachel suddenly gave a loud popping suck, and that nearly sent him over the edge. "I'm close," he warned her. With a nod, Rachel just redoubled her efforts and in no time at all, the orgasm of his life took over him and with a shout he came. And still she kept going while the spasms rocked through him.

Once they were done, Rachel stood up and smiled as if she were the cat who'd swallowed the canary. And in that moment Luke was not going to complain about her looking satisfied with herself. That had been incredible.

"Well?" she asked demurely as she sat down beside him.

"Give me a minute—I can barely think, much less

talk."

Rachel gave a laugh. "I guess that means I earned that A plus."

"And then some," he agreed. Then he grabbed another condom and got ready to show her exactly how appreciative he was of her being such a great student.

"Again?" she asked, her eyes wide.

"Again," he agreed.

Rachel once again had a thoughtful look on her face. "What the hell. This is a once-in-a-lifetime thing. It's not like we plan to see each other again. Let's do it," she said with that same hesitant smile.

Luke decided it was time for less talking, so he kissed her and made sure she couldn't talk either.

SIX A.M. THE next morning, Rachel woke up bleary-eyed, and disoriented as hell. She blinked and had a moment of panic as she realized she had no idea where the hell she was. She'd been drugged, possibly kidnapped.

There was a rustling sound beside her and she bit back a scream. She turned, and when she looked at the man sprawled next to her, last night's memories came rushing back.

Oh God. What the fuck had she done? How could this have happened?

She gave a tortured moan as she remembered the tequila she drank at Wild Saguaro. Tequila—that sneaky bastard had lowered her inhibitions. How could she have forgotten no good came from tequila? Then all of her muscles twinged, reminding her that she's gotten thrown off a mechanical bull less than twelve hours ago. Better and better. She wanted to improve her social and leadership skills, but a wild night of debauchery was an overcorrection of epic proportions.

At least she hadn't lost all good sense last night and given Luke, a complete stranger, her address. What a recipe for disaster that would have been. At least her subconscious had absorbed all the lessons from the hours of murder podcasts she liked listening to and looked out for her. *Thank you, subconscious.* Though ending up in a stranger's bed still wasn't optimal, Rachel took comfort in the fact that there were likely plenty of witnesses at the Wild Saguaro last night, as well as camera footage, even if it was of her getting thrown off the bull. So if Luke had been a serial killer, there would be plenty of leads and her death would be quickly avenged.

The punishing sunlight came glaring through the windows, hurting her eyes. Rachel cursed under her breath as she saw her bra hanging off the lamp across the room. She didn't want to know how it'd ended up there.

As if her dignity hadn't already taken enough of a pummeling, she discovered her panties on the floor beside the bed. The bra and panties didn't match. And she'd been wearing granny panties.

When she'd embarked on her mission at the bar last night, she'd had no idea she'd engage in a wild night of unbridled sex. If she had, she would have at least tried to wear the appropriate undergarments.

Okay. Ninety-five percent of her underwear was granny panties. She believed in comfort above all else. But she would have made an exception for this.

She snuck another peek at her bed companion. Thank goodness his back was still to her, and he looked like he was dead to the world. Gingerly, Rachel threw back the blankets and sheets and got out of bed. Once her feet hit the floor, she took a moment to steady herself.

Damn tequila. No, that wasn't fair. She was a grown woman, and that meant she took responsibility for her actions. Last night was all her. She was going to own this. All of it—good, bad, and ugly.

But tequila was still on her shit list.

As quietly as she could, she tiptoed around the room to gather her clothes, then ducked into the bathroom to get dressed. Despite herself, she looked in the mirror. Her hair was going in ten different directions, her makeup—such as it was—was a mess, her eyes were bleary, and the light was making her head hurt.

Rachel gave herself a shake. She pulled on her clothes and ran the faucet as quietly as she could. She splashed her face with cold water to shock herself awake, then ran her fingers through her hair to tame it as best she could. She cracked open the bathroom door, cringing and cursing again as it made a loud squeak. Poking her head out, she saw that Luke was still inert in the bed.

Perfect. After gathering up the last of her belongings,

Rachel got the hell out as quickly as she could. She tiptoed out to the hallway and let out a huge sigh as the door quietly closed behind her. Leaning back against the door, she closed her eyes. She had misgivings about leaving his apartment door unlocked, but what choice did she have? Worst-case scenario, maybe she could make an anonymous GoFundMe donation if anything got stolen. Then she frowned. By leaving the door unlocked, was she leaving herself open to getting charged as some sort of accessory if anything happened to Luke?

Rachel sighed. She supposed it was a good thing she knew a local lawyer. As far as she knew, Cecily didn't do defense work, but perhaps she could give a referral. Then again, maybe she would be sorely out of luck—no lawyer would want to defend her because she'd let one of their own perish.

Okay, that was enough spiraling and overthinking. If she kept dawdling, she could get caught. Luke might wake up at any moment. It was time to go.

The good thing was, she could go back to her apartment, take a long hot shower, and sleep like the dead. And no one would be the wiser, and it would never be spoken of again. She and Mr. GQ…eerr, Luke, would go their separate ways and never see each other again.

Thank God.

Chapter Five

WITH A GROAN, Luke turned over in bed and slammed the phone back down. The eight thirty wake-up call had been brutal, and he was feeling the effects of last night's overindulgence. He had originally planned to hit the gym this morning, but clearly that wasn't happening. As the brain fog cleared, he realized that something was missing.

Or rather, someone.

He distinctly remembered that he had not fallen asleep last night by himself, but he was very much alone now. In fact, given how cold the other side of the bed was, it was clear Rachel had abandoned him and left some time ago. Normally, Luke was as well versed in the protocols of a one-night stand as anyone else, but somehow, this time, being left high and dry didn't sit as well with him.

She'd ghosted him. He didn't even rate a goodbye or a mere note before she left.

And chances were he'd never see her again. All he had was a first name to go on, so it wasn't like he could track her down. San Francisco was a big city. Not that he wanted to. Of course not. He walked out into the living room, wondering if by some slim chance, she was still there. But no luck. Though he'd been wrong about one thing. Rachel had left him a note. Somewhere, she'd found a Post-it and stuck it to his front door.

> *I had to leave your door unlocked. Sorry. Hope no one came in and stole anything or killed you before you woke up.*

Luke shook his head and gave a small chuckle as he locked his door. Good thing for him his building had reasonably good security and theft and murder weren't serious concerns. It was a shame Rachel had left because that really had been the most fun he'd had in months. Not just the sex, he couldn't remember the last time he'd enjoyed someone's company that much. Too bad she hadn't left her number.

Maybe it was just as well. Perhaps one night of fantastic sex was all it was meant to be. Luke tried not to dwell on why he felt so disappointed as he went about his day.

It was Sunday, which meant it was time for his weekly call home. He was exhausted from his late night, but rules were rules. Ever the dutiful son, Luke sat down at his kitchen table and engaged the video call app on his phone. The weekly ritual had developed when he had moved from Houston to Stanford for law school. His parents needed regular proof of life, and his mother would be consoled that he was eating properly and wasn't wasting away.

By the second or third ring, his mother accepted the call. Naomi Bishop Trudeau's face filled the screen. Elegant and polished as ever with her hair pulled back with a stylish headband, pearl studs in her ears, and perfectly applied makeup.

"Hey, Mama." He couldn't help it, whenever he got home or talked to his family, the Texas slipped back into his voice. There were times he missed hearing that familiar twang, as much as the family and the food.

"Luke, darlin'. How are you sweetie?" Her voice was warm, and her eyes sparkled with happiness.

"Just fine. Same old, same old. How are you and Daddy?"

Naomi rolled her eyes and waved a hand. "Oh you know how he is. If he doesn't get his weekly round of golf in, he gets grumpy. I swear, it's a trial keeping him busy and out of my hair now that he's retired."

Luke chuckled. "Sounds about right. But if anyone can keep him in line, it's you."

"I've been doing it for almost forty-five years now, haven't I?" Her voice was arch and sly. God, he loved her.

"Like you keep reminding us, they grow them strong and tough down in Lubbock."

"Damn straight." Naomi got up from her living room couch, went to the kitchen, poured herself a glass of sweet tea, and sat back down.

"You said Daddy's fine, but how about you?"

"I'm fine, honey. I took my daily walk and did my half hour of Zumba. I'm glad you caught me when you did. I need to head down to the shop." After spending over twenty years as a stay-at-home mother, Naomi decided it was time to put her business degree to good use. Five years ago, she'd opened Trudeau Treasure Boutique, a specialty arts, crafts, and gift store. She was ruthlessly organized with an eagle eye on the bottom line.

"Make sure you have some lunch before you go. We don't need you fainting."

She took a sip of tea and raised a brow. "If I did faint, I would do it in an elegant and graceful manner like any proper Southern woman. That reminds me, I need to take the lasagna out of the freezer. Ben and Viv and the kids are coming over for dinner and so are Lilly and Ryan," she added, referring to his younger brother Ben and baby sister Lilly and their spouses.

Luke shook his head. "I'll pray for your rugs and your china." The last time his parents had a family get-together, his niece Shelby decided to steal a toothbrush from the bathroom, dip it in the toilet, then use it to "clean the TV."

"Don't you slander my grandbabies." There was the sound of a door being yanked open, and then he heard his father's familiar, heavy footsteps.

Clinton Trudeau's face came onto the screen. "That you, son?" Looking at his father was like getting a glimpse of the future. He knew exactly what he was going to look like in thirty years. Even as a child, the family joke had been that Clinton had just used Naomi as an incubator to spawn himself, the resemblance was so strong. There was no denying he was his father's son.

"Yes, sir." Looking hale and hearty, with a tanned face, distinguished salt-and-pepper hair, and slightly pronounced laugh lines, his father looked like exactly who he was—a man happy and content with his lot in life.

"Good. Maybe you can tell your mama to stop starving me." Or maybe not.

Luke's brow raised at the accusation. As always, Naomi dealt with it with grace and aplomb. "Don't mind him. He had his physical two weeks ago, and his cholesterol is a tad high. Dr. Green said he needed to cut back on the alcohol and red meat."

"What's the point of living if a man can't have a scotch or tequila with his steak and potatoes? We live in Texas for heaven's sake. Your mama is feeding me rabbit food."

Naomi gave a light smack to her husband's arm. "You're exaggerating. It was a very nice grilled chicken salad."

"It could be worse, Dad. Out here, they probably wouldn't even offer chicken. You'd have to make do with tofu." Tongue in cheek, he bit back a grin as he watched his father recoil in horror.

"Tell me you're joking."

"Don't knock it till you've tried it. Next time you and Mama come to San Francisco I'll introduce you to tempeh."

"Over my dead body," Clinton sputtered.

His mother gave an exasperated huff and wagged a finger. "Lucas Bishop Trudeau, stop teasing your father."

He did his best to fix his face into a proper penitent expression. "Yes, ma'am."

Naomi's face softened a bit. "Did Vivienne send you pictures of the kids? It's been so long since you've seen them."

"I saw them when I visited."

"Three months ago," Clinton pointed out.

"How about you two come visit me next time? I'll make up the futon and you two can have my bedroom." He saw his parents exchange a look.

"What?" he asked, crossing his arms.

Clinton cleared his throat. "Your apartment is pretty small, son."

"It's San Francisco, Dad. I'm lucky I found a place that's bigger than a closet."

"You've lived there since law school."

"If it ain't broke, don't fix it. Besides, it's close to work and an easy commute. Win-win."

"It's just that we thought you would find a place that's more fitting for you."

"What do you mean?"

"Don't you think you should start thinking about your future? Find a new place, one that you could start a family in one day?"

Luke gave a shudder. "I have time before I have to think about that."

It was Naomi's turn to cross her arms. "You're almost forty. How much more time do you need? Your brother and sister are all settled. Your classmates from high school are married and having kids. It's time for you to grow up."

"If this is you pressuring me for grandkids, aren't you happy with the ones you already have?"

"All I'm asking is for you to keep what we're saying in

mind. You can't be Peter Pan the rest of your life."

Part of him resented the implications of what his parents were saying. Peter Pan syndrome? He wasn't averse to growing up. Far from it. He had a career he was happy with, and his own apartment with his own bills. He had his own health insurance for God's sake, and a retirement plan. How much more grown up could he get?

But being the dutiful son he was, he pasted a smile on his face and nodded in all the right places while his mother gushed about her precious grandbabies and her battle with the deer who were eating up her garden, and his father talked about the marked improvement in his golf game.

It was the least he could do. And the path of least resistance. Hey, if it ain't broke, why fix it?

After the phone call ended, Luke thought again about his tentative plans to open his own firm. And once again, his thoughts turned to Rachel. He remembered her saying she was getting promoted to senior financial analyst. In other words, exactly the type of person who could help him with the projections and research he and Bea had talked about. At the bar, he'd been about to ask her for that help but then she'd proposed they have sex and he'd forgotten all about it. It was a shame she'd left before they exchanged contact details.

For business purposes only. Of course.

TODAY WAS THE big day. Her first day at the new office. As

she walked toward the elevators, Rachel took a deep breath and reminded herself that she was as prepared as she could be. She'd done as much reading as she could, and she'd practiced and rehearsed.

Part of her wished she hadn't spent most of Sunday sleeping and recovering from her ill-advised tango with tequila the night before and the wild sex that ensued. But what was done was done. Besides hadn't Claudia said she was boring and stuck in a rut? She was definitely no longer in a rut.

Getting on the elevator, she made a point of making eye contact and smiling at the other people in the car with her. But not to make conversation. People wanted to be left alone in elevators from what her research told her, and she was all for that.

When the bell dinged for the twelfth floor, she got off and made her way to the front desk. The friendly receptionist Julia promptly took her to see her new manager, Amanda Strickland. After finishing a phone call, Amanda waved her in. She appeared to be a no-nonsense woman in her mid-forties in a smart slate gray suit.

"Welcome aboard, Rachel," she said, sticking out her hand.

"Glad to be here." Relieved that this conversation was somewhat following the script she had prepared in her head, Rachel sat down after Amanda gestured for her to take a seat.

"I don't have a whole lot of time, and I'm sure you want to hit the ground running, but I just wanted to personally welcome you to our office. In general, I have a hands-off policy. I trust my people know what they're doing and leave them to it. That being said, if you have questions, don't hesitate, et cetera." Amanda gave her a considering look. "This is off the record but I'm glad you're here. This field is so male dominated, especially the higher up the ladder you get. Anything I can do to help you succeed, I'm happy to do."

She appreciated the vote of confidence.

"You're probably going to spend most of the day with HR and IT getting set up, but what do you say we meet back at my office at three and we can go over your new assignments?"

"Sounds good."

The two of them spent a few more minutes going over the usual first-day preliminaries before Amanda said it was time to meet her team.

Trying to keep the nerves at bay, Rachel followed her boss down the hall and into one of the conference rooms where five people were already sitting. The minute they walked in the door, all eyes turned toward her.

Oh yeah, they were absolutely sizing her up.

"Everyone, this is Rachel Bai, who's here from the New York office. She's going to be overseeing some of the accounts you're handling and will be taking over some new ones. Rachel, this is Contessina Foscari, Brian Chavez, Randall Ayoubi, Annika Greene, and Jonathan Winthrop."

"Rachel? I'm not good with names or faces but that'll be easy to remember. My wife's name is Rachel too."

Randall, tall with wiry hair and a smooth olive complexion gave her a welcoming smile.

Annika, sitting the farthest away, was hard to miss with her bright red hair. Brian and Jonathan were textbook stereotypes of what you thought of when you pictured men working in finance. Contessina was petite with long dark hair and made her think of the *Mona Lisa*.

"I'm going to let you all get acquainted. I need to get back to work. Rachel, I'll see you later. Remember, HR needs to see you in ten minutes." Without a backward glance, Amanda sailed out of the room and left Rachel standing alone to face down five pairs of eyes, which were blatantly curious and wary.

She took a deep breath, prepared to launch into the welcome speech she'd worked so hard to memorize. But before she could even get started, Annika raised her hand.

"You don't need to do that," Rachel said, confused.

"Would it be all right if I left early? I have a ton of work to catch up on. Maybe we can reschedule this meet-and-greet slash getting to know you?"

The rest of the team murmured their agreement. Well, so much for her speech and trying to get off on the right foot.

"Besides we're going to be spending a lot of time together. Plenty of time to get to know each other, right?" Jonathan said as he stood up.

Rachel cleared her throat. "I know it's going to take me a day or two to get up to speed, but I was wondering if maybe we can schedule a time this Thursday or Friday? We can all sit down and catch each other up on where things stand, so we all get on the same page?"

Brian raised an eyebrow. "That sounds like a good idea. Could be more efficient to make it an email instead of the hassle of finding a time that works for all of us?" Again, there were nods all around.

Seeing how eager all of them were to leave and get back to work and how uninterested they were in her, Rachel figured there was only one thing left to do.

"Can someone tell me where HR is?"

"Two floors down on ten," Contessina supplied.

"Great. Thanks so much, everyone. Good talk."

As they trooped out of the conference room, one thing was made crystal clear to Rachel.

She had a lot of work to do. She was going to need some more help, whether it be to review the books she'd already read to see if she'd missed something or step up her research and efforts. It was probably going to be a combo of all the above.

With a small sigh she made her way to the elevators to head down to HR. So far, her first day could be going better. But it was only day one. Plenty of time to keep working and improving.

"Onwards and upwards," she murmured to herself.

RACHEL PULLED UP to the entrance to Sedgewick Winery with no small amount of trepidation. It was a small winery about an hour outside San Francisco, where Adrienne was holding her birthday party. But the trepidation was also mixed with resolve.

"Adrienne was nice enough to invite you," she reminded herself. "The least you can do is show up, make an effort, and try to make a good impression. You can do this." At the very least, she was going to give it a hell of an effort. Even if this sort of thing was beyond her comfort zone and the likelihood was high that she'd put her foot in her mouth. Though that was probably the point, Rachel mused. This was an excellent opportunity to keep working on her networking and social skills, so really she should be thanking Adrienne for this. This party could be considered a necessary evil.

Then there was the matter of the birthday gift. Rachel had spent days Googling and agonizing over what to buy. There were so many results when she tried to search for foolproof birthday gifts, but all the suggestions seem to have pitfalls. A food or fruit basket? What about allergies? Clothes were non-starters because there was no way she was going to try to guess Adrienne's size and favorite colors or brands or patterns. Candles and flowers were too overdone, bordering on cliché. Thank goodness she'd decided against buying some nice wine because it would be totally redundant in this case. She'd been tempted to go with straight hard cash. That was the way of her people, after all, and who didn't like cash? But then Google suggested cash might feel impersonal, and that she hadn't given the gift much thought. Which was laughable in this case given how much time she'd put into it.

In the end, she went with a spa certificate. She remembered Cecily sent her a thank you gift that included one, so she figured it was a safe option. She'd even asked for a nice fancy envelope for it. Hopefully that would be enough, and Adrienne would like the gift. She didn't need ribbons or anything did she?

Rachel shook her head, got out of the car, and made her way to the entrance. She smoothed the skirt of her plain black dress that she'd dressed up with a red belt, grimacing as the gravel driveway wreaked havoc on the short kitten heels she was wearing. Normally she would have just worn crocs or something more comfortable, but this was an occasion that demanded some effort. She opened the door and was greeted by a tall sleek brunette who introduced herself as Hannah Sedgewick, the manager.

"May I help you?" Hannah asked politely.

"Yes I'm here for a party? Adrienne Arroyo?"

"Right down the hall." In short order Rachel found the room—an open, airy, light-filled space full of rough wooden beams and brick, but with a modern elegant flair. Rustic chic. There was a bar in the far corner already lined up with wine glasses, and the tables were laden with delicious-looking tapas, paella, flan, empanadas, grilled veggies, charcuterie, pernil, and strawberry cupcakes.

"Rachel! You made it!" The birthday girl came up and gave her a hug.

"Happy birthday," Rachel recited. Adrienne's beam told her at least she got that part right.

"Thank you. And thank you for coming. Hope you didn't have a hard time finding the place."

"No, the GPS did a good job."

"Great!"

She opened her purse to hand over the present.

"Hey, put that away. You don't need to pay for anything, it's an open bar," Adrienne protested.

"No, it's your birthday present." She put the small envelope in Adrienne's hand.

"Oh that's so sweet of you. Would you mind if I open this later?" She waved a hand and on cue, a woman who appeared to be a relative walked up to them and took care of the gift certificate.

"Sure, no problem. It's not much, but I hope you'll like it."

Adrienne gave her a reassuring pat. "I'm sure I will. Listen, I have more guests to greet, but go mingle and have fun, okay? Jeffrey and CeeCee are around—go find them. I'm sure they'd love to see you." With that, Adrienne dashed off and left Rachel stranded.

Well okay then. What the hell was she supposed to do now? At least Adrienne had let her know Cecily and Jeffrey were here. She gave a frantic look around the room, trying to locate the couple. After a minute, she found them—Cecily wearing a bright blue dress, strappy heels, with her hair just so and a glass of wine in her hand as if it was the most natural thing in the world. Jeffrey was right beside her, his arm around her, looking dapper in a navy dress shirt and charcoal slacks. Chatting with another couple, they really did look like the picture-perfect epitome of relationship goalz. Rachel bit back the worst of the envy. Just once, it would be nice if she could find someone, anyone, who would look at her the way Jeffrey looked at his fiancée—like he believed she hung the stars and the moon, and he couldn't believe his luck.

Rachel gave herself a shake. That was ridiculous wishful thinking, and she had more important matters to attend to. Actual problems she could tackle and have a reasonable chance of success with. Mainly, trying to put the research she'd done to good use and make conversation like a normal person.

Rachel was debating between barging into the conversation like a bull in a china shop (though she wasn't fond of bull references these days for obvious reasons) or hovering around like a stalker and pouncing when she saw an opening, when fate took the decision out of her hands. Cecily caught a glimpse of her and waved hello. Caught, Rachel waved back awkwardly. After a graceful exit from their current conversation, the happy couple made their way to her. Cecily gave her a quick hug. And then Jeffrey did the same.

"Good to see you. Did you just get here?"

"Yep." For some reason she was all tongue-tied again, damn it.

"How are you settling into San Francisco?" Jeffrey inquired politely. "A cross-country move must have been daunting. You've only been here a week or two, right? Hopefully things have settled down for you a little."

"I don't know. Too soon to say, I think." Rachel frowned in contemplation. "My apartment is still coming together, but there are so many boxes to unpack. And I still need to find the nearest post office, library, pharmacy, supermarket—all that stuff. But at least the furniture I ordered arrived in time. It would've sucked to not even have a bed."

The two of them looked at each other. "That would suck," Cecily agreed. She took a sip of her wine.

"Getting used to a new place takes time," Jeffrey said with a nod. "I'm moving into CeeCee's apartment and it's a whole process. Combining two households into one isn't easy."

"Oh please. You basically already moved in months ago—it was just a formality. He's only annoyed because I made him get rid of his huge man-cave leather couch," Cecily explained with a roll of her eyes.

"I have fond memories of that couch," he retorted with a raise of his brow.

"Stop it, don't embarrass Rachel," Cecily insisted, while elbowing him. But her cheeks were flushed. She took a deep breath and turned back to Rachel.

"How are things at work?"

At that Rachel brightened. Finally, they were on familiar, safe ground. "It's going great. I had to spend a whole day meeting with HR and filling out paperwork, but you know how that goes. Then I had to meet with IT and get set up with my computer. Lots of housekeeping stuff. I met my new assistant Katrina. She seems really nice and efficient. I was also thinking since wine is just a huge industry around here it may be worth looking into as investment prospects for my clients. This could count as tax-deductible research. Wouldn't that be fun?" she asked as she took a breath after blurting all that out.

"I'm always for taking advantage of every tax loophole to pay as little as possible," Jeffrey agreed, with amusement in his eyes.

"Exactly." Rachel beamed. "I'm just excited. But really determined to make this work."

"I'm sure you'll be fantastic. You were really helpful when you walked me through all that financial paperwork when I was working on the Stafford deal." That vote of confidence from Cecily warmed her heart. Maybe she wasn't going to be so bad at this after all. Gathering her courage and deciding to go for broke, Rachel broached her request.

"Actually, I was wondering, since you're here, if I can ask you something."

"Sure. What?" Cecily asked with a raised brow.

"So, you're a lawyer, right?"

"Last time I checked, yes."

"I was wondering how you do it."

"Do what?" Cecily sounded confused, but Rachel was too focused on making her pitch to notice.

"The way I see it, you're a lawyer, so you deal with people all day. You'd know what to do with a difficult client or judge or whatever, and how to get people to listen to you. And I'm sure you can network like a pro."

"There's more to my job than that."

"I know but I'm sure some of those skills are transferable." She was about to ask Cecily if she'd be interested in being her consultant. For pay of course. As far as Rachel was concerned that'd be money well spent. If she was going to embark on this project to be successful at her new job and develop those critical social and communication skills, recruiting the help of experts was an excellent strategy. And having that expert be someone she already knew and was semi-comfortable with was a major plus.

Her enthusiasm took a steep nosedive when she finally took in Cecily's expression and the look in her eyes. Well crap. She'd misjudged and messed up again. But she'd been so sure this would be foolproof. Damn it.

"If I can help, I'd be happy to," Cecily said politely. After exchanging another look with Jeffrey, she explained, "I just saw Adrienne's parents, and I need to say hello. Good talking to you. We'll catch up later?"

"Sure," Rachel said woodenly. Clearly, they couldn't wait to make their escape. Cecily gave her a quick squeeze of the hand before the two of them were off and leaving her alone. Again.

That had been a total disaster, but hopefully Cecily wasn't going to stop talking to her altogether. She'd said they'd catch up later, right? It was time to regroup. Rachel decided the best course of action was to grab a glass of wine and a plate of food. If she was stuffing her face, she wouldn't be forced to make conversation. But then, just as she was about to reach the bar, she heard a very distinct and distressingly familiar voice behind her speak and stop her in her tracks.

"You."

That voice created flashbacks she had no business flashing back on. It couldn't be him. That was a random fluke of a crazy night and it was over, but now it had come back to haunt her. Rachel took a deep breath and closed her eyes and counted to ten while clenching her hands. Maybe if she tried really hard to wish him away it would work. She turned around and opened her eyes. And yep. There he was. Mr. *GQ* aka Luke. Crap.

Chapter Six

LUKE WATCHED WITH an amused expression as Rachel opened her eyes again. "Still here, I'm afraid."

"I'm glad you're not dead," she blurted out.

"No thanks to you," he reminded her, lips twitching. He was still amused by the Post-it note.

"I already said I was sorry," she insisted. Fair enough.

"What a pleasant surprise," Luke murmured. He couldn't help the grin spreading from ear to ear. He'd come to Adrienne's birthday party for form's sake and because he was genuinely fond of her. But running into Rachel again was an unexpected bonus. The universe really was making sure he was catching all the breaks. Now was the time to put his original plan into action. With a twist.

He also took a moment to notice and appreciate just how nicely the black dress Rachel was wearing hugged her curves and showed off her figure. As well as shapely legs that he somehow hadn't paid attention to during their night together.

Meanwhile, Rachel was glaring at him. "What are you doing here?" she hissed. "I was never supposed to see you ever again in life. This was not the plan."

"It would appear fate has decided otherwise. Even if

you snuck out before I woke up. You know how the saying goes, 'Man plans, God laughs.'" As her scowl deepened, he gave an unrepentant shrug. "I grew up in Texas—avoiding God and the Bible is almost impossible." He gave a look around. "Can we find a place to talk?"

Rachel's eyes narrowed suspiciously. "Why?"

"You do like asking that question a lot."

"It's the only way to get answers."

"Well, what would you say if I told you I had a proposition for you?"

"Not interested," she clipped out. "It might have been a while since I had sex, even mind-blowing sex, but I am nowhere near that desperate."

Luke's mind short-circuited a moment at the phrase "mind-blowing sex" as it brought back memories, very pleasant memories, but he gave himself a shake and focused on the issue at hand. And as he replayed his words in his head, he understood where he'd gone wrong.

"I couldn't help but overhear your conversation, and it made me think about our last encounter." As her cheeks flamed, he hastened to reassure her. "My proposition is totally above board and strictly business. Nothing nefarious."

They both stood there silently while she sized him up and decided how seriously to take his offer. It wasn't until she gave a short nod that he realized he'd been holding his breath, anxious for her answer. There were high-top tables scattered throughout the room and he led them to one. But not before Rachel got another glass of wine and a plate of food.

He appreciated a woman who had her priorities straight.

"So what is your offer?" she asked without preliminaries.

Luke pitched his voice low as he spoke. "I know you're working hard to make your promotion permanent, and I can help."

"How?"

"Well, like your friend, I'm also a lawyer."

"You people are everywhere," Rachel grumbled.

"Like bad pennies," he agreed. "But my point is, I can do those things you were asking her about. We can work together to help you develop communication skills, networking skills, and whatever you need to be a good leader and kick ass with your team. I'm a people person," he explained. "This stuff is as natural to me as breathing."

"I've always been suspicious of people who enjoy spending time people-ing. It feels so unnatural."

"Hey, no need to cast aspersions. It takes all kinds, and the world needs introverts and extroverts."

"If you say so. Well, as I told Cecily, I was willing to pay her for her services and the same would go for you. How much were you thinking?" Rachel asked, now in negotiating mode.

"No money—I was thinking more a trade. A quid pro quo type deal."

"I told you sex was off the table."

"And I told you, I'm not going there. Strictly business.

All clothes will be staying on." Much to his regret.

"Then what do you want?" she asked bluntly.

Luke took another look around, making sure they wouldn't be overheard.

"Why do you keep doing that? Is what you want illegal? Because if so, the answer is no. There is no way in hell I'm going to jail for anyone, much less you." Rachel put down her glass of Riesling and crossed her arms.

"My God you're so suspicious. Is everyone from New York like that?" he asked with a shake of his head.

"I just don't know a hundred percent if I can trust you yet," she pointed out in what he assumed she considered a reasonable tone. "For all I know you're trying to get past my defenses and lure me to a horrible death."

Where the hell did that come from? "You think I'm a serial killer trying to trap you with a business deal?"

Rachel's cheek flushed. "I'm a murder podcast fan," she mumbled. "My mind just goes there. But my point still stands. And once again I'm glad you didn't get killed when I left your apartment door unlocked."

So that explained where the content of the Post-it note came from. Running his tongue over his teeth, Luke hid a smile. "I appreciate the concern," he murmured. She gave a short nod in response.

With what he considered admirable restraint, he resisted the urge to point out that most serial killers didn't engage in one-night stands before tracking down their victims again to slaughter them. Instead, he explained. "I am thinking of opening my own solo legal practice and figuring out the finances and logistics has been challenging. That's where you come in."

Luke could see the wheels turning in Rachel's head and her eyes lit at the challenge presented. "I could run some projections, cost-benefit analyses, do some research into the market, how much it'd cost to rent a space, hire staff, and so on."

"Exactly!" he exclaimed with a pleased smile. He took a sip of his merlot and sampled the shrimp ceviche as Rachel thought through the proposal.

"Well, when I said I was willing to do whatever it took to succeed, I didn't have this in mind but what the hell. You got a deal." She stuck out her hand.

"Excellent," he said with a relieved laugh as he shook her extended hand. Then he frowned. "But there is one thing we need to take care of first."

"What?" she asked, confused.

"I never got your last name. That seems important."

Rachel blinked in surprise. "Oh, it's Bai. Rachel Bai."

"Nice to meet you properly, Rachel," he said, amused. "I'm Luke Trudeau."

"Nice to meet you too." Then after a pause she continued. "So what next? How do we do this?"

"How about we take the next few days to brainstorm, and we meet up next weekend to come up with a game plan? At a public place of course." Whatever it took to make Rachel comfortable. While her fears about serial killers were probably far-fetched, better safe than sorry, he supposed. He couldn't wait to spend more time with her.

In a strictly professional capacity to help each other achieve their respective goals of course. It had nothing to do with her fabulous eyes or tempting lips. Or memories of their night together that he still couldn't stop thinking about. Nothing at all.

"Sounds good." They exchanged phone numbers and decided to meet next Saturday afternoon.

"Oh, there you are," a voice interrupted them. A vaguely familiar woman walked up to them arm in arm with a man who appeared to be her significant other, and she greeted Rachel. "I know you don't know people here, so I wanted to check back in on you to see if you're okay. So, who's this you're chatting with?" The woman turned to him, and the polite smile fell from her face and was replaced with a slight look of horror.

"Oh crap."

As Luke finally placed who the woman was, he raised an eyebrow. Oh, crap indeed.

RACHEL WATCHED IN confusion as Cecily's cheeks flushed beet red. Meanwhile, Luke just seemed amused more than anything else. There was clearly subtext flowing but she couldn't make heads nor tails of it, and that was frustrating. What the hell was going on?

"What a pleasant surprise," Luke drawled.

Meanwhile, Jeffrey was clearly as confused as Rachel was. At least she wasn't alone. "You two know each other?"

he asked his fiancée.

"Not really," Cecily mumbled.

"Now that hurts my feelings," Luke murmured. "We spent a lovely evening together months ago. I wouldn't call that nothing. Besides, our companies are merging so we're technically co-workers now."

"Okay, someone needs to explain what's going on," Jeffrey demanded.

"I take it this is him?" Luke asked with a head tilt in Jeffrey's direction.

Cecily threw Luke a dirty glare and gritted her teeth. "Luke is a fellow lawyer over at Bradford Long and Price aka the firm Harmon Burke is merging with. So yes, we're co-workers of a sort. But that's it really."

"And that lovely evening?" Jeffrey's tone was suspicious.

"A blind date that didn't go well and that's all I want to say about that," Cecily insisted. To cut off her fiancé's protest, she went on. "It was last spring after we both came back from Brooklyn." Apparently that explanation was good enough to keep Jeffrey from prying, though he still didn't look happy.

As far as Rachel was concerned, she wasn't sure how to process that information. But at least it sounded like things hadn't gotten further than a blind date. Rachel wasn't sure of many things when it came to social interactions but one thing she knew full well. There had to be nothing worse than finding out that you and your friend, acquaintance, someone you want to turn into a friend had slept with the same person. Talk about fucking awkward.

"Congratulations by the way," Luke piped up, gesturing toward the ring sparkling from Cecily's left hand. It was a nice diamond though she knew nothing about cut, clarity, or any of that stuff.

"So what were you two talking about?" Cecily said, obviously desperate to change the subject.

"Luke just finished propositioning me and I agreed."

Silence descended on the group.

Cecily's eyes widened and her mouth dropped. Very uncharacteristic. Rachel always thought of her as someone who'd always kept her composure. It was good to know that even Cecily could get flustered. Duly noted.

"It wasn't what you're thinking," Luke interjected.

"I sure as hell hope so," Cecily huffed once she got a hold of herself.

"Not that we're judging," Jeffrey said. "We're all adults here." Rachel wasn't sure whether he was joking. It was a coin flip, really.

Her brow furrowed. Had she said something wrong? Perhaps she needed to clarify. "We were talking about a business arrangement. Simple exchange of services. Nothing personal. I already told him sex was off the table."

"She did," Luke confirmed.

Cecily narrowed her eyes. "How do you two know each other anyway?"

"CeeCee, I don't think that's any of our business," Jeffrey interrupted.

"Rachel is my friend," Cecily insisted. "I want to make sure she's okay."

"I'm fine," Rachel assured her. It was nice to know someone cared.

"Are you sure about that? I know a cross-country move can be disorienting and all but this is a lot. I feel responsible for you. If anything happened to you, I'd never hear the end of it from our parents."

Was she a friend or an obligation?

"Oh look, it's time for singing and cake." Jeffrey gave his fiancée a speaking glance. It was clear Cecily had more to say but refrained.

As they walked away, Rachel sighed and shook her head. Luke on the other hand gave her an interested look.

"What?" she asked. He wasn't bailing on her already, was he?

"Sorry about that. I should have probably jumped in and tried to help, but I wanted to see for myself what you were talking about when you said you needed help with people skills. I now have a better idea on how to help."

"If you say so," Rachel said skeptically. The man had to know by now he had his work cut out for him.

"Let's try to enjoy the rest of the party."

The remainder of the evening passed in a blur of candles, cake, and wine. Luke left soon after, wanting to beat the traffic. At the first opportunity, Rachel made her excuses and made her way back into the city. But not before she caught Cecily and Adrienne in a huddle with Cecily making dramatic hand gestures. When she'd gone to them to say her goodbyes they had immediately clammed up. It didn't take a genius to figure out what or who they were talking about. Despite that, Adrienne's "Thanks for coming" still seemed genuine and Cecily had given her a hug and a "Let's get together soon." For whatever that was worth.

Ninety minutes later, Rachel entered her apartment. With a sigh of relief, she kicked off her shoes and practically ran into her bedroom so she could finally get out of the dress and bra and put on a T-shirt and pajama pants. She grabbed a notebook and sat down at the kitchen table.

Today's foray into developing communication and social skills had produced mixed results to say the least. She got the impression she hadn't totally blown her friendship with Cecily, and that was a relief. Rachel was determined to make the most of this new job and opportunity and build a new life for herself in San Francisco. Ideally, she wouldn't end up friendless and alone in the process. It would really suck if the only person willing to spend time with her outside of work was Luke. She had to do better.

But speaking of Luke, assuming he could deliver on what he promised, having someone more experienced willing to help and coach her would be an excellent boon. Surely with his guidance she'd be able to achieve her goals and earn that promotion in no time.

So what if this was the guy she'd had the most amazing sex of her life with? It didn't seem to bother Luke, so it sure as hell wasn't going to bother her. You weren't supposed to mix business with pleasure so, moving forward, pleasure would be taken out of the equation completely. She wasn't going to let anything detract from her objectives, orgasms be damned. They could just forget all about it, put it behind them, and focus on the task at hand. Pretend like it never happened.

How hard could that be, really?

Chapter Seven

IT WAS WEDNESDAY evening and Rachel was making her way home from work when her phone pinged.

Hey. So are you free Friday? Happy hour with you, me, and Adrienne?

Rachel read the text with surprise. She'd assumed when Cecily said they should get together soon it had been a rote offer that she didn't mean. Come to find out, not so much.

I can make Friday work.

Great! Let's say 6 or 6:30 at Jasmine's? I can text you the address.

Six or six thirty? That was so unhelpful. How was she supposed to allot enough time to get there if she didn't know when the meet was? She frowned as she texted back a reply.

Is it 6 or 6:30? Can you be specific please? For planning purposes.

There was a pause. Rachel bit her lip, worried that she'd come off as rude. But she still felt her request wasn't unreasonable. Punctuality was important.

Let's play it safe and make it 6:30. I waffled because I'm not sure when I'll be done with the deposition I have scheduled. I'll let Adrienne know. See you then?

See you then.

Then for good measure she added another text.

Thanks for the invite. Looking forward to it.

She got a thumbs-up emoji in response. At least Cecily hadn't taken offense and revoked the invite. And she really was looking forward to meeting them for drinks.

Life in San Francisco was looking up.

That Friday, at six thirty sharp, Rachel walked through the front door of Jasmine's and took in the atmosphere. Jasmine's was modern and minimalist contemporary with sconce lighting and lots of glass, metallics, black and white and abstract art on the walls. Definitely not your cozy neighborhood pub where you meet up for a pint at the end of the day. She saw Cecily and Adrienne at a booth poring over the menu. Rachel took a breath and gathered up her courage. She could do this, she reminded herself. They had asked her to come after all, so she wasn't going into hostile foreign territory.

"Great! You're here." Adrienne beamed as she saw her approach. She scooted over so Rachel could sit next to her.

"Glad you could join us," Cecily said. She gave a brief smile then turned her attention back to the menu.

"Ignore CeeCee," Adrienne said with an eye roll. "She skipped lunch so she's hyper focused on food right now."

"I need at least two orders of bacon-wrapped shrimp and the pot stickers and the chicken skewers look awesome. Oh! Sliders..."

"How about we just order one of everything?" Adrienne asked, amused.

"That'll work as a starter. You hungry, Rachel?" Cecily asked as she put down the menu.

"Uh, I'm fine. I think that should be enough food."

She had leftovers at home if she was still hungry.

"Okay. But let's get you some booze."

Rachel gave a quick glance and settled on an IPA. They gave their order to the waiter and Cecily and Adrienne exchanged glances.

Oh hell. What now? Was this some sort of intervention? Though for the life of her she had no idea what they would be intervening about. She didn't smoke, didn't gamble (gambling never made sense to her. The odds were too lopsided toward the house. Why bother?), and the strongest drugs she'd ever taken were doctor-prescribed antibiotics. So what was this about?

Cecily cleared her throat. "So, how was your week?"

"Fine." She'd learned her lesson from last time. Don't go into details, keep it short and simple. "Still setting in and getting to know my co-workers and whatnot." Then she paused. "You didn't ask me here to talk about my work, did you?" She was definitely getting a feeling that there was an agenda here.

"Honestly, no. We just wanted to formally welcome you to San Francisco."

"You did that when I visited last time and we had dinner together," Rachel pointed out.

Adrienne leaped on that opening. "Yes. I was telling Cecily that I was looking forward to getting to know you better now that you've moved here."

Oh. That was nice.

"By the way, thanks so much for the spa gift certificate. I'm looking forward to using it. I went to their website and can't wait to try out the treatments. I already know I want a ninety-minute massage."

"My pleasure," Rachel said, relieved her gift had passed muster.

"Are you still unpacking? We've been planning to drop by. Ma reminded me to get you a money tree as a housewarming gift." Cecily took another sip of her drink.

"I'm making progress."

The two of them exchanged another glance.

"You're the one who's dying of curiosity," Adrienne said.

"He's your friend," Cecily tossed back.

"Can someone just tell me what the hell's going on?" Rachel demanded. Of course, that was the moment their waiter decided to come drop off her beer and the food. She gave them a few minutes to load their plates then gave them a nudge. "Well?"

"All right all right," Adrienne grumbled. She looked Rachel dead in the eye. "We're just wondering about you and Luke."

"Please don't be upset," Cecily cut in. "We're just concerned and want to make sure you're okay."

Adrienne snorted. "Girl, please. We're being nosy as hell and you know it."

"Those two things aren't mutually exclusive." Cecily gave a sniff. Both of them then turned their eyes to Rachel.

She gulped hard. "What do you want to know?" she asked hesitantly.

"Well, I called him, and he explained why he was asking you for help. I was surprised, honestly." Adrienne took a big bite of her slider.

"Why?" Rachel asked, curiosity getting the better of her.

"I always pictured him as someone who'd work his way up to partner once he got his foot in the door. A straight clear path. If you asked me to pick which of my friends would be most likely to strike out on his own, he definitely wouldn't be on the list," Adrienne mused.

Oh.

"But when I asked him what you were asking in return, he clammed up."

Rachel relaxed a bit. If they were talking business, this was happily familiar terrain. "I have six months to prove myself with this promotion. So, I really want to nail it. I bought new furniture, got a new library card, and signed up for the rewards program at the new Asian supermarket and everything. I'm here to stay."

"You really don't want to go back to New York, do you?" Cecily asked, her tone amused. "But I respect the commitment."

She had no idea. "Guess I'm just following in your footsteps." Rachel shrugged.

"Always happy to be a trailblazer," Cecily murmured while Adrienne gave an undignified guffaw.

"So anyway, my boss tells me I'm going to be leading my team, and meeting with clients more. I'm used to working on my own, so I figured I needed help with developing my networking skills and learning how to deal better with people so I can impress clients and work with my team effectively."

Adrienne and Cecily exchanged a look.

"What?" Rachel asked, a bit defensively.

"Why didn't you ask one of us?" Cecily asked bluntly. "At the party you were asking me about networking skills, but I didn't realize you were really asking for help."

"Luke offered first. And I figured it was for the best." At the look on her friend's face, Rachel realized her words had come out wrong. Again. Damn it. "After thinking about it, I didn't want to mess up our friendship with business," she explained. Plus, Cecily had her own demanding work schedule and was planning a wedding on top of it. Now Rachel was glad she hadn't made the offer because she didn't want to impose. But Cecily's shoulders relaxed, and her expression softened slightly. Rachel figured she was out of the woods.

Then she turned to Adrienne. "And I didn't think we knew each other well enough to ask such a huge favor." She got a nod in response, which made her feel better.

"Well I get that. I know we didn't get much of a chance to talk at Adrienne's birthday, but I am glad you're here and I'm sure you're going to be great at this new job," Cecily said sincerely.

"And we're more than happy to help," Adrienne added. "Whatever you need."

"I think I'm good with Luke for now. But if it doesn't work out, I'll let you know." The way she saw it, it was best not to have too much competing and contradictory advice.

Better to pick one path and move forward.

"There is one other thing we were wondering," Cecily said.

"What?"

"How did you two meet? It's obvious you met before the winery."

Oh crap.

"There's not much to tell," Rachel said, trying to hedge.

"It's that juicy?" Cecily asked, leaning in.

"I don't know if that's the word I'd use," Rachel mumbled.

"Let us be the judge of that," Adrienne said.

"I should let you know I cornered him before you both left and I threatened him," Cecily said, then popped a bacon shrimp in her mouth.

"What? Why?"

"I just wanted to make sure he wasn't taking advantage of you or doing anything nefarious."

On the one hand, part of Rachel bristled at the idea of Cecily intervening. She was a grown-ass adult and could make her own decisions. But mostly, her heart warmed that Cecily cared enough to look out for her. Even if it was only to get out of trouble with her family. Plus her concern seemed genuine. As did the rampant curiosity.

"Well, thanks," she mumbled, for lack of anything better to say.

"So come on, spill. You can trust us," Cecily assured her.

"Totally. The Girl Code applies here. Anything you say goes into the vault."

Rachel was skeptical. "Why are you two so curious?"

"You're a friend," Cecily said, as if that explained everything.

"But are we friends who talk about our personal lives and spill our guts?"

"Only if you start talking," Adrienne said, tossing back her cabernet sauvignon.

That made sense, Rachel supposed. But it struck her as slightly unfair that she had to go first with the spilling of the guts.

"I'm going to need more booze for this," Rachel muttered.

Without a word, Cecily signaled their waiter and ordered another bottle of white wine.

"Whenever you're ready," she said, with a roll of her hands in the universal go ahead signal.

"We met last weekend. It was a long day of packing, and I needed a change of pace. So I ended up at this bar. He bought me a tequila and dared me to ride the mechanical bull."

"How'd you do?" Cecily asked, leaning in, her eyes fascinated.

"I barely lasted eight seconds," Rachel said wryly. "Even after all the physics, calculus, and geometry calculations I did. It wasn't fair. He's from Texas—I should have gotten some sort of handicap."

"There's a bar in the city with a mechanical bull?"

Adrienne asked, her nose wrinkling.

"Maybe we should all go. I wouldn't mind trying it out," Cecily mused.

"I wouldn't recommend it. Getting thrown off that thing hurts like hell. So anyway, I still blame the tequila for this even though I only had two shots. I asked if he wanted to have sex, he said yes, so we went to his apartment."

Rachel had to admit the sight of her two friends' jaw dropping was funny.

"You did what?"

"I hope Luke helped San Francisco make a good impression on you," Adrienne cracked.

"And you were saying you didn't want to mix business and personal," Cecily said, lips quirking.

"Anyway, I got up early, left before he woke up, and was certain I'd never see him again. Then I saw him at the winery, and you know the rest."

Cecily's brow creased in confusion. "But, wait. You said he propositioned you at Adrienne's birthday. How did he know you were looking for help?"

"Oh, before the bull, he asked what I was doing at the bar, so I explained I had just moved there for my job, and that I was nervous about it."

"You didn't say anything to us about that." Cecily frowned.

"Sometimes it's easier to dump on a stranger. It's not like I thought I'd ever see him again," Rachel said.

"Girl has a point," Adrienne acknowledged. Cecily gave a bad-tempered shrug.

"I do feel bad about one thing, though."

"What? Was the sex bad?"

"No comment."

"Withholding the juicy stuff," Cecily muttered, shaking her head.

"So what did you feel bad about?"

"Well, I didn't want to face him the next morning so like I said I snuck out. But that meant I left his front door unlocked for I don't know how long. Part of me was worried he'd get robbed, or someone would sneak in and kill him. Happily, neither happened. So win-win."

Adrienne and Cecily paused for a moment, then burst out laughing, making her feel like an idiot.

"You are the best, Rachel," Cecily said through the peals of laughter.

"I love it," Adrienne wheezed, trying to catch her breath.

Maybe she wasn't an idiot after all.

"So that's it. Can we move on now?"

"I'd love to say no and continue this cross-examination, but my fiancé is insisting on my return. Jeffrey is waiting for me at home. A foot rub, slice of strawberry cheesecake, and my favorite pajamas are calling."

"You just like saying fiancé," Adrienne accused.

"Guilty," Cecily responded with a cheeky grin.

"But I'm the only one who spilled my guts," Rachel complained. It wasn't fair.

"We promise to make it up to you," Adrienne said with a reassuring pat on her shoulders. "Next time we can compare notes on one-night stands or something."

"Besides, we definitely want you to keep us posted on what happens with you and Luke," Cecily said as she grabbed her wallet to pay the bill. She raised a warning brow at Rachel. "Don't even think about fighting me. My treat; I insist."

It was at that moment that Rachel knew she was a bad Asian because she wasn't even tempted to make a move to steal the check.

"We want updates for sure," Adrienne agreed. "Besides, you're still new here, and it can be hard to meet new people and get situated. We're here for you."

"Absolutely," Cecily said, signing the credit card slip.

She hadn't scared them off? They actually intended to invite her out again? Would wonders never cease.

"All right, I gotta head out. CeeCee gets to go home and be pampered by her man but I got a stack of depositions calling my name." Adrienne sighed as she stood up and grabbed her purse.

"Don't even. That's going to be me tomorrow," Cecily said with a roll of her eyes. Then she turned to Rachel. "Text me when you get home okay?"

"Will do. Text me too. You too, Adrienne. We all need to make sure we didn't get killed on our way home." It was a basic safety rule after all.

"Absolutely," Adrienne said, her lips twitching. As the three of them made their way out of the bar and went their separate ways, Rachel couldn't help but marvel at how well the evening had gone, all in all. She'd put her foot in her mouth more than once, but it seemed no harm done. It gave her more confidence in her ability to tackle the Mt. Everest in front of her as far as her new job was concerned. She wasn't completely hopeless after all. Maybe. Possibly.

Chapter Eight

THE NEXT DAY, Rachel returned to the scene of the crime. Figuratively speaking that is. Despite earlier plans to meet in a public place, they had decided they needed privacy for this meeting, given the sensitivity of the topics they were discussing. Luke's doorman had buzzed her in, so now she was at his front door. She swallowed hard and gave a hesitant knock. Her huge tote bag was loaded down and digging into her shoulders, and she was awkwardly trying to readjust the straps when he opened the door.

She suppressed a sigh at the sight of him in a casual polo shirt unbuttoned to show off some nicely sculpted chest and khaki shorts that clung to a great pair of legs. Rachel took a moment to enjoy the view before reminding herself to snap out of it. Even in semi-casual wear the man was still a thousand times prettier than her and more attractive and appealing than he had any right to be. And she couldn't even be mad about it. What was the point of being angry about a simple fact of life?

"Come on in," he said as he ushered her inside. Now in the light of day and not panicked, Rachel took a moment to take in her surroundings. The apartment was the epitome of a bachelor pad, though not obnoxiously so. There was the requisite leather couch and big TV, the furnishings were sparse, but it didn't scream college frat bro. Just a man who had a busy career and didn't tend to think about decorating and turning a house into a home.

She turned around to thank him for inviting her over when she saw him make a point of locking the door.

"I already said I was sorry," she muttered, her cheeks reddening a bit.

"Hey, I was just kidding," he assured her with a smile. "Can I get you something to drink? Water? I have beer in the fridge."

Best to avoid alcohol when she was around him. "Just water would be fine."

"Coming right up. Go make yourself comfortable," he said, gesturing to the couch.

Rachel walked over to the massive black couch and busied herself for a few moments emptying the contents of her tote bag and setting up her laptop.

"Wow," Luke said in an impressed voice as he walked over and set down two glasses of water. Rachel's brow furrowed as she saw him carefully put them on top of coasters.

Noticing her surprise, he said drily, "I was raised by a Southern mother. Part of my training."

Oh.

"So do you want to get started first?" he suggested as he sat down beside her.

Rachel cleared her throat and opened her laptop. "You

didn't go into details about what you were looking for, so I just did some basic research and projections," she explained, pushing up her glasses. It wasn't precisely the sort of work she did every day, but she'd made do. She tilted her head and looked at him quizzically. "What sort of law do you do, anyway?"

"Employment discrimination defense."

"So what does that mean? You defend employers when someone claims they didn't get a promotion because they're a woman, or gets fired because they complained their boss came on to them?"

"It's a bit more complicated than that, but basically, yes. I've never really heard my job boiled down that succinctly," Luke remarked, lips twitching.

"Why employment discrimination?"

"Why not?"

"That's not an answer." She frowned. "Cecily does business and commercial law. Adrienne does anti-trust. What interested you in this field?"

"I'm good at it." He shrugged. Was it really that simple?

"That's it? You're good at it? Do you even like the work? Or your clients? I mean what made you pick employment law over, I don't know, being a criminal defense lawyer?"

"It's hard to develop any feelings for a company so no I don't get attached to my clients," he joked. "And I like the work just fine and my co-workers are fine. It pays the bills. I don't need it to be any more than that." His answer took her aback. Rachel loved her job, and it was fascinating to her that someone wouldn't have the same amount of passion and dedication to their work and just saw it as a paycheck, a means to an end.

"Then why are you wanting to open your own firm? Why not stay where you are?"

He gave a thoughtful pause. "You know, you're right. Guess I'm not as happy as I thought I was with where I am." He took a deep breath. "I think I like the idea of being on my own because I get to call the shots, set my own hours, take on the clients I want."

Rachel gave a nod of understanding. "So you'd like more autonomy. I get that."

"I didn't even realize that until you asked me that question," Luke admitted with a blink. "So thank you."

Unsure of how to respond to that, Rachel kept going. "I did some analysis of the legal market here in San Francisco, you know, the rates firms are hiring, mergers, closures, things like that. Now that I know what area of law you practice, I can do more specific data gathering. I also did a work-up for prices for renting office space. Coming from New York I thought I was prepared but it still gave me sticker shock," she admitted.

"Real estate in the Bay area is insane," he agreed. Then he picked up the file she'd set up and began thumbing through it. "This is impressive," he said, admiration coloring his tone.

"It's what I do, sorta," Rachel said with a simple shrug.

"Don't be so modest. This is fantastic."

She tried not to blush. "I still don't know the city well but if you can tell me what neighborhoods or areas you're looking at renting office space from, I can run some specific numbers for that too. Do you want to stay in the Financial District?" she asked.

"I'm not sure," he admitted.

"Have you looked into zoning, what licenses or permits you'll need? We're going to need to add that into the cost of the potential investment too. Not to mention setting up things so you can pay and file taxes."

The guilty look on his face said it all.

Rachel frowned. "How did you not think about zoning and licenses and permits?"

"I've never done this before," he pointed out. "I just assumed you needed to fill out a few forms and you'd be set. I didn't realize it would be such an elaborate undertaking."

"Then it's a good thing you have me," she said before she realized it.

He looked deep in her eyes. "A very good thing," he agreed. Butterflies started fluttering in her stomach that she had to ruthlessly quash.

"Maybe we should meet again next week?" she suggested. "Why don't you start looking into what permits and things you'll need from the city, and I'll print out the IRS documents and state tax stuff too." Rachel rolled her eyes at the look on Luke's face when she brought up taxes. "I know, taxes are evil, but they're a necessary evil. We'd have no roads or schools or fire departments without them."

"So they say," he mumbled, but nodded his assent.

"I think that's all I have for now. Your turn." She had to admit her curiosity was piqued. What coaching was he about to provide?

He gave her a small crooked smile. "I thought we'd start off with something simple. But first let me ask you, how many people do you have working under you on your team?"

Rachel's brows furrowed in confusion. "Five. Why?"

"I have a homework assignment for you," he explained. "By the time we meet next week, I want you to tell me something new you've learned about each member of your team."

With a bit of relief, she let out her breath. "Oh, that's easy. I can look up their profiles on the company website."

"No, no, no," he said with a shake of his head. "I don't want anything that you can just Google. Something personal, like their favorite color, where they met their spouse, their favorite band, where they grew up. I want you to talk to them. And the fact has to be something interesting, something personal that you got them to tell you about themselves."

Now she was confused. "How is this supposed to help me?"

"It'll help you establish a rapport with them, and to get to know them as people, and for them to get to know you. Doing this will let them know you are interested and care about them. They're not just cogs in the company machine to you. What better way to build morale and trust?"

"That does make a lot of sense," Rachel admitted reluctantly. "But do I really have to talk to them and make conversation? Can't I just send them an online survey?" At his look she crossed her arms. "Fine."

"This is for your own good," he said solemnly.

"Now you sound like my mother forcing me to do math and language arts workbooks during summer vacation when I was a kid," she complained.

"There's a method to my madness, I promise."

If he said so. "How exactly am I supposed to do this? I mean I can't just go up to them Monday morning and be like 'Hey, Brian, how was your weekend? You mind telling me what your favorite color is?'"

"We should try to go for a little more subtlety than that," he said, amused. "But in that example, listen to Brian's response. If he tells you he went out to play golf with his college buddies, or went over to Oakland to celebrate his grandmother's eightieth birthday, there you go. You just got your interesting personal fact."

Letting the other person speak first and take your cue from them. Interesting. Rachel made a mental note of it because damn it, that really was a good tip. "So then what? Won't he think it's weird that I'm asking?"

"You can follow up. Say something like 'Your grandmother's birthday? That's great. My grandmother just turned seventy-five.'"

Rachel frowned again. "But both of my grandmothers are dead. Wouldn't that be a downer on the whole conversation if I tell him that?" Then she paused. "But I went to

Adrienne's birthday party last week. Maybe I can say I went to a friend's birthday party. That'd be fun, not depressing."

"There you go." Luke beamed at her like she was a star pupil and part of Rachel felt as if she'd actually gotten a gold star sticker.

"Think of it as an opportunity to play Sherlock Holmes," he suggested. "Look around, put your powers of observation and deduction to work. If someone always has fresh flowers at their desk, they're probably into gardening. If one of your co-workers always wears a blue tie, that's probably their favorite color. People also like putting pictures of their families on their desk—that's always a goldmine. Though just comment 'Nice picture' to start off with. Don't want to make any assumptions."

When put that way it didn't seem that baffling or difficult at all. If someone had explained it to her like that and had given her concrete examples, she wouldn't dread small talk as much as she did.

"Try it on me," Rachel said, eager for a demonstration. "Ask me questions and get me to tell you something about myself."

"I don't have to, I already know something," Luke replied, his brow raised.

"Oh yeah? What?"

"You like Alanis Morissette."

Her jaw dropped. "How the hell do you know that? Can you read minds?"

"You were humming 'Hand In My Pocket' under your breath while you were setting up. Like I said, it's all about observation. And you're a true fan because most people's go-to is 'Ironic.'" He said it matter-of-factly as if it were obvious.

"She was the first concert I ever went to. I was sixteen," she murmured.

"So you're an indie rock girl. Let me guess, Fiona Apple, Ani DiFranco, The Cranberries?"

"Love all of them." It was truly spooky the way he did that.

He just gave her a pat on the shoulder. "Don't worry, you'll get the hang of it soon enough."

Rachel appreciated his faith in her, but she was definitely going to have to work up those observation muscles to even get anywhere near his league.

"I really did pick the right coach for this," she admitted. "Thank you." His technique may be unconventional, but she could see the merit in it. Like he said, she felt more seen and understood when he guessed her favorite music artists.

Luke beamed. "Any time. And trust me, you'll be taking your team out for happy hour and hosting gatherings at your place for them in no time." The horror she felt at the prospect must have been telegraphed on her face because he then hastened to assure her, "We'll work our way up to that. Baby steps."

Thank God. Because honestly the idea of her hosting a gathering was enough to give her hives. "You have any other assignments for me?"

"No, that's it." Luke then tilted his head and studied

her. “I bet you haven’t seen much of the city yet have you?”

“Been too busy with work,” she admitted. “But it’s fine. I saw the major tourist hot spots when I visited here months ago.”

He shook his head in disappointment. “Nope, not going to cut it. I know what your next assignment is. Leave your stuff here and follow me. We’re heading out.”

“Where?” she demanded as he pulled her up from the couch.

“You’ll see.”

What the hell did he have in store for her now?

Chapter Nine

MONDAY

Rachel: *You were wrong.*

Luke: **raises brow* Excuse me?*

Rachel: *Brian doesn't play golf. He plays basketball on the weekends with his college buddies.*

Luke: *1) It was purely a hypothetical I was using as an example so I wasn't wrong. But 2) Congrats! See, I told you it wasn't going to be as hard and painful as you thought.*

Rachel: *I just did what you said. I asked him how his weekend went, and he told me he almost got a black eye because one of his friends elbowed him.*

Luke: **nods in approval of his star pupil* But ouch. I once had to show up in court with a black eye. Wasn't fun. The judge, the client, and the partners weren't happy with me at all.*

Rachel: *Were you playing basketball too?*

Luke: *My nieces were fighting, one of them threw a Barbie doll at the other. I was unfortunate collateral damage.*

Rachel: *That sounds painful.*

Luke: *It was.*

Rachel: *Then I did what you said and took his lead for the conversation. I told Brian I played poker, not basket-*

ball. He says he's not a fan because he has two kids to put through college. So now I also know he has two kids. Do I get bonus points for that?

Luke: *No.*

Rachel: *But now I also know you have two nieces and once got a black eye too. Come on, that has to count!*

Luke: *Look at you being an overachiever.*

Rachel: *Why settle for an A when you can get an A+?*

Luke:

Rachel: *Why did you send me that emoji?*

Luke: *Do you not remember the last time you said that to me?*

Rachel: *Shit. Get your mind out of the gutter!*

Luke: *You took it there first.*

Rachel: *But I didn't mean to!*

Luke: *As much as it pains me to agree, you're right. We need to keep this professional.*

Rachel: *All clothes are staying ON.*

Luke: *No need to remind me. Now, go talk to your next co-worker.*

TUESDAY

Rachel: *Contessina's family was originally from Florence.*

Luke: *That's a pretty name.*

Rachel: *I was in the break room and saw her using one of those language apps. She's learning Italian because she's going to visit Tuscany next summer. She wants to be fluent.*

Luke: *Good for her. You're doing great so far!*

Rachel: *She said her mother is a genealogy fan and did tons of research so that's how she knows what area of Italy her family's from.*

Luke: *Roots are important. Now I'm wondering if I'm distantly related to the Canadian Prime Minister. That'd be kinda awesome actually.*

Rachel: *I have no idea where my family is from. I mean Taiwan, obviously. But I don't know if our roots go back to a certain area in Taiwan or province in mainland China, or if we have any aboriginal ancestry or what. I mean, the Portuguese and Dutch were in Taiwan for a while too. So I may be part European?*

Luke: *If you are a mix of all those things, you're all American. Very cool.*

Rachel: *But the way the European ancestry came into my family tree may not be as cool.*

Luke: *Colonialism and imperialism suck.*

Rachel: *Indeed.*

WEDNESDAY

Luke: *Hey, where's my daily update?*

Rachel: *Sorry. Was swamped at work today. Phone never stopped ringing and it was one meeting after another.*

Luke: *No worries.*

Luke: *So what did you find out today?*

Rachel: *That Randall is a cheating bastard.*

Luke: *WHAT??!!*

Rachel: *I'm pretty sure he's having an affair. This counts right?*

Luke: *Sure, sure. But why do you think he's stepping out on his significant other?*

Rachel: *Because I overheard him talking to someone named Mandy, saying he couldn't wait to see her tonight, and to put on the negligee he likes.*

Luke: *Maybe Mandy's his wife?*

Rachel: *Nope. When we met, I specifically remember him saying he'd have no problem remembering my name because his wife's name is Rachel too.*

Luke: *Well well well. Sounds like Randall's been a naughty boy.*

Rachel: *On behalf of all Rachels everywhere, I'm disgusted and horrified.*

Luke: *Understandably so.*

Rachel: *But the way I see it, it's none of my business. So…*

Luke: *Agreed. Unless his wife and Mandy come to the office and confront him, this has nothing to do with you.*

Rachel: *I'm never going to look at him the same way again.*

Luke: *It occurs to me that today's bit of personal info shouldn't count because you eavesdropped instead of engaging in conversation with him. But I'll allow it.*

Rachel: *I mean, I could try to ask him what his favorite color is. Maybe that's the color of Mandy's negligee.*

Luke: *Rachel.*

Rachel: *What??*

THURSDAY

Rachel: *I have good news and bad news.*

Luke: *Let's start with the good news.*

Rachel: *Really? I would think it'd be better to get the bad news first, get it over with.*

Luke: *Don't decision-shame me. I get to choose how I digest my news.*

Rachel: *What? Decision-shaming? No way that's a thing.*

Luke: *MOVING. ON. What's the good news?*

Rachel: *I had a nice convo with my boss this morning. We got into the office around the same time. Amanda was asking me how I was settling in. It was nice of her.*

Luke: *Nods.*

Rachel: *Anyway, she's a major foodie. She gave me some great restaurant recommendations. And told me she's been doing research. Her wife Tam's from Thailand and she's been secretly learning how to make Tam's favorite dishes from her mother-in-law. Their anniversary is coming up so it's a big surprise.*

Luke: *And they say love isn't real.*

Rachel: *It's quite sweet. Unlike that cheating bastard Randall.*

Luke: *I thought we were going to forget about him.*

Rachel: *UGH. Sorry you're right.*

Luke: *So what's the bad news?*

Rachel: *I had to stop by Jonathan's desk to talk to him about something. He had Red Hot Chili Peppers playing on Spotify. I asked if that was his favorite band. He said yes. Then I told him I like Alanis. Then he gave me this look and said, "If you ever want recommendations for music that's actually good, let me know." So that was a bust.*

Luke: *It wasn't a bust. He was being rude. That's totally on him.*

Rachel: *I guess.*

Luke: *No guess. You did good today.*

Rachel: *Sigh. Well I got one more day to go.*

Luke: *I have faith in you. Go get 'em, tiger.*

Rachel: *You know I've never understood that phrase. Why compare someone to a tiger? Or if they're talking about actual tigers, going after one sounds scary. And very unwise.*

Luke: *It's supposed to be encouragement and motivation.*

Rachel: *Encouraging someone to get mauled?*

Luke: *Tigers have also been traditionally been seen as a sign of virility and sexual prowess.*

Rachel: *I thought we agreed to stop talking about sex.*

Luke: *Merely providing information.*

FRIDAY

Rachel: *Jonathan dropped by my office and brought me a cherry Danish this morning. He apologized for what he said yesterday. Apparently he got off a stressful phone call with people yelling at him.*

Luke: *Well good for him. Was the Danish good?*

Rachel: *It was a Starbucks Danish.*

Luke: *Enough said.*

Rachel: *It was the thought that counts. Anyway, Annika also stopped by my office. She just adopted a new puppy that is currently destroying her house. The puppy's cute though. I got to see pictures.*

Luke: *What kind of puppy??*

Rachel: *Annika said it was a rescue so she's not sure.*

Luke: *#adoptnotshop*

Rachel: *She also said she was looking for one who'd be chill at home alone. Guess there was a miscommunication.*

Luke: *Eh, it's a puppy thing. I grew up with dogs.*

Rachel: *I remember my sister and I wanted a pet when we were little. But my parents said no, even after we swore we'd walk it and take care of it. They didn't believe us. So no pets for me.*

Luke: *What a poor deprived childhood you led.*

Rachel: *At least I never came home to find dog poop in my shoes.*

Luke: *Love how you always look on the bright side of life. But congratulations on completely crushing this homework assignment. You did good.*

Rachel: *Thank you.*

Luke: *Let's reconvene next Saturday. I found a possible rental space. Wanna meet me there and take a look with me?*

Rachel: *Okay.*

AS SHE WAS making her way home, Rachel's phone buzzed. She pulled it out of her bag, then suppressed a groan. She'd had a long day and all she wanted was to go home, eat some delicious Thai takeout, and cue up the latest episode of the *Murder in the City* podcast. But instead she now had to deal with Claudia and whatever the wedding crisis du jour was.

"Yes?" she asked. She crossed her fingers in vain that this conversation would be short. It had been a week since she'd completed Luke's homework assignment and she'd prefer to not talk to people unless she absolutely had to.

"Your bridesmaid dress came in," Claudia said without preamble. "Ma wants me to ship it to you so you can go get alterations done. I'll send you the tracking info once I send it off. And send me photos when you're done. Make sure you find good lighting and try to put some makeup on because I want to get the full effect before I approve everything."

"Anything else?"

"I'm sending it priority so you should get it by Friday. Take it to the seamstress this weekend. I found a couple. I'll text you the list of acceptable places." Because sure, why not? It wasn't as if she had a pile of work she'd hoped to catch up on that weekend and had nothing better to do than run wedding errands for her sister. Rachel took a deep breath and reminded herself that there was a light at the end of the tunnel. Claudia's bridezilla act would come to an end eventually. Hopefully.

"Anything else?" she asked again. Surely her sister wasn't calling just to talk about the wedding. Claudia was also going to ask how she was doing, how she was liking San Francisco, right?

"No, that's it. I'll send you the details for the shower and bachelorette when I have them. But you probably won't have to worry about it. Not your thing." Claudia's voice sounded distracted, as if she was just checking off her list, half-listening. Then she spoke again. "You are coming to the wedding, right? Your company won't give you any problems with taking the days off?"

"It's already been approved," Rachel said in a flat voice, trying to hide the hurt. Her own family couldn't even be bothered to check in and ask how she was doing. And even if Claudia was right, that the shower and bachelorette wasn't her cup of tea, she was still her sister for God's sake. She would have sucked it up and put in the command performance to celebrate her sister. But no worries, her presence wasn't expected or required. Wow.

"Are you doing okay?" Claudia asked. At that, Rachel's heart lifted a little. "I told Ma I was calling you today and she told me to tell you to make sure you're eating properly. And getting fresh air and exercise instead of being cooped up at work and your apartment 24/7."

"I'm fine, thanks." Beginning to feel a little better, Rachel walked up the block to get to the entrance of her apartment building. "I went to the museum two weeks ago as a matter of fact. A friend suggested the outing." That was what Luke had wanted to do after their first meeting and he'd given her her first homework assignment. They'd spent the rest of the afternoon at the San Francisco Museum of Modern Art. She still couldn't claim to understand Pollock (if you asked her a toddler throwing paint cans could do the same thing) but she appreciated Luke helping her see more of the city and broadening her horizons. And, as he pointed out, it gave her something to talk about Monday morning in the break room.

"It was nice of Cecily to invite you on an outing," Claudia replied.

"I didn't go with Cecily," Rachel said with a frown.

"Oh it's good you're meeting new people. Glad you're getting out there more. But be careful."

"I will, thanks."

"I mean, the alterations could be expensive, so make sure you don't gain or lose too much weight so the dress will fit. And I want all of my bridesmaids to have a nice tan so try to get some color."

Rachel was beginning to seriously wonder if her sister had been taken over by a body snatcher. Did nothing exist in the world besides the wedding?

"Thanks for your concern," she clipped out.

"Sure. You're my sister after all," Claudia said, oblivious to the sarcasm. "Anyway, who is this friend? Maybe she can introduce you to someone. There may still be time to shuffle things around if you magically score that plus-one."

Okay, enough was enough. "I'll have to ask Luke if he has any friends I can hook up with. I gotta go, bye."

It was with no small amount of satisfaction that Rachel ended the call while hearing her sister squawk: "Luke? Who the hell is Luke?"

Chapter Ten

IT WAS SATURDAY night and his monthly poker game. It was a ritual he'd established with some of his law school friends, and it was sacred. No outsiders were allowed. But for Rachel, an exception had been made. Though not before he had to suffer through the requisite teasing and taunts about making him look bad in front of his new girlfriend by winning all his money. Despite his repeated insistence that Rachel was just a friend. A friend he'd seen naked and wouldn't mind seeing naked again, but that was neither here nor there. It was a few days after the office visit that had unfortunately gone awry. Since then, Rachel had made great progress with her team, and he was looking at better office options in the Financial District. Things were looking good.

So the six of them were sitting around his kitchen table, with guac and chips, wings, pretzels, and pizza on the island. Everyone had a bottle of beer next to them, and their game faces on.

Terry Quinn was dealer tonight and laid down the rules "No-limit Texas Hold 'Em, blinds are fifty for the small, a hundred for the big. Let's do this." He shuffled and dealt out the cards to everyone.

Luke shot a glance at Rachel. Who merely blinked and gave nothing away. When it was her turn, she simply said, "Fold." Which she did for the next three hands.

He couldn't help rolling his eyes a bit. What was the point in playing it safe? But then the next round, she raised a hundred.

Bea immediately folded. Roger Green took a puff of his cigar, then looked at Rachel. With a heavy sigh, he threw down his cards too.

Soon, it was just down to her and Aimee Garcia. Aimee checked. Rachel raised again. The problem was the five of them had spent years playing together, could try to figure out each other's bluffs and tells. Rachel was new, and no one knew her strategy or tells. Or if she even had any.

With regret, Aimee also folded. "This round goes to the newbie."

Rachel raked in her winnings with barely a smile.

Dying of curiosity, Luke had to ask, "So what did you have? Pocket aces?"

"A three and nine off suit." The rest of the table stared in shock. It was a garbage hand and she hadn't even been able to make a pair.

"You bluffed me?" Aimee croaked.

"It is considered a legitimate strategy, isn't it?"

Roger shook his head. "Damn she's good." The rest of the table murmured in agreement.

"It's always best to sit back the first few rounds to observe your opponents. And plus, this early in the game, stealing the blinds can be quite useful. Those fifties and hundreds start to add up." She said it with a shrug, which just added insult to injury.

"I told you it was a mistake to let other people play," Bea grumbled.

Luke just shook his head. When would he learn to stop underestimating her? And for the next two hours, Rachel systematically cleaned house.

The final hand of the night was a heads-up between him and Rachel. She had a healthy stack of chips in front of her, while he was down to his last hundred.

He had a pair of aces and there were a pair of kings on the table. He had this in the bag.

Rachel studied her cards, pushed up her glasses, and pushed some chips into the middle of the table. "I'm putting you all in." The rest of the table oohed.

He looked at his cards again, and what was left on the table. Besides the two kings, there was a seven of hearts dealt in the flop, and a four of spades, and a queen of clubs for the turn and the river. Rachel probably had a queen, and thought she had the better hand.

Or she was bluffing again. Either way, he was staying in.

"Call," he said confidently, putting the rest of his stack into the pile.

"All right, let's see what you got. Turn over your hands," Terry announced.

With a triumphant smile, Luke turned over his two aces. "Looks like I'm about to double up," he gloated. The rest of the table laughed.

Without a word, Rachel turned over her cards. "Not so fast there." She had a four of diamonds and the four of clubs.

"Hate to break it to you, sweetie, but aces beat fours. Better luck next time." He couldn't help the glee in his voice.

"Uh, bro?" Bea gave a polite cough. The rest of the table went silent.

Horror dawned as he looked at the five cards on the table again. The four of spades jumped out at him like an evil taunt.

"Shit. You got a full house."

"I'm afraid so. Better luck next time." When he recovered, he'd make her pay for throwing his words back in his face. For now, he was still trying to process what happened. He'd never been so thoroughly spanked in a game of poker in his life.

Poker night concluded, the group got ready to leave. Terry took an extra slice of pizza to go, and Aimee grabbed the rest of the beer. There was the usual requisite ball busting on the way out. But they also made certain to include Rachel.

Roger pointed at Rachel and said in a firm voice, "You're not allowed to play anymore." But there was a teasing glint in his eye. "Listen, I don't like losing my shirt, but props to anyone who can take down Trudeau the way you did tonight." He stuck out his hand, and Rachel shook it with a shy smile.

"I agree," Bea said.

The rest of them also said their farewells, leaving him and Rachel, who had volunteered to stay behind and help him clean up. Really, it was the least she could do. They made short work of the leftovers and Luke was putting the food away while Rachel wiped down the table and counter.

"You lied to me," he accused. He sat back down at the kitchen table and crossed his arms.

She turned to him in surprise and put down the microfiber cleaning cloth. "What are you talking about? I never lied to you. I'm genetically incapable of lying. Ask anyone."

"You should've told me you were a shark."

"I'm not a shark." Rachel frowned. "I said I liked to play; you're the one who assumed I wasn't good and couldn't keep up with you and your friends. That's on you." She turned to the counter again and went back to work. The vague dismissal irked him for some reason he couldn't explain.

"You're practically a professional!"

"That's exaggerating. But it is true my family has banned me from playing poker and mahjong. Decided it was unfair."

"And the reason you withheld this information from me?"

Finished with the counters, Rachel took the towel back to the sink, rinsed it, put it on the edge of the sink, and washed her hands before joining him at the kitchen table.

"I'm going to need to spend a ridiculous amount of money on my sister's wedding, so my bank account's taken a bit of a hit. Why give up a strategic advantage?" She blinked, the total picture of innocence.

"How much money could you possibly need to pay for things for your sister's wedding?" Recognizing a loaded question when he heard one, Luke shook his head and held up a hand. "Forget I asked."

Rachel slid him a look. "That reminds me."

"Yes?"

"So I told her how you and I went to the art museum together a while back. She was impressed that I managed to make a friend so quickly and suggested that maybe you can help set me up with someone who could be my date for the wedding. What do you think?"

She looked at his open-mouthed expression and cringed slightly. "Sorry, that was inappropriate, wasn't it? Forget I asked, okay?"

"No, I was just surprised, that's all." For reasons he couldn't articulate, the idea of combing through his mental Rolodex to find a date for Rachel didn't sit well with him. In fact, it made his stomach churn and his jaw clench.

"Hopefully, the money you made tonight will help pay off the dress, shoes and whatever else you need," Luke offered, after he counted to ten to calm himself down.

Rachel shrugged. "I've been banned from the game, so worst-case scenario I find another solution if I need money. Maybe take a quick trip to Vegas or something." At his look, she shrugged again. "What? It's not that hard. You just have to know some basic probabilities and statistics. Easy math."

"The reason I went into law is so I wouldn't have to

deal with numbers," he mused.

"But don't you deal with settlements for your clients? Isn't that dealing with numbers, and figuring out how much to pay?"

"Fair enough," he conceded. "Anyway, I hope you had fun tonight."

"I won six hundred dollars—of course I did." She frowned at his snort. "What?"

"Well I can tell you my friends loved seeing you beat me."

Rachel tilted her head. "I've been meaning to ask. How do you know all those people? Are they co-workers?"

"Well Bea is, but we actually all went to law school together. We formed a study group our 1L year and stayed in touch. Impressive considering it's been ten years. And the fact we're all in the same place."

"How did you end up working in California anyway? Why didn't you want to go to school in Texas?"

"I wanted a change of scenery and thought California might be fun and interesting. Luckily, Stanford accepted me, and I got a full ride. And Roger's uncle is a partner in one of the firms here, and he helped get me an interview when I graduated, and well, I've been here ever since."

"Just like that?"

"What do you mean?"

"You decide to go to law school in California on a whim, get accepted to a top law school, and your friend helps get you a job after graduation. Things just seem to work out for you, huh? Like when your friend helped you find that rental space."

Luke frowned at the memory. He had asked his relator friend to find him a possible office space, and he'd been so excited. It was everything he'd been looking for. Or so he'd thought. When Rachel showed up to take a peek, she'd pointed out things he'd neglected to consider—like accessibility, proximity to public transportation and parking, maintenance and utilities. In the end, they both agreed to keep searching, though it had been a bit lowering for him to realize he'd had all those blind spots.

But things seemed to just work out for him? What was she implying? "Well not exactly. I'm still looking for a possible space, and I had to work to get and maintain the grades to get through school and get hired. And as for the job, it wasn't a big deal. Roger wanted to do patent law, and our firm doesn't do IP, so in a way I was doing him a favor, helping him get his uncle off his back."

"Don't be so defensive. I'm not saying you didn't deserve any of it. It's just interesting how things seem to work out for you and the stars align. Not everyone's that lucky. I certainly didn't have a friend of a friend to get me in the door at my firm." She shrugged.

"You act like I grew up with a silver spoon in my mouth," he protested. "I'm not some Boston Brahmin family who came over on the *Mayflower* and has a shit ton of money."

"Of course not. You're from Texas, not Boston. But that's not the point. Stop acting like I'm accusing you of something. All I'm saying is, you're a straight white guy.

Things tend to work out for straight white men. Statistics don't lie."

"I'll have you know I graduated in the top ten percent of my class at Stanford, and won moot court awards."

"Well, good for you. Congratulations."

"I take on any number of pro-bono cases."

"Aren't you legally required to do that?"

"And I mentor three to five first-year associates every year at the firm. I give back."

"This isn't a job interview. You don't have to rattle off your résumé." Puzzled, Rachel drummed her fingers on the table, which only served to irritate him further.

"I just don't want you thinking I'm some sort of spoiled douchebag."

"If I thought you were a spoiled douchebag I wouldn't be here."

"And like I said, I applied and got accepted like everyone else. No special treatment—I didn't have a dad who called up the admissions office and got me in."

Rachel frowned. "I really don't understand what this is about."

"Despite what you think, I am not some over privileged white guy. I worked hard to get where I am. I don't like the implication otherwise."

"So you want me to know you're a good guy, who earned his place and deserves to be where he is? That you aren't some spoiled, entitled schmuck?" Rachel said slowly.

Luke breathed out a sigh of relief. Finally, she was getting it. "Exactly."

Rachel took a beat, then gave him one of those patented stares that made him feel like a pinned moth.

"I never said anything about you being a douchebag or that you didn't deserve to be where you're at. All I was saying is that not everyone is as lucky as you to have been born with a Willy Wonka Golden Ticket and catch all the breaks in life. Who are you trying to convince? You or me?" With that, she got up and collected her things and made her way to the door. Her hand paused on the knob and she turned back to look at him. The expression on her face was a combination of sadness and confusion. And a bit of irritation. Vintage Rachel.

"Thanks for a fun night. I'm sorry if I said anything to spoil things. I didn't realize this was such a sore point. I won't make that mistake again." Without another word, she left and the door closed softly behind her.

At those words Luke blew out a breath and grabbed another beer from the fridge. God knew he needed one.

How had the evening gone off the rails like that? It had been all fun and games, literally. Then an innocent comment from Rachel sent him into a tailspin and the conversation devolved into him being an insecure idiot.

And there was the matter of Rachel's final words. For someone who claimed to be better with numbers than words, she sure knew how to pack a verbal punch.

God damn.

"YES, MA. I already made the plane reservations to fly back for the wedding. No I didn't buy travel insurance—it's a waste of money. It was only four hundred dollars round trip. I have a ninety-minute layover in O'Hare. Yes I looked into direct flights—none were available. Unless you think I should pay an extra hundred fifty for it. Yes I get it's a risk but with the move and everything else Claudia is making me buy for the wedding, I'm looking to save and cut corners where I can. No, I am not blaming Claudia. Yes it was my decision to move to California so it's my fault. It's always my fault. No, I don't need someone to pick me up from LaGuardia." Rachel rolled her eyes and gave thanks that her mother couldn't see her. "No, I'm not rolling my eyes. No I'm not copping an attitude. Dui bu qi."

She listened to her mother ramble on for another ten minutes, interjecting with a random hao and dui and okay and yes. Part of her started to zone out. It was the same thing again, nothing ever changed. Rose would always find something to nitpick and nag about.

"Sorry, Ma, but I'm going to need to let you go. I have work to do. No, I am not working the whole weekend. Yes I am going outside and getting fresh air. No, I am not turning into an antisocial hermit. Claudia's there? Tell her I said hi. No, I don't have time to talk to her—she can email me if it's urgent."

There was a pause as Rose passed over the phone. Damn it.

"Hi, Claudia. Yes, I am picking up the dress from the

seamstress next week. Yes, I will send pictures. Yes."

Then as if her day wasn't already going to hell in a handbasket, she heard a knock on her door. Looking through the peephole she scowled. A scowl that only deepened when she saw who was on the other side.

A scowl that turned into confusion when she saw the bouquet of flowers in his hands.

"What are you doing here?" she asked, brows furrowed.

"I come with a peace offering." He presented the flowers to her with a flourish. It was a lovely mix of purple, blue, and white lilies and hydrangeas. Her heart tried not to skip a beat at the gesture and the expression on his face with his trademark charming grin. Rachel couldn't remember the last time a non-family member gave her flowers. And she couldn't deny how happy she was to see him. But first things first. Rachel held up her hand and turned her attention back to the phone. She switched to Mandarin in order to ensure some privacy and finish the call as soon as possible.

"No, I wasn't talking to you. Someone just came in the door. Yes, I checked who it was. No, it isn't a stranger. For God's sake, Claudia, do I look like the sort of person who'd open my door to someone I don't know? Yes I know people here in San Francisco now. Why do you sound so surprised? No, he's not a co-worker. What the hell kind of cliché do you think I am?" she demanded in a huff. She then saw the look on Luke's face and flushed. So much for privacy.

"I already told Ma I made the plane reservations. I

promise your wedding will be perfect. No, I don't have a date yet. But what else is new, right? Anyway I gotta go. Bye." With a great deal of satisfaction, she ended the call.

"Is this a bad time?" Luke inquired politely.

Immediately, Asian manners and protocol kicked into gear. "I'm sorry about that. I should've called them back later. And I hope I wasn't being rude."

"Don't worry. I hope it wasn't anything serious."

Rachel rolled her eyes. "Just more wedding drama. You would think it was a matter of national security with the way my sister and mother are carrying on."

"I plead the fifth," he said somberly.

"Stop joking."

"No, I mean it. I remember when my siblings got married. I learned early the best thing I could do is just stay out of it." He offered her the flowers again. "Do you have a vase to put these in?" At the look on her face, he shook his head ruefully. "I should've guessed. We can go get one later. But first I need to apologize."

Now this was interesting. "For what, exactly?"

"My behavior after the poker game. I was rude and I'm really sorry. You didn't deserve to have me lash out at you like that."

Rachel stood there, frozen as a statue. This was unprecedented to say the least. She'd expected him to send her a polite text saying their arrangement had run its course, thanks so much for your help and hope you have a great rest of your life, et cetera. She honestly didn't know how to react. First the flowers and now the apology. Part of her was tempted to reach out and pinch Luke because he was too good to be true. But of course that would be rude and totally unacceptable behavior.

"I hope you can forgive me." he said, his eyes earnest as a puppy's.

How the hell was she supposed to say no to that?

"You're fine. I appreciate the apology. And I probably shouldn't have pried into your personal life like that anyway." She waved him in and gestured for him to take a seat on the couch while she got them something to drink.

"No, don't do that. I was the one in the wrong, not you."

That stopped her short. "Well, okay if you insist."

"I do. Are we good now?"

She nodded and set down their drinks on the coffee table.

"Whew. What a relief. I came over to apologize and brainstorm to see what our next steps should be. But it sounds like you have bigger problems at the moment." At her confused look he explained, "That conversation with your family—it sounded intense."

"Oh, my sister was making a point of reminding me what a loser I am because I don't have a date for her wedding. She already gave my plus-one away," she said with a frown. "Though she said, quote: 'If by some miracle you do find someone to bring, I'll make it work,' end quote."

"She was the one who suggested you ask me if I could set you up with anyone, right?"

Oh yeah. How could she have forgotten about that? "Yep," she confirmed with a wince. "But don't worry about it—you're so not on the hook for that. Totally beyond the scope of our arrangement."

He gave her a look, then said quietly, "I'll do it."

She blinked. "You're going to set me up on a blind date? I don't think I'm ready to tackle the dating scene here. I already have enough on my plate."

Luke shook his head vehemently. "No, I meant me. Tell your sister you have a date."

"I appreciate the gesture but it's truly not necessary. If you're still trying to make it up to me, don't. Because the apology and flowers are sufficient. Are you Catholic? Are you dealing with some sort of guilt complex?"

"Why do you assume that? Why can't I just be a friend who wants to help a friend?" he asked, looking intently in her eyes.

"Because we're friends. Offering to fly cross-country and attend a wedding is above and beyond the call of duty. Especially since we barely know each other."

"Maybe I just have a yen to visit New York City. I've never been." He shrugged.

Well that made sense. And his offer was unbelievably kind. "So you're saying this is some sort of kill two birds with one stone thing? You get to visit New York and rack up another IOU?"

"What IOU?"

Rachel scoffed. "Come on. That totally creates an imbalance in our arrangement. So you get to call in another favor whenever you want? Not that I blame you—you'd deserve one for doing this."

"Does everything have to be transactional to you?" he asked, puzzled.

"In my experience, there is usually something for both parties in something like this. Most people don't do something nice for the hell of it," she replied.

"Well then maybe that's something else I can teach you. Friends do things for each other and don't keep a ledger. Accept help when it's offered and offer help when you can. Trust that eventually it'll all even out, even if you don't keep score." His voice was light, but his body language was telegraphing something completely different. Rachel couldn't quite put her finger on it. It felt as if he was a bit insulted that she would question why he would make such a generous offer.

But she was telling the truth. In her experience, most people weren't nice just for the hell of it. Except for Cecily. Her overtures of friendship seemed genuine. Though part of that was probably to prove their parents wrong and thumb their noses at them for pitting them against each other all those years. See? There was something non-altruistic there. She was right after all. Even though she didn't blame Cecily a bit and was totally on board for the nose thumbing.

"Okay, if you're sure you want to do this."

"Just let me know the date and I'll put it on my calendar and take the time off."

"I'll pay for the plane tickets. It's the least I can do.

And I can book you a hotel room."

Luke shook his head. "I'll pay for my hotel room. And we can split the cost of the plane ticket. Like I said, it's not like I'm not getting anything out of it. I want to visit the Statue of Liberty and all the clichéd tourist stuff. That's my final offer." At her look he just raised a brow. "Take it or leave it."

"You are so damn stubborn," she muttered, crossing her arms.

"My mama tells me I get it from my dad's side, so blame him," Luke said, lips twitching. He extended his arm. "So, do we have a deal or not?"

"Fine, if that's how you want to be about this." She'd figure out some way to even the balance. Maybe she could figure out a way to throw him some business without him knowing, refer him some clients, or help him get some publicity. Or, worst-case scenario, she could learn pick-pocketing and stuff a couple hundred dollars in his wallet. She shook his hand.

"If you insist, maybe you can buy me lunch while we're there," he offered.

"You like seafood? Maybe I can get a reservation at Le Bernadin."

He shook his head and wagged a finger. "Oh no you don't. I see what you're trying to do. No, I said clichéd tourist, remember? You can take me to Katz's deli."

"Why? You just want a meal from a deli?"

"Don't tell me you've never seen *When Harry Met Sally*?" He looked horrified.

She shook her head.

"Okay that's it. We're ordering lunch and we're going get it on streaming. We're fixing this egregious knowledge gap right now."

"This better be good," Rachel muttered as she gave in and joined him on the couch.

"Don't worry. You'll be saying I'll have what she's having like a pro before you know it."

"What?"

"Just get the movie off Amazon. I'm ordering lunch."

"Fine."

Chapter Eleven

SHE DIDN'T KNOW what sins she'd committed in a past life, but she was definitely being punished for something. Rachel rolled over to the side of the bed, gave a pathetic moan, grabbed the trash can, and emptied her stomach for the third time in as many hours.

Her hair hurt. Her throat was on fire, and she was freezing. Her body ached.

Yep, the flu had hit her like an eighteen-wheeler Mac truck. She'd come home from work Friday night, tired and a little run-down, but nothing out of the ordinary. This was after she had helped Luke finalize a budget to see how much he could afford to pay an office assistant and two paralegals. Then at three a.m. the gates of hell opened, and she'd been in sheer misery ever since.

Honest to God, she didn't even know how it happened. She was always super conscientious and washed her hands often and used hand sanitizer like it was going out of style. She'd even gotten a flu shot, for all the good that did her.

Due to how busy she'd been, she hadn't had a chance to hit the nearby CVS to stock up on ibuprofen, Band-Aids, basic first aid stuff. And cold and flu medicine. She was so screwed. She was also running out of tissues. She'd meant to buy more but hadn't had the time. Damn it.

She could barely muster the strength to get out of bed, much less make it all the way to the pharmacy to get supplies.

She was slowly coming to peace with the fact that she was about to die. Really it would be more merciful to go now than prolong her suffering. She was thirty-six. She'd lived a good life. What more could one ask for?

Rachel curled up into the fetal position and waited for the inevitable.

Miracle of miracles, she'd managed to doze off for an hour or so before her phone woke her up again.

Already planning to haunt whoever it was from beyond the grave, Rachel grabbed the phone, glared at it, then croaked out: "What do you want?"

"Well hello to you too." Luke's smooth voice came over the line and sounded way too cheerful and chipper. She tried not to resent him for it.

"What do you want?" she repeated.

"Are you always this cranky in the morning?"

"I am when I'm about to die."

"What?" Amusement fled from his tone, and she snorted.

"I have the world's worst case of the flu. I'm pretty sure I won't last the day."

"Do you need anything?" The concern was touching really, but she didn't want him to feel obligated to hover over her.

"No, don't come here. Spare yourself." With that she

hung up the phone. Then let out a groan when she realized she still needed orange juice, soup, and most importantly meds. But she couldn't handle that right now. Maybe she could text Cecily later and hope her friend would take pity on her. That was part of the Girl Code, right? Or she'd see if she could get a delivery.

She tried to fall back to sleep, to no avail. Two hours later, she finally gave up, and became even more cranky while cursing Luke under her breath. She was resigning herself to a daylong *Law and Order* or *NCIS* marathon when she heard a knock on the door.

For a brief moment, Rachel wondered if it was Cecily. Did the Girl Code come with instructions on telepathic powers? Maybe Cecily sensed her mental and emotional SOS. She hobbled her way to the front door and peeked out. When she saw Luke's piercing blue eyes, she bit back another curse. Then closed her eyes and sunk to the floor with her back to the door.

"Open up. I know you're in there and you saw me. Closing your eyes and hoping I'll go away didn't work last time, and it won't work this time." His voice was firm and brooked no opposition.

Muttering under her breath, Rachel threw open the deadbolt, and let him in. Her hair was going in twenty different directions. Her eyes were bleary, her nose resembled Rudolph's, and she probably didn't smell so hot. At that moment, she couldn't give less of a damn. She'd warned him. He had no one to blame for this but himself.

"Why are you here?" she demanded with as much force

as she could muster. There he was, looking better than he had any right to, in a dark T-shirt, jeans, sunglasses, and running shoes. She tried not to hold it against him.

"As a gentleman, I must answer the call when a lady is in distress." She was trying to formulate the necessary withering response when she noticed the two bags of groceries in his hand. She nearly wept at the sight of the bottle of Tropicana orange juice.

"You brought me juice?" she croaked.

"Yes, of course. And all the fixings for my mama's chicken soup. Guaranteed to knock that virus out in forty-eight hours or less. She swears by it." After a quick reminder to take off his shoes, Luke brushed past her and made his way to her tiny kitchen and started emptying the bags. She saw two packages of chicken, a bag of carrots, another of celery, and two of the biggest onions she'd ever seen. And a bag of egg noodles. "Where are your pots and pans?"

"In the oven."

He looked over at her. "Wow, you really do look terrible." She resisted the urge to stick out her tongue. Luke put the chicken in the fridge then turned to her. "Listen, why don't you go get comfy on the couch?"

Before she knew it, she'd been plied with tea, and blankets, and he'd brought over her measly box of tissues. He handed her the remote. "Just sit and relax. When do you need your next dose of meds? If you fall asleep, I'll wake you up so you don't miss it."

His eyes narrowed at her guilty look. "Don't tell me," he warned.

"I haven't gone to the pharmacy to buy medicine yet. I never got around to stocking the medicine cabinet," she admitted in a small sheepish voice. Luke stuck out his hand toward her, palm up.

"What?"

"I need your keys."

She was so baffled that she turned them over to him without a thought.

With a shake of his head, he grabbed his keys and wallet, started putting his shoes back on, and headed out the door.

"What are you doing?" she asked.

"What does it look like? There's a RiteAid three blocks away. It's around the corner from the flower shop where I got you that bouquet," he said nodding toward the lilies and hydrangeas that were still hanging in there after a week and a half. "I'll buy you some over-the-counter stuff."

"You don't have to do that."

"If not me, who?" Grumbling to himself about her needing a keeper, and putting him behind schedule with the soup, he opened the door.

"Can you get me some more tissues too? I'm running out."

He opened his mouth, took a beat, then closed it again. Then shut the door and left.

Not ten seconds later, the door opened again. "Do not get off that couch for any reason."

Rachel huffed out a breath and blew her nose. What was his damage? No one asked him to come, and he was being all surly.

Pouting a bit, she turned on the *NCIS* marathon. Nothing like a good formulaic procedural to help take your mind off having contracted the plague. Not even fifteen minutes later, she felt her eyes getting droopy. She decided to just rest her eyes for a few minutes.

Three hours later, she woke up groggy and disoriented. How was she back in bed? She'd crashed on the couch. And where were all those delicious smells coming from? She threw back the blankets and gingerly made her way to the living room. The sight that greeted her stopped her in her tracks.

"What are you doing?" she asked, bewildered.

Luke's head popped up from the pot on the stove he was stirring, and he frowned at her.

"You keep asking that. It's starting to get concerning. And what are you doing out of bed? Go lie down," he ordered.

Rachel shuffled her way over to the stove where the smells were beginning to make her stomach rumble.

"You made me soup?"

"What did you think I brought all the ingredients for?" When she lifted the pot lid, he slapped her hands.

"This still needs thirty minutes. Don't touch." With a proprietary look, he put the lid back on.

"I didn't think you'd go to all this trouble."

"Why did you think I mentioned my mother's recipe?"

"I don't know—maybe just to drop off a recipe card with the raw ingredients?"

Luke scoffed. "Please. Naomi Trudeau's chicken soup is a sacred, guarded family recipe. I had a look through your cabinets and had to make a second trip to the supermarket to get other stuff I needed. We need to discuss the importance of a properly stocked pantry and fridge. One can't live on takeout alone." He gave her a look and she couldn't deny it. Guilty as charged.

Rachel cleared her throat and blinked her eyes. "I don't know what to say."

"Don't say anything. Just go back to bed. I'll bring you a bowl when it's done."

She wasn't sure if she approved of this bossy side of him, but she couldn't deny she didn't mind being fussed over and taken care of.

Then she noticed the backpack on her couch. "What's that?"

"Oh I went back to my place to grab some extra clothes and a few other overnight things. Does your couch convert? It looks like a futon."

"What? You're staying here tonight?"

"You need someone to look after you and make sure you get liquids and rest. And take your meds."

"I'll be fine by myself."

Luke let out a breath. "God save me from cranky patients. The point is, you don't have to go through the flu by yourself. Let me take care of you." At her blank look, he furrowed his brows. "Haven't your parents ever stayed home with you when you were sick from school? Fed you soup, changed your sheets, made you watch *The Price is*

Right while sipping Sprite and nibbling on Saltines?"

"No." Her parents had always been too busy working. Her mother would drop by during lunchtime to check her temperature or give her a call to make sure she was okay, but for the most part, she'd been home alone. They'd take her to the doctor's of course, but the idea of either of her parents missing work to tend to her was unfathomable.

He gave her a look that was tinged with pity, which she hated. "Well that changes now." He turned toward the fridge, opened it, grabbed the OJ, and poured her a glass. He stuck the glass into her hands and pointed toward the table with the DayQuil and NyQuil medicine. She meekly acquiesced and dutifully swallowed the juice and caplets.

"Thank you. I feel bad you're going to all this trouble though. You really don't have to stay the night—the couch may be really uncomfortable."

Tapping a wooden spoon against the lid of the pot, Luke tilted his head. Then he grabbed a mug from her cabinet.

"New rule. Every time you thank me, or keep insisting you'll be okay by yourself, you put a dollar in the mug. After you have your soup and rest, we'll come up with a plan to work on this 'I have trouble accepting help from others' thing. And I'll be fine on the couch—I've slept in worse conditions. Tomorrow, we'll re-evaluate. If you get some more color, and stop looking like I can knock you over by breathing on you, I'll leave you alone."

"All right. But don't blame me if you end up getting sick. I'm probably contagious as hell right now."

He gave a small grin. "Duly noted."

"And if you do get sick, don't expect homemade soup. I can bring you medicine, and I'll buy you takeout, but I can't cook worth a damn."

"That's mighty generous of you." Luke gave a quick glance at his watch. "The soup still needs a few minutes. Why don't we find something to watch?"

Rachel squinted at the clock on top of the stove. "Sure. The *NCIS* marathon is still going. It's almost the top of the hour so we can start with a new ep."

"Well that makes sense. Matches up with your obsession with murder podcasts," he said under his breath.

"I'm going to ignore that."

"I said what I said."

They settled on the couch and watched the past exploits of the *NCIS* gang. When the timer went off, Luke got up and went back to the kitchen. Rachel tried to get up to help but the look he shot her had her sitting back down.

He found a makeshift tray and brought over two bowls, with napkins and spoons.

Rachel took as deep a breath as her lungs would allow her. Despite the congestion, even she could tell the smells were incredible.

"This looks amazing," she said, picking up her spoon.

"Tastes even better," he assured her.

"Someone is damn sure of themselves."

"It's my mama's recipe," he reminded her. "As a Southern boy, it'd be blasphemous to speak ill of your mama's cooking. I'd go straight to hell."

Even she couldn't help but give a chuckle. With an inhalation and a small breath to help cool down the soup, she took a taste.

"My God," she mumbled.

Luke's satisfied smirk was evident in his voice. "See? I told you."

"I'm ready to offer your mother any amount of money to give up the recipe."

Rachel looked up as he gave a scoff. "Never going to happen. It only gets passed down to family. And didn't you just say you can't cook?"

"I'm willing to give the recipe to someone who can cook and pay them for it."

"Ummm...hello?"

She looked up from a mouthful of soup.

"I'm right here."

She frowned. "Okay, maybe we can renegotiate our agreement to include soup." She took another bite. "This really really is amazing."

"It was one of the first things I ever learned how to make."

"You're a real cook?"

"Every Trudeau man is taught how to cook at least one signature dish."

"I thought you all just grilled or did barbecue."

"That's a stereotype," Luke said with a mock frown. "I expected better from you."

"Whatever. Just give me more soup."

With a smile and shake of his head, he complied.

"So it's almost five. I have some ham and turkey in the fridge and bought some kaiser rolls. We can have sandwiches later if you're up for it."

"No, I want more soup. All the soup."

"I'll have to tell Mama she made another convert."

His statement took her aback. She wasn't sure how she felt about the idea of his family knowing about her. It just felt weird. Why would he feel the need to mention her at all? And how would they react?

Suddenly a hand was waving over her face. "Hey what are you thinking?"

"Nothing." The look he gave her told Rachel he wasn't buying it, but thankfully he let it drop.

"What do you want to do the rest of the evening?"

She shrugged. "The marathon is on for at least another six hours." At his scrunched-up face, she pointed out: "You're the one who insisted on staying."

"Fair enough. Let me clear the table." He took the dishes to the sink and came back with a glass of water and a glass of OJ for her.

Rachel adjusted the blankets and patted the spot next to her on the couch. "Come on, the new ep is starting. Let's see who Mark Harmon head-slaps in this one."

"You're hilarious," he deadpanned, setting the glasses on the table. Which turned to a disgusted recoil. "Oh my God, is that a decaying corpse?!"

"Shhh!!! Quiet!"

THE NEXT MORNING, Luke woke up with a huge crick in his neck. Despite his protests to the contrary, he really couldn't sleep everywhere. The futon was lumpy and uncomfortable as hell. But that was a small price to pay to make sure she was okay.

It still stunned him that she was prepared to suffer alone, that she wasn't used to having someone look after her.

What sort of parent left their poor defenseless children alone at home when they had the flu? True there were some families who both had to work, but to him it was still unthinkable.

He pulled his laptop from his backpack and booted it up. He had his headphones plugged in, listening to music, and going over emails. He groaned when he saw that his assistant had scheduled a meeting with Eddie from accounting first thing Monday morning. Eddie was a pain in the ass and fought him tooth and nail over every receipt.

If he was able to open his own practice, one of the biggest perks would be he no longer had to justify expense reports to Eddie. Then Luke remembered the staggering number of spreadsheets Rachel had sent him. Instead, he'd be justifying expenses to a CPA who could handle the finances for him. Thank God Rachel had worked that into the budget. Luke shuddered at the notion of having to deal with all that himself.

He was just getting in the zone and answering client emails when he saw the door to Rachel's bedroom open. She looked kinda adorable actually. Her eyes were bleary, her hair was a tousled mess and she was wearing a Harvard sweatshirt and flannel pajamas pants.

"Hey there, Sleeping Beauty."

Without missing a beat she scowled and said, "Shut up. It's too early for this."

"How'd you sleep?"

"Fine."

He got up, walked over to her, captured her cheeks in his hands and scanned her face.

"You look a little better. Are you feeling more steady?"

"I'm fine," she insisted.

Obviously they'd entered the cranky portion of the recovery program. In all honesty, her color was better, and a good night's rest had worked wonders. But she was still nowhere near out of the woods.

"So, what do you want to do today? Is there another *NCIS* or *Law and Order* marathon you want to watch? Or we can stream a movie—I have my laptop."

Her brows knit in confusion. "You said you'd leave today."

"Only if you're feeling better," he reminded her.

"Which I am."

"I think I better stay the day just in case. I'll leave tonight."

"You don't have to do that."

"What did I say about that? That's a dollar in the mug."

She narrowed her eyes and hissed.

"Wow you really aren't at your best in the morning, are

you?"

"I've never been a morning person."

"How about some more juice and fruit for breakfast? Bananas? That should be soft and easy to eat if you have a sore throat. Or yogurt?"

"I don't have any of that in my fridge."

"I can run out and get some, no problem."

"Now you're making me feel bad." She sighed.

"Don't. Tell me what you want. We still have plenty of soup for lunch."

Giving up, Rachel plopped on the couch. "Fine." Then she gave him a sheepish look. "Thank you. I promise to not be so awful for the rest of the day."

"You have the flu; you get a pass. I'll get breakfast."

After a breakfast of juice and soft oatmeal, they were settled back on the couch. For the first time, Luke noticed something bright hanging on a rack on the opposite side of Rachel's bedroom door.

Following his gaze, Rachel made a face. "It's my dress for my sister's wedding. Claudia's been on my case making sure I went to a seamstress and got it tailored in time. Let me just say, having to stand still while people are pointing pins and needles at you isn't fun."

"Doesn't sound like it," Luke agreed. "I know you're not looking forward to the wedding but hopefully it'll be fun."

She wrinkled her nose. "It'll be fine. Mostly I'll be glad when it's over so Claudia can stop giving me grief because I'm so far away and thus making everything more difficult for her."

"We can always make a run for it and grab an earlier flight home if things get too rough," he suggested, only half kidding.

Rachel shook her head vehemently. "That's not going to work. At the very least, the looks on everyone's faces when you and I show up may be worth it. We may need paramedics; people may keel over from the shock that I brought someone. When I told Claudia I had a plus-one after all, I thought the video had frozen and her mouth dropped wide open."

"Well, we'll just have to show them how much good being in California has done for you," he suggested gamely, though he really didn't like when she talked about herself that way. She was great and she didn't seem to realize it.

"True. But time to find something to watch." Rachel flipped through the channels.

When he saw the familiar logo, he groaned. "Please, no more. I beg of you."

She looked over at him and pouted. "But I'm bored," she whined.

Without a word, he reached over and grabbed his backpack, and removed an important item from one of the pockets.

"What's that?"

He turned around and showed her. "A deck of cards. I want a rematch."

IT WAS ANOTHER weekend afternoon, which meant it was time for him to call and talk to his family. He'd been lucky that his immune system activated and prevented him from catching Rachel's flu. She was now fully recovered. Good thing he'd already had his morning run, so the endorphins were going, and he was in a relatively good mood. In fact, he'd even downloaded some of the podcasts Rachel had recommended and listened to one of them while he ran.

He didn't know whether to be intrigued or disturbed that Rachel was such a fan of grisly murder podcasts. All he knew was, she knew way too much about how to effectively dispose of and hide a body. And the other day he'd caught himself turning on an *NCIS* episode for the background noise.

His phone went off and gave him a start. Due to his hectic work schedule, he was usually the one to call the family, not the other way around. But nevertheless, he accepted the video call.

"Hi, Uncle Luke!" His nieces' faces filled the screen, and despite himself, his grin widened.

"Hey, munchkins. What are you doing?"

"Saying hi before we have dinner. We're at Nana and Pop Pop's house!" To prove the truth of their words, they started tearing around the living room, waving the phone and camera everywhere.

Luckily, his brother Ben grabbed the phone before he started getting motion sickness.

"Mama's gonna skin you alive for getting them all hopped up on sugar before bringing them over to her house."

"She's not going to do anything to me with witnesses present," Ben retorted. A few more minutes of fraternal verbal abuse were volleyed until both of them got it out of their systems.

"Anyway, what are you doing? What are you up to?"

"Catching up on work, as usual. Reading over this deposition for a case. Boring—nothing that'd interest you."

"Listen, I spent the day listening to *Elmo's World* on a loop. A deposition sounds frigging fascinating right now."

"That actually sounds…painful." Luke winced.

"Bro, you have no idea. Total effing nightmare."

"Benjamin Clayton Trudeau, how many times have I told you about using that sort of language in my house?"

Luke couldn't help but snicker as Ben winced at their mother's tone.

"Yes, ma'am," he mumbled. "I'm sorry."

"You got in trouble," Luke singsonged.

Ben's eyes narrowed and promised retribution in short order.

Short order meaning less than ten seconds later when his brow rose in confusion.

"What's that?" he demanded, pointing an accusing finger at his older brother.

"What are you talking about?"

"That, on the table beside you."

For a moment Luke panicked. What embarrassing or incriminating thing had his damn brother noticed? As far as he knew, he was in the clear. After all, it only took that one time when his mother found a string of condoms in the drawer of his night stand for him to do a pre-family sweep before every call or visit.

"Is that a book?" his brother asked in the same tone one would ask: "Is that a venomous viper?" or "Is that an oozing gangrenous pus-filled wound?"

Looking around in confusion, his eyes finally landed on the object of his brother's fascination slash horror.

"Yeah. It's a book."

"What are you doing with a book?"

"Reading it," he said slowly.

"What's it about?"

"It's a biography of Aileen Wuornos."

"Who's that?"

"Oh a serial killer from the eighties."

"What?" His brother's eyes widened in confusion.

"A friend recommended the book to me. I have to admit, not my usual thing, but it's a fascinating read."

Rachel had insisted that if she was being forced to explore hobbies, he had to do the same and show interest in one of hers. Fair enough, in his opinion. The way the author delved into Aileen's childhood and psyche and charted the path of her turning into a murderess was gripping.

"You never read unless you have to."

"Hey, I'm not a total philistine."

"How many times have you complained about the amount of writing and reading you have to do for work? And that you don't want to read unless you have to and get paid for it?"

Okay. Busted. He totally had said that before.

"I chose to make an exception in this case. Can't a person change his mind? Besides, it's been fun talking about the book with her." The minute the word *her* slipped out, he immediately regretted not holding his tongue.

"Mama! Luke met a girl!"

God damn it.

"Are you thirteen?" he hissed.

"Someone's in trouble," Ben sang as their mother grabbed the phone from him.

"Who's the girl?" Naomi demanded, with no preliminaries.

"There's no girl, Mama," Luke said with a sigh.

"Liar!" Ben yelled. "You said she."

Brothers sucked.

"Don't make me ask again. If you've met someone, how could you keep that from your family?"

Giving an internal roll of his eyes, Luke gave up.

"Her name is Rachel. But really we're friends. Nothing more." Friends who'd seen each other naked roughly two hours after they first met, but that was neither here nor there. A girl who fascinated him like no one else with her unique insights and her sheer determination to achieve her goals. Who he couldn't stop thinking about. Which again was beside the point because they'd decided to just be friends.

"How did you meet?"

Oh crap. "We met about two or three months ago."

Luke saw the wheels turning in his mother's head.

"Wait a minute. Is this the same friend you made my soup for?"

Shit Fucking Hell.

"Yes, ma'am."

"Then I'm afraid I'm going to agree with your brother. This is no friend."

"I told you, Mama. She's a friend I'm helping out with a work thing, and she's helping me with my idea to open my own firm." When he'd told his family about his plans, they'd been pleasantly surprised. And he and Rachel had been making progress. He'd arranged meetings with several of his colleagues to see if they were possibly interested in jumping ship and joining him, and talking to other business leaders and officials to drum up some word of mouth.

It was all exciting, but something still wasn't sitting quite right with him. It just felt like the same old, same old. When Luke had started this endeavor he'd expected it to feel like...more. That he'd feel different now that he was taking ownership of his career and striking out alone. He saw the passion Rachel had for her work and wanted some of that for himself. But maybe it was just the stress of planning everything that was dampening his spirits.

"I stand by what I said."

"Friends make soup for each other!"

Naomi just raised one elegant brow. "Benjamin, have you ever made soup for Derek?"

With the biggest possible shit-eating grin, his brother replied with a cheery: "No, ma'am."

"I know Lilly made soup for her roommate!" There.

"That's different."

"How?"

"It just is."

"But you know who I did make soup for?" Ben really did have a smug, punchable face. How had he never realized that until now?

"Don't start..."

"Vivienne. When we first moved in together and she caught a cold. Fixed her right up."

Naomi gave him a look that screamed: *See*?

"So when do we get to meet her?"

"When hell freezes over."

"Lucas."

"We're just friends," he insisted for the thirty thousandth time. But even to him it was starting to sound hollow. Though damn if he wasn't going to ride that one to the grave.

"We'll see about that," Naomi murmured. At that Luke's heart sank and the red flags were waving as though they were blowing in a gale.

"What are you planning, Mama?"

"Goodness, son, relax. Why are you acting like I'm plotting and scheming?"

Luke just let the silence speak for him, lest he got himself into even more trouble.

"I'm thinking it's about time your father and I came to visit you. It's been too long. And we'd love to have dinner with you and what did you say her name was? Rachel?"

"Yes, ma'am," he replied with a sigh, giving in to the inevitable. He should have known better than to even try to go up against his mother—it was a losing proposition.

"Lovely. I'll talk it over with your father and let you know some dates. Looking forward to it," Naomi said, beaming serenely.

"Same," he said through gritted teeth.

"Well, time for dinner and I need to check on the pot roast. Talk to you next week, darling." With a wave, Naomi ended the call and left her son sitting back in his chair wondering what the hell had just happened. All he knew was his parents were going to descend and visit him sometime in the near future and there was nothing he could do to stop it. Then a terrifying thought had him swallowing hard.

How was he going to explain this to Rachel?

Chapter Twelve

A LITTLE NERVOUS, Rachel knocked on the door of Cecily's Palo Alto apartment. She'd received the invite earlier that week.

Hey, I kicked Jeffrey out Saturday. Wanna join Adrienne and me for movie night at my place? I'm providing the wine, takeout, and Netflix. Feel free to pack your pajamas and an overnight bag if you want in case we hit the vino too hard. You're welcome to stay the night.

Cecily had also texted a link to the restaurant she was planning to order from and asked for Rachel's selections by Friday afternoon at the latest so she could place the order. The level of meticulous planning warmed Rachel's heart. And a strong bout of optimism had her carrying a backpack, which was serving as her overnight bag for the evening.

The door swung open, and true to her word, Cecily was in a tank top and pajama pants, with her hair up in a messy bun and with no makeup.

"Welcome! Come in. Glad you could join us." She ushered Rachel in and gave her a brief hug. Remembering her manners, Rachel handed over the white bakery box.

"I went to a nearby bakery and bought us some cupcakes. I got two each of vanilla, chocolate mocha, lemon, red velvet, maple bacon, and Samoa. It's supposed to taste like the Girl Scout cookie." She'd gone with a variety, figuring better safe than sorry. Surely with that assortment there would be something for everyone.

"You didn't have to do that," Cecily protested as she set the box aside on the kitchen counter. "But it's really sweet of you."

"You know the rules." Rachel shrugged. The Asian code said to never show up anywhere you were invited empty-handed. Good guests always provided a small gift. A quick Google assured her that bringing over baked goods was a pretty safe bet. And so far, so good. Thank you, Google.

"The only problem is whether we can manage to finish these before Jeffrey gets home tomorrow afternoon. Otherwise he'll demolish the rest of them." Cecily grinned.

"Did you really kick him out?" Rachel asked, curious.

Cecily waved a hand and rolled her eyes. "Okay I may have exaggerated slightly. He's over at his friend Greg's house overhauling a script. He'll be fine."

"I thought I heard voices," Adrienne said, coming down the hallway to join them in the living room. She was decked out in a navy blue satin polka dot pajamas set, but also with hair up and face makeup-free. "Rachel! Glad you're here," she said with a hug and big smile. Then she frowned. "Are you not staying?"

Rachel held up her backpack and Adrienne's frown relaxed.

"She also brought cupcakes," Cecily informed her.

"I knew I liked you."

"Rachel, you wanna go get changed and get comfy while we set up here?" Cecily pointed down the hall Adrienne appeared from.

With a philosophical shrug, Rachel found the bathroom and quickly got changed. When they were teens, Claudia was always the one who had friends over for sleepovers and whatnot, while she'd never been invited to those sorts of things. This was her first real, honest to God girls' night. She was both excited and terrified.

"You'll be fine," she said to herself in the mirror. "You've got this. They wouldn't have invited you if they didn't like you. So don't blow it." She pulled on her T-shirt and drawstring gym shorts and joined them back in the kitchen.

"I placed the order, and it should be here in about forty-five minutes," Cecily informed her. In addition to the cupcakes, there was a bottle of red and a bottle of white wine on the counter, a bowl of white cheddar popcorn, and a meat and cheese platter with two sleeves of crackers.

"How appropriate. You provide the salty and Rachel brings the sweet," Adrienne cracked. Rachel blinked her eyes as Cecily shot Adrienne an evil look. Then Cecily broke down and snort-giggled too.

"No one ever called me sweet before," Rachel mused.

"Compared to CeeCee? You're a veritable angel," Adrienne assured her.

"Stop making fun of me," Cecily said as she started pouring the wine. "Red or white, Rachel?"

"Red please." In short order she was handed a nice glass of cabernet sauvignon.

"I mock because I love." Adrienne's cheeky grin stayed even as she started sipping her wine.

"Remind me why we're friends again?" Cecily rolled her eyes as she poured herself a chardonnay.

"Because I'm amazing."

"So what movie are we watching tonight?" Rachel asked, unsure how to contribute to the current conversation.

"*Downton Abbey*." Then she saw Cecily's eye roll and Adrienne's smirk.

"Uh, okay." She didn't watch a lot of period dramas, but what the hell. She'd be willing to give it a shot. Her move to San Francisco was full of new experiences to say the least.

"She's being a smart-ass," Cecily explained. "The first time she met Jeffrey, that was what she and I were watching. We were having movie night, and he surprised me. I didn't know he was coming."

Rachel tried to picture Jeffrey watching *Downton Abbey* and couldn't quite get there. "Naturally, he disappeared into the bedroom while we finished watching the movie. Then I had to go home."

"For the record, no one asked you to leave. You were welcome to stay," Cecily interjected.

Adrienne snorted. "Yeah right, like I was going to stick around and witness something I'd rather not."

Rachel shrugged. "He is a sex god after all."

Cecily looked at the two of them and shook her head. "I'm beginning to regret inviting the two of you." But her lips were twitching and Rachel decided it was safe to assume she was just kidding.

"Grab a plate and let's get this party started," Cecily said, waving a hand over the spread.

Soon enough the three of them sprawled on the couch.

"But seriously. What movie are we watching?" Rachel asked, curious.

"How about the Ocean trilogy? I found it on streaming."

Adrienne shrugged. "Sure. Always up for eye candy and a good slick heist movie."

"Works for me." Rachel nodded.

Cecily picked up the remote then set it down again. "Speaking of eye candy..." Her tone was sly and arch and Rachel immediately went on alert.

"That was a hell of a segue," Adrienne quipped.

"How are things going with your arrangement with Luke?" Cecily's expression was too innocent for Rachel's liking.

"Is that why you invited me? You just wanted to gossip and pump me for information? You didn't really want me here tonight, did you?" It was happening again. She shouldn't be surprised but it didn't diminish the hurt.

"Of course we wanted you here! You think I'd invite just anyone to join us on movie night and to sleep over? Please," Cecily scoffed. For some reason Cecily's response reassured Rachel and made her feel better than any effusive declarations.

"But we're also nosy as hell and want the tea. It's not a mutually exclusive proposition. So like that girl in the commercial used to say: 'Why not both?'" Adrienne's mischievous smile glinted with humor, not malice, and that helped put her at ease too.

"We're friends. It's what we do." Cecily shrugged.

"We are? I mean I know we had dinner together awhile back and we've met up since I got here, but didn't want to assume," Rachel stammered, with her heart beating a mile a minute.

"Like I said, I don't invite just anyone to a sleepover and Adrienne doesn't invite just anyone to her birthday," Cecily said. "We've known each other basically our whole lives even though we only stopped hating each other not that long ago. We may be getting to know each other better now that you're here but I like the cut of your jib. That's enough vetting for me," she joked.

"How about that," Rachel murmured.

"Now can we go back to the eye candy and Luke?"

Rachel took a breath and decided to take a chance. "Considering you have a fiancé, should you be noticing other men and calling them eye candy?"

There was a long, wretched silence while Cecily and Adrienne just looked at her. Then they both burst into laughter.

"Oh CeeCee was so right about asking you to come tonight," Adrienne said, wiping away a tear and grabbing a handful of popcorn.

"I told you I have good taste in people. And as for the other thing, I'm engaged, not blind," Cecily said cheekily. Then she held her left hand up to admire the ring. "Besides, Jeffrey knows I'm stupidly in love with him."

Once again, the glow and joy on Cecily's face brought a pang of envy in Rachel's heart. She wished there was a possibility of someone out there who could make her feel that way. She thought back to Luke and the butterflies in her stomach whenever she saw him. But that was different. They'd already decided to just stay friends. Even though there were times when he looked at her and her knees turned to jelly, and she had to remind herself to breathe. Which was her problem to deal with, because she didn't want to ruin the good thing they had going.

Hugging a pillow close, Adrienne made a go ahead motion to Rachel. "So tell us what's going on."

Rachel frowned thoughtfully. "I have to admit, his methods have been unorthodox, but they work. He even invited me to his poker night. Trying to network in a less formal setting," she explained.

Adrienne looked at her, the surprise on her face evident. "You got to go to poker night? Poker night is sacrosanct. I never managed to get invited."

Rachel shrugged. "He was kinda annoyed that I beat him and took all his money."

"Of course you did," Cecily said, nodding her head. "I would expect nothing less from you."

"We sorta got into a fight because he was being an ass. But then he came over and gave me flowers to apologize."

The two of them looked at each other and exchanged glances. Glances Rachel couldn't interpret.

"What?" she demanded. If those flowers meant something she wanted to know.

"Nothing. I just find it interesting, that's all. But go on," Adrienne encouraged.

"Well I have to say one thing for Luke. His timing is impeccable. I was on the phone with my mom and Claudia and they were going on about the wedding and giving me crap because I don't have a date. Luke volunteered to go to the wedding with me," she said with a shrug.

At that Cecily choked on her chardonnay and Adrienne's jaw dropped.

"He what?" Adrienne asked when she managed to speak again.

"I know, I thought it was weird too, but he assures me it won't be a problem. And he says it's a good excuse for him to visit New York, since he's never been. So that helps explain why he'd offer to come with me. I feel a bit guilty though. The scales seem really imbalanced—I am getting way more out of this arrangement than him."

"I wonder why," Cecily murmured.

"What do you mean?" Rachel asked, her brows furrowed in abject confusion.

"Let me put it this way. I got flowers from Jeffrey when he was trying to apologize and get back in my good graces. And no way in hell I'd volunteer to go to a wedding for someone as a favor."

"Me neither," Adrienne agreed as she popped a piece of

cheddar in her mouth. "Especially cross-country."

"I think it's obvious what's going on here. Luke likes you."

"Well of course he does. We're friends."

"Likes you as in I want to rip your clothes off and jump you like you."

"He doesn't see me that way," Rachel protested. "And didn't you hear me say he's doing this to visit New York?"

"Bullshit. You told us how you two met, remember?"

"Okay so he doesn't see me that way anymore," Rachel rebutted vehemently. To quote Cecily, she wasn't blind. Of course she was attracted to Luke. Who wouldn't be? Besides the dazzling good looks, he was kind, and thoughtful, and didn't make her feel like the constant awkward turtle she was. Around him, she felt…funny, interesting, more comfortable in her own skin. Normal. Someone who was capable of capturing a man's attention instead of being an object of pity or ignored completely. But it was a moot point. It didn't matter how she felt about him when he had nothing but platonic feelings for her.

"Yeah right. I beg to differ," Adrienne objected. "I don't know who you're trying to kid, you or us, but we're not buying it."

Cecily gave her a piercing look. "You like him too don't you?" she said quietly.

"It doesn't matter what I feel. The point is we both agreed to keep things strictly business."

"Last time I checked, flowers and weddings don't fall under any definition of strictly business that I've ever run across," Cecily said, brow arched.

Damn lawyers always doing their lawyer thing and talking in circles.

"Okay you're right. But I also said we'd become friends. And I'd like to drop the topic and move on to something else please?" Because this line of conversation was making her think and speculate and maybe hope for things she had no business hoping for. It was not going to happen—such things weren't in the cards for her. Luke was just doing her a favor. Period.

At that moment, the door buzzed. "Food's here," Cecily said as she popped up to go tip the delivery person.

"Saved by the bell," Adrienne murmured.

Rachel barely resisted the urge to stick out her tongue. Her first girls' night was off to a hell of a start.

Rachel: *Adrienne wants you to know that you're on her list.*

Luke: *What did I do this time? By the way, thanks for reminding me to look into IT guys who can help set up the internet and computer system for the new office.*

Rachel: *No problem. I had a girls' night with her and Cecily. I told her how I kicked your ass at poker. She's mad because you never let her come to poker night.*

Luke: *Well you can tell her she's still not getting an invite. Did you have fun?*

Rachel: *Yes, actually.*

Luke: *Why the actually?*

Rachel: *I was convinced I'd do or say something and they'd kick me out. But that didn't happen. I'm just getting home now. Cecily went out and got croissants and made mimosas for us for breakfast. Felt very fancy.*

Luke: *Of course they didn't kick you out. Dollar in the jar for having so little faith in yourself. And my coaching.*

Rachel: *Easy for you to say. You're not an awkward turtle like me.*

Luke: *An awkward turtle sounds adorable. Do they come in stuffed animal form? I may buy one for my niece's birthday.*

Rachel: *Anyway, I'm taking a nap then catching up on some work.*

Luke: *Send me the info for the wedding so I know when to ask for time off and buy tickets.*

Rachel: *Will do. I'll see you on Wednesday at the reception right?*

Luke: *With bells on.*

Rachel: *That sounds distracting.*

HEAD DOWN READING over opposing counsel's settlement agreement with a fine-tooth comb, in the zone, Luke almost didn't hear the perfunctory knock on the door before it swung open and the last person he expected stood in front of him.

"We need to talk," Cecily Chang said, the expression on her face serious.

"What are you doing here?" he asked, puzzled. Despite

the merger between their firms, there was no real reason for her to drop in on him during business hours. But ever the gentleman, he stood up, and gestured for her to sit. He had a feeling about why she was there, so out of an abundance of caution, he also closed the door before sitting back down.

"I had business over this way and thought I'd take this opportunity to drop by," Cecily said primly, her tone all business. "Your assistant said you were available until your next appointment at three."

Luke made a mental note to have a discussion with Gavin about being so helpful and willing to volunteer information to all and sundry.

"What can I do?" he asked, hoping to get this over with.

Cecily nailed him with a look. "What's going on with you and Rachel?" Her tone was blunt and direct, warning him not to bullshit her. Her nails were drumming on the arm of the black leather guest chair.

"I think that's between me and Rachel," he replied carefully.

She gave a wave of her hand. "Stop with the chivalry. And Rachel is my friend. I want to make sure she's okay."

"And here I thought you and I were friends too," he murmured. "At least that's how I interpreted your offer of coffee after our dinner," he couldn't resist pointing out.

"Let's pretend that never happened. And we aren't friends. You declined my coffee invitation, and we never saw each other again until Adrienne's birthday party."

"Fair enough."

"We're getting off track. Now please answer my question."

"Since Rachel's your friend, shouldn't you be asking her?"

"No, I felt it was better to come straight to the source." Cecily crossed her arms.

Luke sighed. "What exactly do you want to know? I assume she told you about our arrangement?"

She nodded. "She said she's helping you do some research for some potential job opportunities, and in return you are helping her work better with her team so she can officially get that promotion."

"Exactly. So what's the problem here?"

"Oh none whatsoever," Cecily said pertly flipping her hair over her shoulder. "But that was before I found out you also agreed to accompany her back to New York and be her date at her sister's wedding."

Oh, yeah. That.

"That does seem to be beyond the bounds of a professional business relationship, wouldn't you say?" Then she held out a hand. "Before you answer that, you should also know that I am well aware of how you and Rachel met."

Luke swallowed hard. At first he'd been bemused and intrigued, curious to see where Cecily was heading with this talk, but now he found none of this funny.

"It seems to me Rachel has kept you well informed," he said in an attempt to rally.

"Don't play games with me. Rachel is a friend, and I

feel responsible for her. I like her. I don't want to see her hurt."

"You think I'm going to hurt her?" he asked, baffled. That took him aback. In what universe could she possibly think he'd be a threat to Rachel?

"I think you're giving her mixed signals," Cecily tossed back frankly. "She's convinced you two are just friends now, despite how you met, and that you're not interested in her at all."

"We are friends."

"Friends who've known each other only a few months don't just volunteer to fly cross-country and play wedding date," she pointed out.

"I caught her while she was talking with her family about the wedding. She seemed upset, and I just wanted to help. This wedding seems to be difficult for her. I don't know how else to explain it," he said honestly.

At that Cecily's expression softened. "That was a nice gesture on your part," she conceded.

"I have my moments," he said drily.

"If you're interested in her, tell her now," Cecily insisted. "Don't play games and toy with her. Rachel doesn't deserve that."

"Who said I was interested?" Luke said, but even to him the protest sounded weak as hell.

Cecily rolled her eyes. "Friends slash business acquaintances don't take the time to make homemade chicken soup from scratch and insist on staying over to make sure they're okay."

With an inward wince, Luke tried to school his features into not giving anything away. First, Mama was on his case about the soup, and now Cecily.

Sometimes, to paraphrase Freud, soup was just soup. No need to read into it.

"You mean you never dropped by to check in on Adrienne when she was sick?" he tossed back.

"Don't be stupid, it's not the same at all," Cecily said, rolling her eyes again.

"How?"

"Because Adrienne and I are just friends."

"So are Rachel and I," he insisted. "And besides I'm also getting a chance to visit New York City for the first time. You're reading more into this than there is."

"God save me from the stupidity of the Y-chromosome," Cecily muttered.

"Hey, no need for insults." Seriously, he had much better things to do with his time than listening to this character attack.

"You're right. I suppose you can't help it." She sighed. Then she gave him that look again. "But what I said still stands. When I talked to you before and threatened you, I was only mostly kidding. I'm not kidding this time. Don't hurt my friend. It was one thing when you were only working together to help each other out. With the wedding, now her family is involved. The stakes are totally different. You're going with her to a wedding and meeting her relatives. Feelings are going to get involved; it's going to be messy and complicated. Tread lightly." While he still didn't appreciate being interrogated and threatened again, Luke had to admire Cecily's loyalty. Rachel was lucky to have such a good friend.

"That is the last thing I want to do."

"Do you even understand the minefield you're walking into?" Cecily asked, tilting her head and studying him like a specimen under a slide.

"It's a wedding." He shrugged. "It's a happy occasion. I'll sit in the pew, smile, ooh and aahh at the bride's beautiful dress, eat the chicken or fish at the reception, smile some more, get on the dance floor, and make small talk with the people around me. What's the big deal? It'll be fine." It was what he'd done at his siblings' weddings. He knew what to do and how to play his role as the supportive friend.

Cecily blinked then shook her head slowly. "You really have no idea," she murmured.

"I get that her family is Asian and I've never gone to an Asian wedding before," Luke admitted. "But the basics will still be the same, won't they? What's there to worry about?"

"You poor sweet summer child. I'm going to remind you of this conversation after the wedding," she decided. "Let's see how well you'll actually hold up." She then muttered under her breath something about nosy aunties and descending like vultures and mincemeat.

He blanched a bit. Cecily was just messing with him. That was the only reason she was making it seem like he was a lamb being led to slaughter, right?

Instead Cecily gave a sigh and shrugged philosophically. "Guess some people just prefer to touch the hot stove." At his confused look, she shook her head. "Example is the school of mankind and they will learn at no other. Edmund Burke, Irish economist and philosopher." While Luke blinked, trying to process the implications of what she was saying, Cecily glanced at her watch and stood up. "I gotta go. It was nice chatting with you," she said, sticking her hand out.

"Is that what that was?" he murmured, with a raised brow. But he shook the proffered hand. The manners ingrained in him wouldn't allow for anything less.

"Remember what I said," Cecily tossed over her shoulder as she opened the door and got ready to leave. "Don't mess this up. You better know what the hell you're doing." With that, she sailed out and made her way to the elevators.

Taking a page from Rachel's book, Luke just closed his eyes and tried to pretend the last ten minutes hadn't happened. To no avail. Cecily's words kept running in his mind in an endless loop. Because as much as he hated to admit it, she was right. The wedding was kicking things up a notch and who knows what would happen. And despite what he said to his family and Cecily, Rachel was probably the only person he'd do this for. Thinking back to his prior relationships, Luke couldn't think of a single other woman he would have agreed to attend a family wedding for, much less cross-country.

Luke gave a deep sigh and decided it was time to be honest. He hadn't offered to go to New York with Rachel out of pure friendship. He was interested in her—seriously interested in her. She was unique, interesting, and kept him on his toes. Who wouldn't find that appealing? He wanted to ask her on a proper date and see where things went. Hopefully back to the bedroom.

But now wasn't the time. He was still working on getting his potential new business off the ground, and Rachel was focused on earning her promotion, as she should be. So for now, things were going to stay the way they were. Once things settled down, when Rachel had settled into her role, and he'd figured out his new business plan, then he could ask her out for real. It wouldn't be a problem to convince Rachel to give whatever they had between them a shot. Their first date could be them celebrating and toasting to their mutual success. Despite their decision to keep things platonic, the chemistry between them was too strong to ignore.

Until then, he was going to behave himself, no matter how hard it would be. After all, they still had her sister's wedding coming up and he was determined to help Rachel navigate that weekend, no matter how messy things got. She deserved support and didn't need him muddying the waters.

He was also more than a little disturbed that Cecily seemed to be privy to all the details about his relationship…er, friendship with Rachel. In theory he sorta knew and understood women told each other everything. It was quite another to have theory turn into practice and smack him right upside the head. And if his knowledge of the women in his family and his previous dealings were any indication there wasn't a damn thing he could do about it.

However, there was one thing he could do, and he was going to do it right now. He pressed the intercom. "Hey, Gavin. Can you come in here for a second? We need to talk."

Chapter Thirteen

HIS BRIEFCASE IN hand, Luke made his way to Courtroom 256. He and Aimee had lunch plans, but court had wrapped up a bit earlier than expected for him, so he was dropping by Aimee's turf at Family Court. Luckily, Aimee seemed to be finishing up too because he heard the judge say court was adjourned. He pushed the door in and saw Aimee still at the table talking with her client. The woman had tears streaming down her face and Aimee reached over to give her a hug.

"Thank you, Ms. Garcia," Aimee's client said over and over. They spoke for a few more minutes, and then the woman got up and left. Aimee was on her way out too before she saw them.

"Oh," she said, surprised. "I thought we were meeting at the restaurant."

Luke shrugged. "My meeting wrapped up early and I had time. Is everything okay?" he asked, tilting his head toward the door.

"Fine. More than fine. I'm fucking fantastic. She hired me two years ago after her nasty divorce with her husband. He's been putting her through hell and was threatening to sue for sole custody and prevent her from having visitation with her kids."

Luke blinked. That sounded incredibly intense. "Well, I heard her thanking you over and over so I'm guessing you didn't let that happen."

"You bet your ass I didn't. She has full custody." Aimee's smile was triumphant, but he could see the strains of stress and worry etched on her face.

"Better you than me," he murmured. Truly, he had no idea how Aimee did this sort of work. The stakes were immense, lives and futures were on the line, and the idea of a mistake or failure on his part having such massive repercussions was enough to make him break out in a sweat. He couldn't imagine shouldering the responsibility of determining whether or not a parent would ever see their child again, or whether or not his client might die depending on whether the restraining order was approved or not.

But that being said, it was clear the work Aimee was doing mattered. Maybe that was what was missing. The current work he was doing felt like going through the motions. If he could find a way to focus on the importance of his work, Luke could feel like he'd done a good day's work when he went home at night, instead of merely figuring out how to maximize his client's settlement.

"Thanks," Aimee responded with a roll of her eyes. "Hey, since I'm hosting poker night soon, remember to ask your girlfriend what kind of pizza she likes."

Immediately on guard, Luke gave Aimee a suspicious look. "What girlfriend?"

"Rachel of course," his friend replied, elbowing him in

the ribs.

"Not you, too," he groaned. First Cecily's ambush the other day and now this. It was one thing that he was finally honest with himself about his feelings but it was sort of embarrassing how obvious he must have been if everyone knew what the deal was before him.

"You brought her to poker night," Aimee said, as if that explained everything. "The last time we had an outsider was when Roger brought Nicola three years ago. Six months after that, they eloped and got married."

"This is a totally different situation," Luke protested. "Rachel wants to be friends and that's how it's going to be." For now.

"So Rachel wants to just be friends?"

"She keeps reminding me that all clothes are staying on," he said wryly. He tried not to be offended at Aimee's snort of laughter. Personally, he was looking forward to convincing Rachel to repeal that particular rule.

"I was a fan when she kicked your ass at poker. Now I really like her," she said as she caught her breath.

"Ha ha."

Then she gave a thoughtful look. "Considering the other women you've dated in the past, Rachel is a major step up for you. You'd be lucky to get her to date you."

"Hey, what's wrong with me?" he protested.

"Just saying, if you want to date a high-quality person, you gotta be high quality."

"And I'm not? In principle, I agree with you," he said with a shrug. Part of him wished Rachel saw herself the same way—she didn't give herself nearly enough credit a lot of the time. But Aimee's words gnawed at him. There was more than a kernel of truth in what his friend was saying. Rachel was working so hard and showing such grit and determination, he was beyond impressed. It was truly admirable. And made him feel slightly guilty about how he didn't always put in the same effort when it came to his own career.

But no matter. He could make it up to her by working hard to help her achieve her goals. Then plan a romantic gesture to officially ask her out. That way, everyone won.

"I'm a catch," he insisted when Aimee rolled her eyes.

"Yeah sure whatever you say. Let's go eat."

LUKE KNOCKED ON the door of Rachel's apartment, curious. He had gotten a text from her out of the blue, asking him to come by her place after work, saying that it was important. There were no emojis, exclamation points or anything to give him any context clues about what was happening. Maybe something had happened at work and she wanted some advice on how to navigate it, or she had more info or research to share. Or something had happened with her family and she needed to talk about her sister's wedding.

He reminded himself, depending on how things went tonight, to ask if Rachel was willing to help him look over the loan application one last time before handing it in.

Despite being a lawyer, even he was taken aback at the pile of paperwork needed. The bank seemed to want his full life history before they'd even consider giving him a penny. It'd make him feel better if Rachel double-checked everything. Filling out the forms really made everything seem more real.

Rachel threw open the door, and she was beaming. So okay, whatever it was, was good. What a relief.

"Come on in," she said, ushering him inside. He saw a bottle of wine and Japanese takeout on the kitchen table. He took a step into the living room before Rachel stopped him by putting a hand to his chest. His breath caught and he immediately froze. He hoped she couldn't feel how fast his heart was beating.

"What?" he asked thickly.

"Shoes off," she reminded him, sounding slightly out of breath herself. And if he wasn't mistaken, her eyes were a little hazy too.

Maybe she'd gotten a head start on the wine.

"Oh, sorry." Dutifully, he slipped off his shoes and followed her to the kitchen. "Sushi?" There were double orders of gyoza and edamame, shrimp tempura, and a variety of makis still in the containers. His mouth began to water.

"I went for the good stuff tonight," she said over her shoulder as she went to grab plates. "I even sprung for green tea cheesecake for dessert."

Luke gave a low whistle. "What's the occasion?"

Rachel poured them both a glass of red. "We are celebrating a major win tonight—that's what we're doing!" Her eyes were sparkling and her smile was from ear to ear.

He picked up the glass and took a sip. "Nice," he commented.

"I thought about getting some saké but thought it'd be overkill." At his look she relented. "Fine, I was running late and didn't feel like making a trip to the store," she admitted. "But the wine is really good! It's my favorite and I only break it out on special occasions." Luke looked at the label and was taken aback. It really was the good stuff. He wasn't any sort of wine connoisseur, but it looked like the real deal from Burgundy, France.

"I didn't know you were a wine snob," he commented.

Rachel's brows furrowed. "I'm not. I just did some research on wine and asked the shop owner. The Machard Gramont seemed to be a good deal."

The two of them sat down and started filling their plates. For a few minutes they ate in silence. But then Luke couldn't take the curiosity any longer.

"So don't keep me in suspense. What're we celebrating?" He took a bite of a spicy shrimp and lobster roll with cucumber and avocado and eel sauce and nearly rolled his eyes to the back of his head in bliss.

"Remember that thing we went to last week?"

"You mean the reception with the chamber of commerce and the mayor's office?"

"Yeah. So that guy I was talking to, Graham DeKay, actually runs a small chain of gourmet specialty food shops."

"Fancy pasta that costs twenty bucks for five ounces of flour, water, and salt?"

"Actually he told me he focuses more on imported wine, meats, and cheeses. Apparently his sausages are quite impressive."

Luke considered it earning brownie points with the angels and a sign of his maturity that he didn't latch on to the sausage remark.

"I got a call from Regina—she does corporate analysis for the firm. Graham set up a meeting with her. Basically she'll be doing for him what I'll be doing for you. Graham wants to take his business national and wants Regina and the company to help him do it!"

"Rachel, that's amazing," he said, genuinely thrilled and proud. Rachel had come a long way since they first started. It was like being a mama bird pushing your baby out of the nest and watching them soar.

"I mean it doesn't exactly help me and my team but it's still a win for the company. Amanda's happy."

"Of course she is."

"Then there's this." Rachel pulled out her phone, tapped on it for a few moments and showed it to him. "It's from my old boss—Jake."

Rachel,

Just wanted to drop a line saying I'm hearing great things about how well you're doing out there. I talked to Amanda today and she is happy with the progress you're making. Keep up the good work. It sounds like you're going to be there for a good long while. We're going to miss you. I knew you could do it.

Jake

Luke put down the phone and grinned. "That calls for a toast." They clinked glasses. Then Rachel put hers down and frowned.

"I appreciate the vote of confidence, but I can't help but feel like Jake's tempting fate. Nothing's official yet. I could still end up in Omaha. No one wants to end up in the Omaha office."

He shook his head. "Rachel. Take the win."

"I don't like corn or cows," she insisted. "I mean I like eating them fine, doesn't mean I want to be surrounded by them."

"What did we say about stereotypes?" he said with mock severity. "Dollar in the jar."

"Does Nebraska not have corn or cows?"

Giving up, he grabbed his own phone and put it on speaker, then pulled up Katrina and the Waves' "Walking on Sunshine." He walked over to Rachel and pulled her to her feet.

"Come on, let's celebrate!"

He twirled her around a few times, and pulled her into an impromptu boogie.

"You're crazy," she said with a breathless laugh. "I'm no good at this—I'm gonna stomp all over your feet. You'll be lucky to have any toes left if you keep this up."

"You need to let go and have some fun," he retorted, then spun her out and spun her back in.

Rachel finally got into the spirit and began dancing with him with gusto. For someone who claimed not to be good at dancing, she had a pretty decent sense of rhythm. And his feet and toes remained intact. Which didn't surprise him. No one could resist the lure of "Walking on Sunshine." And it felt good to cut loose a little bit and convince Rachel to do the same. Maybe she was right that her former boss was getting ahead of himself, but there was no reason not to celebrate a win whenever you got a chance.

Still grinning he watched Rachel give a little shimmy then took her hand, spun her in, then dipped her. When she came back up, suddenly they were flush up against each other, nose to nose, mouth to mouth. He was staring straight into those dark chocolate brown eyes. That was one of the unexpected good things about Rachel being as tall as she was. They lined up perfectly and he could look right into her eyes. He would barely need to tilt his head down if he wanted to capture her lips, as he so desperately wanted to do now.

The music seemed to fade away and the only thing he could hear was the beating of his heart. Rachel stood still, and suddenly it wasn't fun or games anymore. Of their own volition, his hands cradled her face and Rachel's eyes widened. Afraid that he was misreading the situation, he started to step away, but then her lips parted slightly.

It would be so quick so easy to close that distance and give them both what they so clearly wanted. He was just about to taste those luscious lips again when the song switched and Billy Joel's "We Didn't Start the Fire" started blaring.

First of all, Luke had to wonder what the hell kind of algorithm would play that song after Katrina and the Waves, but he wasn't going to complain. Nothing like a four-minute mini history lesson in song form with constant references to war, disease, famine, and nuclear annihilation to put a damper on the sexy vibes. Thank goodness he'd snapped out of it before he'd ruined everything by giving in to his momentary desires.

Second, he had a plan and he was sticking to it. No matter how much willpower it took, he was going to wait and do this properly. He'd never forgive himself if he took things too fast and ended up ruining things for Rachel or put any of her goals in jeopardy. Besides, he needed a little time to figure out the best way to ask her out. He was going to behave himself until after the wedding and the promotion becoming permanent. It was for the best. Rachel had set the ground rules and he was going to respect them. She was worth it.

"I think we better get back to dinner," she blurted out. "It's seafood—it probably shouldn't be at room temperature for too long. And I still need to warm up the cheesecake for dessert."

Luke let out a breath. Thank God he'd stopped himself in time. But just in case, he gave a sheepish grin. "Sorry. What can I say? I love dancing and got carried away."

"Sure. Carried away," she said slowly as she sat down again. Her face was impassive, her tone flat.

"Hey is everything okay?" He frowned. Rachel had been the one who'd put a stop to things, and he'd backed off, no questions asked. So what was the problem?

"Sure. Everything's great. Why would anything be wrong?" Rachel asked carefully as she started to eat again.

"You don't sound like you're fine," he ventured hesitantly.

"I've had a day, still trying to process it all, I guess," she said. Her eyes cleared and when she smiled this time it reached her eyes. Luke gave a sigh of relief.

"So enough about me. What's going on with you?"

"Never mind me. Tonight is your night," he insisted.

With a frown, Rachel kept pushing. "No, I want to know. If it makes you feel better, getting an update from you is how I want to celebrate."

Shrugging, he acquiesced. "I spent the past few nights downloading and printing out forms. I even applied for an EIN."

"That's great!" She beamed. "I also saw you talking to some people at the reception. Did you get some business cards? Maybe they can refer you or talk about putting you on retainer for their company."

"Actually, we just talked about Steph Curry and the Warriors' prospects next season," he admitted sheepishly.

Rachel shook her head. "Sportsball completely eludes me." Excuse me? He couldn't have possibly heard right.

Luke put a hand to his heart. "The fact you use the word sportsball wounds me more than you can know."

"Not liking sportsball is not a crime."

"It damn well should be. I get season tickets every year. You and I are going to a game."

"I don't think that's necessary. Besides, basketball is a winter sport right? This arrangement will have ended way before then. No need to take me."

"Maybe I just want to take you to a game." Was that really such a foreign concept to her? That he enjoyed her company outside of their arrangement? Maybe he needed to do a better job of showing her that. Luke put that on his mental list of possible future dates.

"Okay, I guess if you insist."

He nodded firmly. "I insist." Then he paused. "Maybe it'll be how we celebrate you nailing that promotion and not getting sent off to Omaha."

"Hold on. Going to a basketball game is one thing. But that's not going to be how I celebrate if I officially get the promotion."

"Fine, we'll do whatever you want," he said with a breezy wave of his hand.

Rachel's frown was thoughtful. "I've always wanted to do an escape room. Maybe we can do that. And a nice dinner out, of course. And prosecco. Maybe Adrienne, Jeffrey, and Cecily could come too."

"Sounds like a plan." He smiled gamely. "The more the merrier." He'd hoped they could do something just the two of them, but if that was what she wanted, that's what she'd get. Escape room, here they come.

"But maybe the basketball game won't be so bad. Something to talk about in the break room right?"

"Sure. Sports has always been a way to build bridges and forge common ground. My friend Chris aced his interview because he's a huge golf fiend, and so was the guy interviewing him. They go golfing together once or twice a month."

"Which probably helps when it comes to promotions and getting the good job assignments," Rachel pointed out.

He shrugged. "Probably."

"But what about the other people Chris works with who don't get that face and bonding time on the golf course? Especially the women? I bet a lot of those golf clubs are snobby and exclusive as hell. So that probably also puts the minority employees at a disadvantage too."

"I don't know the details," he said, squirming slightly. He'd never thought of it that way before.

"It's like that episode of *Friends* when Rachel pretended to be a smoker so she could get in better with her boss. Not everyone can afford a fancy set of golf clubs and become BFFs with the higher ups."

"Even I'd draw the line at starting up a potentially deadly habit in order to advance your career."

"You said they bonded over golf. Remember how I found out Brian plays basketball with his friends? What if one of my bosses overhears him talking about it and asks to join. Not like Brian can say no. Do you think it's fair that Brian gets that leg up just because they have a hobby in common? One that's not open to me and other people?"

Upon seeing the look on Rachel's face, he could muster only one response. "The patriarchy sucks?"

"Just like colonialism and imperialism."

"Duly noted."

SHE WAS IN the zone. It was time for her monthly deep clean and Rachel was making excellent progress. The Roomba had already run its course, so now she was mopping the floor. Her hair was up in a bandana, she was wearing a ratty T-shirt and gym shorts, and she had one of her favorite podcasts going. The dishes were done and she'd dusted the tables and furniture. All that was left was the laundry, and the bathroom—her least favorite chore.

Cleaning was a pain in the ass, but she had to admit the results were worth it. A clean living environment was always soothing, and there was something about the scent of the citrus cleaning products in the air to signal a job well done. Besides, having a podcast to listen to while cleaning made the time go much faster and the whole process less painful.

Rachel saw a dried soy sauce stain on the kitchen floor and frowned. How did that get there? With a sigh, she shrugged and attacked it with vigor, putting her shoulders into it. She gave herself a mental cheer and high five when the brown spot disappeared.

That was more like it.

She blew out a breath and looked around. "Not bad," she murmured to herself. Another hour or so and she'd be done. Then she could watch that Netflix documentary she'd been meaning to get to for months. She'd earned it. Order in some takeout, and her day was set.

Then she heard her phone ring and almost reflexively

glared at it. She had her whole day planned out and now someone was interrupting it. She walked over and groaned when she saw who it was.

"Hi, Ma."

"Rachel. What is wrong with you? How could you keep something like this from us?"

"What did I do now?"

There was a pause before Rose spoke again. "What is that?" Her mother's voice was strained and shocked. Then the podcast hostess's voice registered.

"So Gordon Walters' body was found exsanguinated in the bathtub. His throat was slit, and his eyes had been gouged out. The killer had also cut his tongue out, and left it for police to find in Gordon's bedroom, along with the family jewels, so to speak. The stomach, spleen, and intestines were stuffed into the mattress. Needless to say, when investigators finally arrived, it was a nasty bloodbath to wade through."

Oh, that. "Just listening to a podcast while I'm cleaning. It helps the time go faster." Reluctantly, she turned off *Murder in the City*.

"You couldn't find some decent music? What's wrong with some Mozart, Bach, or Chopin? Or Andy Lau or Teresa Teng? Why do you have to listen to something so gory? What will other people think?"

"I like murder podcasts," Rachel said through gritted teeth.

"No wonder your sister says you can't find a nice boy," Rose said primly.

"That assumes I'm trying to find a nice boy," Rachel tossed back, knowing full well that she'd basically just committed blasphemy as far as her parents were concerned. The idea of one of their children not fulfilling their filial duty to provide grandchildren was unthinkable.

"Don't get fresh," Rose warned. "Anyway, that actually leads to why I'm calling you."

"What did I do now?"

"What did I just say about your tone?" Rose's tone was calm, but it did nothing to lessen the threat.

"Sorry," Rachel muttered. "So why did you call?"

"Claudia said you told her you're bringing someone to the wedding. A boy named Luke."

"Yes."

"Who is he? We don't know anything about him." Again, her mother's tone was all polite inquiry, but Rachel knew better. All decorum and manners in public, but a whole different story when they were home, and it was time for tough love and discipline. Though in Rose's case, she let Ray be the one to drop the hammer. So many times growing up, "Wait until your father gets home" was Rose's ultimate threat.

"His name is Luke Trudeau. He's a lawyer."

"A lawyer." The approval was immediate. So clichéd. "Does he work with Cecily? Is that how you met? Did she introduce you? She's such a nice girl—you're lucky she's your friend."

"No, they don't work together, but they will be. Well, sorta. It's complicated."

“Then how did you meet this boy?”

There was no way in hell she was going to tell the real story. And she sent a quick prayer that Cecily wouldn’t blab on her. Because if she did, Rachel may end up being the topic of one of the episodes of her favorite podcasts.

“I ran into him at Adrienne’s birthday party.” Technically true. Part of her was actually proud of herself for being able to think on her feet like this. Luke really was a good teacher.

“Oh. How long have you been dating him?”

“We’re not dating, Ma. He’s a friend and he offered to escort me to the wedding.”

“But he’s a stranger.”

“I thought you and Claudia would be happy. Now I won’t be the sad lonely pathetic spinster who can’t land a date and sticks out like a sore thumb.”

“Sarcasm is unattractive, Rachel. Stop it.”

“I wasn’t being sarcastic.”

“Why do you always act like Claudia and I are attacking you? It’s not true. We care about you and want to help. We want the best for you.”

By gleefully pointing out everything they thought was wrong with her? But that was very much the Asian family way. “We nag, push buttons, and poke at wounds because we care.” Not exactly the best fodder for a cross-stitch or embroidery sampler.

“I know.”

“But wait a minute. What did you say his last name was?”

Immediately, the alarm bells began ringing. "Trudeau."

"So he's not Asian." Which meant she'd just earned another black mark.

"Who knows? Maybe he has a random ancestor somewhere."

Rose sighed. "Why am I not surprised you're making things more difficult than they have to be?"

"I'm not making anything difficult! He's just a friend I'm bringing to the wedding. Don't read more into it than there is."

"Rachel, marriage is hard work and a big commitment, even when the couple has a solid foundation with similar values. Dating a wai guo ren just makes things harder than they have to be. Why couldn't you find a nice Asian boy to date?"

"I'm not marrying Luke!"

"But is he going to understand all the different aspects of the wedding ceremony? Is he going to be respectful? Is he going to fit in? You're going to have to spend a lot of time explaining everything, and that's a lot of work."

As much as Rachel hated to admit it, her mother had a point. Claudia and Dennis planned to have a traditional marriage ceremony as much as possible, and a lot of it would be brand new to Luke. She knew he would be respectful, but there was a high possibility he would be lost during the course of the day and not understand what was happening or why. They would have to have a deep dive before the flight to New York.

"I'll take care of it," she assured Rose. "And he'll be

nice. He won't gawk or be rude, if that's what you're worried about."

Rose tsked. "It would be so much easier if you could have stayed here in Brooklyn. I talked to Mrs. Chow last week. Her nephew Brandon got a new job and is back in New York. He would be perfect."

"Ma, it's not like that."

"I'm just saying Brandon would be a much better fit for you. And the family. Assuming you don't do anything to scare him off, like you always seem to do."

It was on the tip of Rachel's tongue to retort that she didn't seem to have scared Luke off and they'd been together…or working together over three months now. So maybe the problem wasn't all her. Then her mind flashed back to their dinner last week. She'd been so excited to share the good news with him and celebrate. Then he'd gotten her to loosen up and dance, something she never did. But then that moment after he'd dipped her remained seared in her mind. The way he was looking at her, the way her body instinctively responded and the way her heart was pounding like crazy, Rachel would have sworn he was about to kiss her, and she'd been ready to throw caution to the wind and let him.

But at the last minute, fear and doubt got the better of her, and she'd blurted out the asinine comment about the food. And thank God she did. Luke had just gotten caught up in the music too, and it was clear she'd totally misread the signs. He hadn't been about to kiss her at all. She could only be grateful her instincts had kicked in before things went too far and she'd made a fool out of herself again.

Why did she think he'd want to kiss her? Stupid.

"I've already invited Luke and it'd be rude to back out now. He'll be coming with me to New York." And knowing Luke, he'd no doubt charm the pants off her entire family and everyone at the wedding and have her mother eating out of the palm of his hand.

"You always were so stubborn," Rose muttered. "But you're staying with us. And Luke will need to find his own accommodations. The hotel block we reserved for guests is already full."

"We'll find an Airbnb nearby. He'll be fine."

"Maybe I can ask Judith if he can stay with the Changs. Or Pam and Martin. They probably have a spare room or bed your friend can borrow."

Oh God no. Cecily and Jeffrey would probably never forgive her if her mother did this.

"Please, Ma, I'm begging you, let me handle this. Don't meddle."

"What meddling? I'm trying to help. Why waste money on a hotel or stranger's place God knows where when he can stay with family and friends right here in the neighborhood?"

"It's my money to waste. And I'm sure Luke would be more comfortable in his own space instead of staying in a stranger's house."

"How's that different from an Airbnb? Don't be silly." Rose sounded genuinely baffled, as if she couldn't understand the difference. Which were massive. Huge.

"Just trust me, it's better this way."

"See right here? This is what I'm talking about. Americans, wanting privacy, their own space. A good Chinese boy would know that it'd be better to stay with friends and family. Now you understand why I want to set you up with Brandon?"

"I. Don't. Want. To. Date. Brandon," Rachel gritted out. She was ready to bang her head against the wall.

There was a long pause. When Rose finally spoke again, her tone was low firm and even.

"I see you've decided to be unreasonable and difficult. There's no point in talking to you when you're like this. Do what you want. You always do, after all." With that, Rose ended the call, leaving Rachel staring at her phone, trying to get her blood pressure under control.

"Unbelievable," she muttered. She really wished she knew the magic formula to smooth things over with her family but it wasn't meant to be.

But on the bright side, at least this conversation had two silver linings. One: she knew to be on guard for a possible setup. Rachel made a mental note to be sure to never be left alone anywhere with Brandon. She wasn't stupid enough to believe this would be the end of it. And two: she made a note to have a sit-down with Luke and explain all the ins and outs of a Taiwanese/Asian/American fusion wedding.

That was going to be interesting, to say the least. She hoped Luke wouldn't come to regret his extremely generous offer.

Chapter Fourteen

"THANKS FOR THE invite, boss," Annika said as she raised her beer in a toast. With a nervous smile, Rachel returned the toast. Part of her still wasn't sure how the hell she'd ended up here, but this was happening. Despite Luke's promise to let her gradually wade into the deep end of the pool, he'd thrown her off the high dive and was letting her fend for herself.

Though technically, this was less Luke's fault and more of that cheating bastard Randall's fault. The other Rachel had indeed come into the office and caused a scene. It appeared she had found out about Mandy and wasn't taking it well at all. Rachel could hardly blame her. But the result was that in a last-ditch effort to save the marriage, Randall and the other Rachel were moving to the Milwaukee office, closer to her family. And now Teddy Pierce had taken Cheating Bastard Randall's place on the team.

Luke had convinced her that hosting a happy hour slash dinner as an icebreaker and to welcome Teddy properly to the team was essential. So here she was. Frankly, she'd been surprised that the rest of the team was so eager to come. But then again, people rarely turned down free booze.

"I had to pay out the wazoo for a last-minute babysitter but totally worth it," Brian added.

Rachel frowned. "I'm sorry. I didn't realize you're having to pay for extra childcare for this."

"Oh it's not what you think," Brian explained with a grimace. "My in-laws live nearby. My mother-in-law was practically in the car and on her way to the house before my wife got off the phone to ask. But we had no choice. No way was I missing this, and Marissa has book club tonight."

"Your mother-in-law charges you to babysit?" Contessina asked, surprised.

"Nope, it just means I can't avoid going to their place for Sunday dinner. So now I have no choice but to force down her overcooked tough-as-hell pot roast and do it with a smile."

Well, that was a lot of pressure to live up to for her group happy hour/dinner. At least Amanda wasn't there, due to a previous engagement. The only thing worse than her being a total awkward turtle around a bunch of her coworker/teammates was doing so in front of the boss and really making an idiot of herself.

But so far so good. Everyone was just drinking, making small talk and leaving her out of the conversation. If this kept up, she could probably get through the evening unscathed. She'd have to thank Luke for that. The books she'd read and Goggle searches helped, but he was a huge part of it. She was beginning to feel more comfortable with the group.

That was, until Jonathan turned to her and decided to bring her into the conversation. Crap.

"So, boss, thanks for inviting us out."

"Sure," she said carefully.

"You know it occurs to me we don't really know that much about you. I mean you know that I love the Red Hot Chili Peppers and you like Alanis, but beyond that you're a mystery."

"A riddle, wrapped in a mystery, inside an enigma," Annika agreed.

At that Rachel had to give an unladylike snort. Though part of her wasn't sure how she felt about having that Churchill quote used on her. "Please, you're making me sound way more interesting than I actually am. I am so boring, there's really nothing to know," she insisted.

"Now I'm even more intrigued," Contessina said, raising her brow.

Rachel looked around the table. It was clear the gauntlet had been thrown down because every single one of them was looking at her with expectant expressions on their faces.

She took a deep breath. "How about this? You each get to ask me one question. Any question you want." The mischievous look on Teddy's face had her include a quick caveat. "Any sex-related questions are out. Other than that, ask away. Make it good." Her heart was pounding a mile a minute because this had the potential to go off the rails very quickly and badly. She hoped she wasn't making a huge mistake. Things had been going well and she hoped she wasn't about to undo all the progress she'd made.

There were sighs and eye rolls all around, but the team acquiesced.

"How old are you?" This was from Brian.

"Brian, you know better than that. You never ask a lady her age," Contessina admonished.

"No that's fine," Rachel said, relieved. "I'm thirty-six."

"When's your birthday?" Jonathan asked.

"February thirteenth. And yes, my birthday is almost always overlooked because of Valentine's Day."

"Ohh an Aquarius. They're the best!" Annika said with a big smile.

"Thanks?" Rachel knew nothing about astrology, so she had no idea what being an Aquarius meant. But as long as Annika approved, she'd roll with it.

"Yeah," Annika continued. "My best friend from college is an Aquarius. We were roommates freshman year. We pledged Delta Sigma Nu together."

Interesting. "You don't strike me as a sorority-girl type," she mused.

Annika gave a blink. "What do you mean by sorority-type girl?"

With a sinking heart, Rachel realized she's screwed up and put her foot in her mouth big time. "I just meant, when people say sorority girl you tend to think..." she stammered in a futile effort to apologize and walk back her insulting remarks. Fumbling as she stood up, she excused herself and practically ran to the bathroom.

Nearly hyperventilating, she got her phone out of her

purse, hands trembling, and pulled up Luke's name.

"Please pick up, please pick up," she muttered.

"Hello?" As soon as she heard his voice on the other end of the line she nearly collapsed in relief.

"I'm in serious trouble," she blurted out.

"What's wrong? Aren't you supposed to be having drinks and dinner with your team? What happened?"

"I happened, that's what," she hissed. "I put my foot in my mouth and now everyone hates me."

"Slow down," he said in a soothing voice, as if he was trying to calm down a skittish bridezilla who was having a meltdown because the sash on the flower girl's dress was maroon, not burgundy. Which, to be fair, wasn't far off. "I'm sure whatever it is, it's not that bad. Back up and tell me what happened."

"It was going fine at first. They were talking amongst themselves and leaving me out of it. Then they decided they wanted to get to know me better and ask me questions. And that's when it all went to hell in a handbasket."

"Surely you're exaggerating."

"I surely the hell am not. Annika asked me a question, mentioned that she was in a sorority, and I said I didn't think she was the sorority girl type, and she asked what I meant by that. So I have now mortally offended her and now she hates me because I insulted her."

"Maybe, maybe not. I'm sure she knows you didn't mean to offend her."

"That doesn't matter! What do I do now? I can't move to Omaha. I can't. I already spent so much buying new furniture and things for my apartment here!" She heard herself. Part of her brain realized she was going off the deep end and that she was very close to hyperventilating and a panic attack but she couldn't care less at the moment.

"You're getting a little ahead of yourself aren't you? Breathe," Luke said, still calm and soothing as any yogi at a new-age retreat. He counted with her to ten and her panic abated slightly.

"Rachel, you need to keep it together. This isn't as bad as you think it is."

"Easy for you to say. You weren't there, and you would know what to say to get them to laugh and forgive you everything."

"Look," he said, ignoring her completely, "if you're so convinced you screwed up, the best thing you can do is swallow your pride, own your mistakes, apologize, and ask for forgiveness. A simple but sincere 'I'm sorry' can go a long way."

"But the books I read and the Google articles all say women apologize too much and it undermines them. Am I going to have to add a damn dollar to the jar?"

"That only applies if you're apologizing when you didn't do anything you needed to apologize for. Besides, remember another rule—sometimes it's better to ask for forgiveness than permission."

"All this seems very contradictory," Rachel pointed out with a frown.

"At the risk of you grumbling about it, I need to fall back on another lawyer standby. These things are situation-specific. It depends."

"Fine, you're right. I'll go apologize to Annika. At the very least it'll make me feel better."

"There you go. Go get 'em champ."

"I thought we already talked about how sportsball references elude me."

Luke gave a brief chuckle and sigh. "Okay, now I know you're feeling better. Go back out there. I'll talk to you later."

"Remind me to give you crap about the 'it depends' lawyer thing later."

"Sure, Jan." Then he ended the call. Rachel frowned in confusion. Who the hell was Jan? Then her phone pinged with a text and she saw the gif. As she looked at the gif of Marcia Brady giving the mother of all side-eyes she laughed and blew out a breath.

"Damn it." Trust Luke to make her laugh and ease the situation. Then Rachel squared her shoulders and went back out to join the group.

With her most sincere regretful expression, she immediately dove into her apology. "Annika, I'm sorry that I upset and offended you, even unintentionally. There's no excuse, and I shouldn't have said what I did. I promise I won't do it again, and I hope you'll forgive me."

The whole table fell silent and stared at her again. A celery stick full of blue cheese dressing was halfway to Annika's mouth and stayed frozen there. She put the celery stick down and blinked.

"Oh, wow. Okay."

What the hell did that mean?

"Honestly, I was worried when you ran off like that."

"Yeah, she was convinced you were going to come back and fire her," Brian piped up.

Rachel's mouth opened in a surprised O. "I would never do that."

"And I wasn't offended. The sorority girl stereotype is a thing for a reason," Annika said with a shrug.

"All right. So no harm, no foul?"

"Absolutely." The other woman picked up the celery again and ate, and the tension at the table began to ease.

Rachel's shoulders relaxed and she began to smile. "Great. So anyone want to get one last round in?"

"Oh no you don't," Contessina warned. "You still haven't answered a question from all of us yet."

"Yeah I had a good one ready," Teddy said, rubbing his hands.

"Watch it, new guy," one of the others warned. "You're still on probation."

"But if she really wants to make it up to us, maybe we should make her tell us an embarrassing story from her childhood," Annika said with a mischievous grin.

Rachel's face blanched, and she was ready to ask for any other method of penance when the rest of the group broke down laughing.

"Hell no. You guys had me going there for a sec," Rachel protested. Then with a smile, she crossed her arms. "No sex questions or embarrassing childhood questions. But the rest of you can try to do your worst. Bring it on."

An hour and a half later, Rachel was back in her apartment, crashed out on the couch, relieved that she's survived the whole affair. She'd suffered a setback but she liked to think she'd rallied and come back strong, and that was the important thing. It didn't matter where you start, it's how you finish, and she'd done well if she did say so herself. She picked up her phone, ready to text Luke and debrief him and then suddenly she stopped herself.

When she was going down a spiral and freaking out, he'd been the first person she called. She'd gone to him for support and advice. And now, her instinct was once again to reach out to him first. Not her family, not Cecily or Adrienne, but Luke. He was the one who came to mind and that was no accident. There was a reason why he was the one who she wanted to share all the details with.

Despite their agreement to keep things friendly and professional, there was no denying it any longer. She'd fallen for him. Hard. He was handsome, charming, and had a way of making her feel like she was the only woman in the world when he looked at her in that way when they were talking. He didn't seem to mind her weird and awkward ways and was exceedingly kind and patient while he worked with her to improve her skills and make this promotion permanent.

And, well, it had to be said. Just look at the man. Who could blame her for falling for that? If she was honest with herself, she'd probably started falling for him the minute they first set eyes on each other at the Wild Saguaro and she'd been falling ever since.

With a shake of her head Rachel reminded herself of the rules. All clothes were staying on. Her current revelation slash breakthrough had disaster written all over it. The last thing she wanted to do was something stupid to ruin the current arrangement. She and Luke had a good thing going and it was going to stay that way.

For now, the truth of her feelings was going to stay within the four walls of her apartment. No one would ever know.

Rachel: *By the way, did you check out those links I sent you for graphic designers? They can help you design a new website for your business and business cards. That will be essential for marketing and promo when the time comes. And how are you doing with the permits and stuff?*

Luke: *Yes. I'm also looking at Craigslist and ZipRecruiter and other places to look for paralegals and assistants. Still working on the permits and applications. It's a never-ending pile of red tape.*

Rachel: *It's people like you who created the red tape in the first place. Once you decide on the specifics, let me know and I can update the data and projections.*

Luke: *Will do. I may have also found a few other options for office space. Maybe I can send you some pictures and you can let me know what you think?*

Rachel: *Okay.*

Luke: *So I have a big favor to ask.*

Rachel: *As long as it doesn't involve anything illegal,* *immoral, or suspect, I'm willing to listen. Besides, after you talked me through my freakout at the bar last week, I owe you one.*

Luke: *It involves dinner.*

Rachel: *What about it? Are you asking me to make you dinner? If that's the case, you're better off ordering takeout. I can barely boil an egg. I'm the worst. I only know how to make like three dishes. You'll be better off letting me buy some takeout or giving you cash for it. But you must be desperate if you're asking me for a meal.*

Luke: *No, dinner with my parents. My parents are visiting in a few weeks and they're inviting us to dinner.*

Rachel: *Why would they want to have dinner with me? What did you say to them?*

Luke: *Remember the chicken soup?*

Rachel: *Yes, it was amazing and I still dream about it. Why?*

Luke: *Unfortunately, my mother found out that I made the soup for you when you were sick. And now she insists on meeting you.*

Rachel: *I still don't understand.*

Luke: *Look up* Steel Magnolias *in the dictionary. You'll find a picture of Naomi Bishop Trudeau.*

Rachel: *Is this another movie I need to watch?*

Luke: *Yes, but that's not the point. My mother insists on having dinner with us, and you would be doing me a huge favor by coming. They're harmless, I swear. Well Dad at least. I make no promises about Mama. She still scares the daylight out of me.*

Rachel: *I'm even more confused. Why does she want to*

meet me? Is this some sort of Southern thing because I didn't send her a handwritten thank-you note? Or does she want to size me up and decide whether or not I'm soup-worthy? Because I would need to know the criteria for soup-worthiness before I commit.

Luke: *Trust me, you're soup-worthy.*

Rachel: *According to you or your mother?*

Luke: *Don't worry, they'll love you.*

Rachel: *I highly doubt that.*

Luke: *You're wrong. Will you please say yes?*

Rachel: *Just explain why they want me there.*

Luke: *Like I said, Mama found out I made soup for you and made certain assumptions. Which my brother was more than willing to aid and abet.*

Rachel: *But you told them we were just friends, right? You didn't tell them how we really met?*

Luke: *Yes, don't worry.*

Rachel: *In that case, okay. But you'll owe me one.*

Luke: *I'll make you another batch of soup and put it in quarts and you can store it in your freezer. Will that work?*

Rachel: *Okay. Anything for soup.*

Luke: *Thank you—7 p.m. at the Rose and Crown. Saturday the 25th.*

Rachel: *It's on my calendar.*

Luke: *You are a lifesaver.*

Rachel: *That sounds a little dramatic. What if I'd said no?*

Luke: *I would have had no choice but to bring them by*

your apartment. Mama would insist.

Rachel: *WHAT??*

Luke: *You really need to watch* Steel Magnolias. *That'll explain everything.*

Rachel: *If you say so.*

She took a deep breath and shook her head. What had she just agreed to? Despite Luke's smooth talking and assurance that the Trudeaus would love her, she knew that she was very much an acquired taste. But she couldn't help but be who she was. So what was she going to do? She didn't want to make a bad impression. She could draw on the knowledge she'd gleaned from her reading list and from her lessons with Luke, but those were all in a career and business context. Meeting the parents was a whole different situation.

She needed help. And at the moment, she went with her gut instinct and sent out a group text.

Rachel: *I need help.*

Cecily: *What's up?*

Adrienne: *You need bail money?*

Rachel: *Nothing like that.*

She paused. Maybe asking Adrienne and Cecily wasn't the best move.

Adrienne: *Well don't keep us in suspense!*

Rachel: *What does it mean when you get invited to meet someone's parents?*

Cecily: *Depends on who the someone is. Is it who I think it is?*

Rachel: *Who do you think it is?*

Adrienne: *Don't try to be cute. Did Luke ask you to meet his parents?*

Rachel: *Apparently his mother found out he made her soup for me and now it's a thing.*

Cecily: *And here you were insisting nothing was going on.*

Rachel: *Okay. Maybe you were both right. I may have feelings for him.*

Wow so much for keeping her feelings private. Where had that come from? Maybe part of her wanted help and advice after all. Rachel sighed. Oh well, too late to take it back now.

Cecily: *May?*

Rachel: *FINE. I do. But it doesn't matter because he doesn't feel the same way. He's made it clear he's happy to keep things as they are.*

Adrienne: *Cough. Bullshit. Cough.*

Cecily: *I don't know why you're so convinced he has no feelings for you. You two slept together and have been working together for weeks, months now. Of course there are feelings.*

Rachel: *But I don't want to have these feelings. How do I make them go away?*

Cecily: *That's the thing about stupid feelings. You have to deal with them. Ask me how I know.*

Rachel: *Let me guess, the sex god?*

Adrienne: **Snickers*.*

Cecily: *I'm going to ignore that. But yes, despite me wanting to forget about him for ten years, it didn't work. I still had stupid feelings for him, and now the stupid feelings aren't so stupid anymore. Though I am willing to agree and stipulate that for the most part feelings are indeed stupid.*

Rachel: *Damn it you really are such a lawyer. Both of you.*

Adrienne: *Hey! What did I do?*

Rachel: *You were also cross-examining me or whatever the hell it is they call it. Anyway, I need help.*

Cecily: *With what? (By the way, I am going to take your last comment as the compliment I'm sure it was meant to be.)*

Rachel: *What do I say? What do I do when I meet his parents? I tried to look for books on the topic but that wasn't helpful. Neither were the Google searches. They had good general tips but nothing that works in this situation.*

Adrienne: *I can see how finding info on how to talk to the parents of the guy who I had a one-night stand with, then we decided to be just friends and enter into a mutually beneficial arrangement to help both our careers but now I went and developed stupid feelings for the guy could be difficult.*

Cecily: *But I love that your first instinct was to Google and try to find books on Amazon.*

Rachel: *You two are mocking me, right?*

Cecily: *Not mocking, just snark. We snark with love in the group chat. Don't worry, you'll get used to it.*

Adrienne: *Indeed, it's how we roll.*

Rachel: *Well thanks a lot, CeeCee. Good to know. Not good at snark though.*

Adrienne: *And to answer your question, calm down. Just don't be nervous, be yourself, you'll be fine.*

Rachel: *Did you not read that I said I wanted to make a GOOD impression? I can't just be myself. That's the whole damn fucking problem!*

Cecily: *What's wrong with you being you?*

Rachel: *More snark?*

Cecily: *No, deadly fucking serious.*

Adrienne: *I completely agree with Cecily.*

Rachel: *What's wrong with being me is I have no idea what to talk to them about. Should I do research on Texas? Maybe I can find out what his parents do so I can talk to them about that too?*

Cecily: *That sounds like a plan. And seriously, relax. This isn't a job interview, it's just dinner.*

Adrienne: *You didn't need us after all.*

Rachel: *Actually those were the tips Luke gave me about establishing a good rapport with my co-workers. I guess those are transferable skills.*

Adrienne: *You should give yourself more credit. You're better at this than you think you are.*

Rachel: *You're kind. I've made progress but still have so far to go.*

Cecily: *Doing all this to improve your communication skills and secure a promotion is one thing, but I hope Luke isn't making you feel like a project.*

Rachel: *No. He's saying we're just smoothing out the*

rough edges and making tweaks.

Cecily: *Okay good. Because you know we think you're pretty cool just as you are.*

Adrienne: *Aawww, CeeCee, look at you paraphrasing* Bridget Jones's Diary.

Cecily: *What can I say? That movie came out during a very formative period of my life. And it's Colin Firth, the definitive Darcy.*

Adrienne: *That scene when they're cooking together. Blue soup. Sigh.*

Rachel: *Blue soup? That sounds kinda gross. Wait. That may have come out wrong.*

Cecily: *Cackles. No you're fine. That's exactly the point.*

Rachel: *Though speaking of soup, that's how Luke got me to agree to go to the dinner. He promised to make me more of his mom's soup. That stuff is to die for.*

Adrienne: *But can we circle back to how you now have stupid feelings for him?*

Cecily: *YES.*

Rachel: *Really, I'd rather not.*

Adrienne: *For what it's worth, I think you should tell him. You may be surprised by his answer.*

Rachel: *That is terrible advice. What if he doesn't feel the same way? Then everything is so awkward. Things are working fine now. No reason to rock the boat, even if I have stupid feelings for the guy.*

Adrienne: *If you say so…*

Cecily: *I agree with Adrienne. Trust me, ignoring stupid feelings never works. NEVER. I have the ring and fiancé to prove it.*

Rachel: *Shit.*

Cecily: *I know. Sorry to be the bearer of bad news. But you got this. You'll have fun at the dinner and his parents will love you. You'll do great.*

Rachel: *Fun might be stretching it.*

Adrienne: *Just keep us posted. I wanna know how it goes.*

Cecily: *Same.*

Rachel: *I suppose. If you guys really want to know.*

Cecily: *One thing you should know about lawyers. We're nosy as hell. So yes we want to know.*

Rachel: *Understood. Yes I will report back. If I make it out alive.*

Chapter Fifteen

"STOP FIDGETING," LUKE told her.

"I can't help it. This is a very stressful situation."

He rolled his eyes. "This is dinner with my parents. No big deal."

Rachel frowned and pushed her glasses up. "That's easy for you to say. Everyone likes you. You can talk anyone into anything. That's not the case here."

"Don't worry, they'll love you."

"I wouldn't be so sure about that," she muttered. He'd made reservations at a nearby gastropub, which would have something for everybody.

"Your mom is going to hate me," she declared with a resigned sigh. Despite the pep talk she got from Adrienne and Cecily, she still felt intimidated as hell and in way over her head. Her current game plan was to speak as little as possible and take every opportunity to ask questions and deflect the attention off her. It was safer that way and better for all involved.

He gave a slight frown. "Why do you say that?"

"I've seen the pictures. She looks like the baroness from *The Sound of Music*. I look and feel like Maria. She's going to hate me."

"If it makes you feel any better, Mama never sent me off to boarding school, so she's nicer than the baroness. Besides, she's Southern. She believes in manners."

"Not. Helping," she growled.

"Oh, there they are now."

Rachel saw the couple walking toward them and groaned. "See? What did I tell you? She looks like Grace Kelly."

"If you really want her to like you, you should tell her that."

Naomi walked right over and smothered him in a hug. "There's my baby boy," she murmured with a fond smile. She then turned to Rachel, and while the smile stayed on her face, it didn't quite reach her eyes.

"You must be Rachel. I must say I've heard so much about you."

"It's very nice to meet you, Mrs. Trudeau." She gamely tried to not let her voice quaver, and surreptitiously wiped her hand on her pants before offering it to shake.

"Oh no, that won't do. No need to be so formal, honey. I'm Naomi."

Meanwhile, Luke and his father did the patented handshake into a hug and loud pats on the back combo men who were only comfortable with limited forms of PDA were famous for.

"Clinton and Naomi Trudeau, I'd like you to meet Rachel Bai from New York City."

The four of them took their seats and Rachel tried not to feel like a pinned bug under a microscope.

"You're from New York? Son, you didn't tell us that."

"Yes, I'm a heathen Yankee." She was trying for the snark Adrienne and Cecily seemed to be able to summon instinctively. Judging by the raised eyebrow from Naomi and slight twitch of the lips from Clinton, it was hit and miss.

"Well I suppose you can't help that," Clinton mused.

"I'm so glad we have this opportunity to meet. I've been looking forward to getting to know you," Naomi put in, placing her napkin on her lap with a delicate flip of her wrist.

"So tell us a little about yourself," Clinton said, after taking a sip of his whiskey.

"I grew up in Brooklyn, went to Harvard and Dartmouth, and I'm a financial analyst for Kirkwood Young and Sloane."

His parents looked at each other. "Well, that's mighty impressive," Clinton said, approval in his tone.

"Do you have any siblings, dear? What do your parents do?" This from Naomi.

So much for trying to avoid having to talk. But Rachel supposed this was typical get-to-know-you small talk so she was probably still in safe territory.

"Well, I have a younger sister. She's getting married soon. And my dad is an accountant. My mother helped run his office."

"Worked hard, pulled themselves up by their bootstraps," Clinton said.

"Something like that."

"She's also a fan of murder podcasts," Luke interjected.

"Oh yes. Well that explains a lot. What an interesting hobby."

Rachel was pretty sure she'd just been dissed Southern style by a quintessential belle.

"I like to listen to them during my commute—it helps pass the time."

"She's also an amazing poker player," Luke added. "She came to my monthly game and cleaned everyone out. Roger banned her from coming back."

From the look on Naomi's face, Rachel was pretty sure this tidbit Luke just shared was strike two. His father, on the other hand, looked impressed.

"Is that so? Maybe you and I should play a few hands someday."

"Fair warning, Dad taught me everything I know," Luke kidded.

"Then it shouldn't be a problem to beat him too," Rachel said without thinking.

Luke swallowed a guffaw, while his mother remained silent, observing and judging. Clinton raised an imperious brow. Oh crap. Did she say something rude again?

"I believe that was a challenge. Just name the time and place. I'm looking forward to it." Clinton's chuckle was a huge relief.

Rachel grabbed a breadstick and started munching. It was better to stuff her mouth so she didn't have to talk.

Naomi ran a perfectly manicured nail over the rim of her glass. "Tell us how you two met. I don't think we've heard that story yet."

At that Rachel choked on her bread, and even Luke started looking uncomfortable.

"You know, the usual story," he said in a strangled tone.

She KNEW this dinner had been a mistake.

"Well, we'd still like to hear it, wouldn't we, Clinton?" Naomi slid a look to her husband, who immediately agreed.

The waiter came by to drop off more bread and top off their water, which gave her and Luke a few precious moments of reprieve, but it didn't last long.

"It was a few months ago. I'd just moved here for a new job at my company and ended up at the same bar he was at."

"I saw her throw back a shot of tequila and ride a mechanical bull and knew immediately I wanted to get to know her better."

"We Texas men do appreciate a woman who can hold her liquor," Clinton acknowledged with a nod. "How long did she last on the bull?"

"Eight seconds."

"Not bad, not bad."

"We went our separate ways but then ran into each other again a week later at a mutual friend's birthday party. Rachel and I got to talking, and discovered we had similar interests. And here we are." Normally, she could appreciate the judicious edits Luke was giving to their origin story, but at the moment she wanted the floor to open up and swallow her whole.

"Now see? Was that so hard?" Luke's mother asked.

Not really, Except Naomi probably thought she was a lush who was trying to put the moves on her baby. Rachel took a breath then tried to put her game plan into action. She was beyond relieved when the waiter finally dropped off their food.

"So, Mr. Trudeau, Luke tells me you like to play golf?"

"I play every week," he confirmed. But he was too busy going to town on his moules frites.

"Thank God for that. It gets him out of my hair and out of the house. He'd drive me crazy if he was underfoot all day."

"Maybe I can suggest my dad talk up golf," Rachel mused. Her mother might appreciate the tip when the time came. Ray had been talking about winding down his business and retiring within the next year or two. This could be a good hobby for him to take up to keep active instead of zoning out in front of the TV all day.

"Maybe your dad and I can go golfing when we're in New York," Luke suggested.

"I think he's going to be too busy with the wedding. We all will be. But it's a nice thought."

"Honestly I'm surprised there are golf courses in New York. I would have guessed there wouldn't be enough room," Luke said with a shrug.

"There are tons," Rachel informed him. "Some even right in Brooklyn."

"What's this now?" Naomi inquired politely.

"You can hardly blame me for making the assumption, Mama. Everyone knows how crowded New York City is."

"Not that part. Did I hear that you two will be attending a wedding?"

Oh crap. Rachel gave a panicked look to Luke. *You handle this one.*

"Yes, well, Rachel needed a plus-one, and as a proper Southern gentleman I could hardly say no to a lady in distress who was in need of assistance."

Rachel blinked and frowned. "Hey, I'm no damsel. I was perfectly fine with going to the wedding myself. You're the one who suggested and insisted on coming with me. Not that I'm not grateful for the offer, but let's set the record straight here. I was not desperate. I wasn't," she insisted. She was so focused on getting the true version of events out there that she didn't realize silence had descended on the table.

Oh, shit. She'd done it again. Rachel closed her eyes and wondered how bad it would be if she did a dine and dash and just left. Okay, she would never do that. She would absolutely throw some cash on the table before running, but the urge was strong.

Naomi got up and excused herself, regal and elegant. "Rachel dear, why don't you come with me?" It was clear it was a command, not a request, so the dine and dash was out.

She dutifully followed Luke's mother to the restroom, all the while feeling like she was walking toward her doom.

Rachel came out of the stall and stood next to Naomi

at the sink, who was touching up her lipstick.

She gave a quick look around to ensure they were alone.

"Mrs. Trudeau..."

"Honey, what did I tell you about that? It's Naomi."

"Fine. Whatever you say." The older woman's brow raised at her tone.

"Since it's just the two of us here, we can be honest with each other and drop the act."

"What act?"

"It's obvious you don't like me. If it were up to me, I couldn't care less, but this is important to Luke, so I would appreciate it if we can just be polite for the rest of the evening and not spoil things for him. And I'm sorry about what I said. I wasn't trying to make him look bad or anything, I just wanted him to stop exaggerating."

"What makes you think I don't like you?" Naomi turned to her and gave an assessing look.

"You're kidding right?"

"I'm afraid my sense of humor never ran toward jokes."

Rachel took a deep breath and kept going. "It's clear you wanted to meet me to size me up and to no one's surprise I've been found lacking. But I get it. A lot of mothers don't think anyone is good enough for their sons."

Naomi gave a small laugh. "Oh, you poor sweet, deluded child." She grabbed Rachel's hand and took them over to a small bench and the two of them sat down. "In the interest of full disclosure, maybe you're right. I don't like you."

Rachel gave a look that screamed SEE?

"But that's only because I just met you. How can you like someone you just met? To me, those things take time."

Rachel had to concede she had a point there.

"As for judging you, I think you are a lovely young woman who is refreshingly honest, with an impressive career and interesting hobbies."

"Oh." That was the last thing she expected to hear.

"Speaking of, you really did throw down the gauntlet. I'm afraid my husband is going to insist on that poker game." Naomi gave her that considering look again. "My gut tells me to put my money on you. No doubt you don't need the help, but if you ever want the inside scoop, I can give you a list of my husband's tells."

Rachel blinked. "I would never. That's cheating. If I'm going to win, I want it to count. I'll beat your husband fair and square."

A pleased smile curved Naomi's lips. "I knew I liked you. As for the other bit, I know my son, and believe me, I have no illusions about him. I don't have him on a pedestal. Luke is far from perfect, and I couldn't be happier he found someone like you. He needs someone to keep him humble, kick his behind, knock him down a peg or two when he needs it. Something tells me you're up for the job."

"Wow. Thank you."

Naomi inclined her head. "You're welcome. We good here?" She gave a satisfied smile at Rachel's nod.

"Great. I'm glad we cleared the air. Something tells me

you're going to be around for a while, and I'd hate to have started off on the wrong foot."

"Oh I don't know about that," Rachel protested.

Again, Naomi gave a tinkling laugh. "Oh, honey. Didn't I just tell you I know my boy? And this is the only time I ever heard of him making my soup for anyone, much less a woman."

Rachel's mouth opened in a surprised oh.

"He called to ask if he could substitute dried parsley for fresh, and I wondered who he was making it for. When he told me it was you who he made the soup for and that he was reading a book about Aileen Wuornos you recommended, I knew I had to meet you. And now I find out my son has taken it upon himself to offer to accompany you to a family wedding—that goes way beyond mere friendship if you ask me. Trust me, I'm never wrong about these things."

Rachel's mouth opened and closed a few more times. Naomi just gave her a pat on the hand.

"Close your mouth, dear. Don't let the flies in. And fix your lipstick. I'll let the men know you're on your way." With a wink, Naomi left the bathroom.

Rachel just sat on the bench and didn't move. She was going to need a second. She'd just had her first run-in with a Southern belle slash steel magnolia.

LUKE WHISTLED AS he put his living room in order in

anticipation of Rachel's visit. They were doing one last planning strategy session before their trip to New York. Part of him was looking forward to it (he was serious about being excited to visit New York City for the first time) but part of him was a bit unsettled, which was quite unlike him.

Right on cue, there was a knock on the door. He glanced at his watch. On time as always. He went to the door and opened it. Rachel stood in front of him, jeans, espadrilles, floral print blouse, and an enormous tote digging into her shoulder. Immediately, he reached out to take the tote.

"I'm fine," she insisted, pushing up her glasses. Comfortable in his apartment by now, she made her way to the living room, sat down on the couch, and started unloading the contents of the tote. He joined her, setting down drinks and a small platter of pretzels, hummus and veggies, and chips and guac. He was from Texas, after all.

Rachel looked up and gave a slight frown. "That's a lot of food."

He shrugged. "It'll tide us over until lunch. The bistro around the corner does takeout and they make amazing gourmet burgers. And I got macadamia nut cookies."

Interest piqued, Rachel's eyes lit up. "Do they have sweet potato fries? If so I'm in."

"Sure, I think so."

"Okay then. Sit down and let's get started. We'll have to be careful not to get any smudges on this." Rachel held up a photo album.

"What's that?" He hadn't expected her to bring photos to look at. Were they going to look at photos of office spaces?

"Family photos. I thought we could have a quick crash course on who's who before we get there so you won't be totally lost at the wedding," she explained.

Oh. That was a brilliant idea. Why hadn't he thought of that first?

For the next thirty minutes they made their way through the album and Luke was introduced to a dizzying array of faces and names. There was no way he would be able to remember them all, but he made sure to at least know Rachel's immediate family, the groom's name, and the senior members of the family. He could depend on Rachel to whisper and provide the other names.

"Anything else I should know about the wedding?" he asked. "I don't want to be insensitive, so if there are things I need to do or not do, now's the time to tell me."

"Well, the reception is going to be more a banquet dinner, not a dance party like a usual reception here. And there is a tea ceremony in the morning. Claudia's going to be wearing a white gown, not a traditional qipao. But you really don't have to do anything. Just follow the crowd."

"I'll just stick by you the whole day and be fine. Except during the ceremony at the botanical garden." He nodded.

"You'll have to get there yourself. I'm accompanying Claudia there and holding an umbrella over her head."

"What? You think it'll rain?"

"No. It's a traditional thing. Whenever the bride is

outdoors on her wedding day, she needs to be covered with an umbrella. It symbolizes luck and fertility for the bride and helps ward off evil spirits."

"Interesting. So where do I drop off the gift? Where are they registered? I feel like I should get them something."

"Don't worry about it. You don't need to buy anything."

"I don't need to, but I want to."

Rachel shook her head. "No, you don't understand. Gifts aren't necessary because we don't buy things for the bride and groom. That's not how weddings work in our culture."

This baffled him. Whoever heard of a wedding with no gifts?

"If you want, you can bring a red envelope and give cash. That's what everyone else will be doing. But really it's not necessary."

"Cash. Doesn't that seem sort of…I don't know. Cold and impersonal?" he asked, taken aback.

"I think it's more practical, but I may be biased. Why waste your time on a registry at Williams Sonoma deciding how many ceramic casserole dishes to ask for, when you can use the cash to make a down payment on a house, pay back student loans, or whatever else? Claudia and Dennis can use the money for stuff they actually want and need instead of colanders and napkin rings."

When put that way, it made a lot of sense. And then Luke remembered the opening scene of *The Godfather* where Don Corleone's daughter was dancing with a satchel full of money. So it wasn't that unusual after all.

"That works for me. So should I give them like one or two hundred dollars?"

Rachel frowned thoughtfully. "Well, it depends on how deep into the weeds you want to get with this."

Now he was confused. "It's money in a red envelope. How complicated can it be?"

"Look, you're the one who asked. So the first thing you should know is giving an amount with an even number is preferred. Odd numbers are out. Eight is an especially auspicious number because it represents prosperity, et cetera. But not four."

"Do I even want to ask?" he murmured.

"It's bad luck because the number four in Mandarin sounds similar to the word for death. Not a good omen."

"Okay. So two hundred and eight dollars? That'll work?"

"Perfect. But make sure they aren't old crumpled bills. They should be in as good condition as possible." At his look, Rachel gave a shrug. "My people are superstitious and anal. I didn't make up the rules."

"Can I just put a check in the red envelope?"

"I can ask my mother. You and I can head into Chinatown and get the red envelope. Make sure it's wedding appropriate and not one for New Year's or anything."

"This is turning into quite a production," Luke said with a shake of his head.

"You're the one who asked," Rachel pointed out. "Like I said you don't have to do this if you don't want to. It's fine."

"True. But thank you for filling me in on the details. I appreciate it," he said sincerely. Who knew gift giving at Asian weddings was filled with so many pitfalls? Even when just giving straight hard cash?

"Sure. It's actually really nice of you to offer. Enough about the wedding—let's move on to you."

"Okay," he said with a shrug.

With a smile, Rachel opened her laptop and booted it up. She pushed her glasses up and went into total business mode. "The last thing I want to go over with you is the marketing and promo for your new firm."

"I wasn't planning on doing any commercials or ads or anything." In fact, he had been wondering what sort of marketing and promo he should be doing besides word of mouth.

"Let's not get ahead of ourselves. Being at the beginning. How do you envision your business?"

"Huh?"

"Branding. Remember when we talked about a designer for a new website? What services are you offering, your expertise—you know, stuff like that."

"You already know the kind of law I practice."

Rachel sighed. "Yes, employment discrimination defense. I'm talking more about intangibles here. There are hundreds of attorneys and dozens of firms that do employment discrimination. So what are you bringing to the table? Do you specialize in some sort of subset of cases, like sexual harassment? What makes you special? Why should they come to you to represent them instead of someone else? You need to stand out from the crowd. It's not like you can say, 'Hey hire me. I have good looks and charm—you can count on me.'"

Luke winced a bit inwardly at Rachel's last sentence because the truth of the matter was, for most of his career, he had relied on his ability to win people over. He'd never had to really hustle for business. Now Rachel was asking the hard questions, wanting to know what exactly he brought to the table besides a basic level of competence.

"I'm good at my job," he offered. "I have an excellent rate of getting good results for my clients."

"How's that different from any other firm? Or any other lawyer?"

"You're right," he admitted. "Maybe striking out on my own wasn't such a great idea after all."

"Don't give up now," Rachel protested. "You've already come so far. I've invested so much time and energy into this and so have you. Don't you dare throw it all away. If you want to do this, then do it."

"You're right though. If I can't figure out what I can provide that other firms or attorneys can't, there's no point."

"Well you have time to think about it," she pointed out. "It's not like you're having a ribbon-cutting ceremony next week. You can figure it out. Maybe you speak Spanish, or can learn it, or Mandarin. I could even help with that. Or hire someone on staff who can speak a different language. San Francisco has a significant Hispanic and Asian population. Tapping into that can be an excellent way to stand out."

"That is actually a great idea." Luke sat back, astounded and impressed.

"Thanks," she said with an awkward smile. "That's why they pay me the big bucks, after all."

"You've definitely given me a lot to think about. We should talk more about this after we get back from the wedding."

"That sounds like a plan. Once we figure this part out, we can really start to think about when you want to put this plan into motion. At some point you have to stop talking and planning and start executing."

"Let's put a pin on that and talk about it later. Now it's time for lunch."

"Works for me."

As Rachel put away her things, Luke had to admit he was feeling a bit unsettled. For ages, he'd thought about striking out on his own, and like he'd originally told Rachel, he'd been attracted to the idea because he liked the idea of being his own boss, setting his own schedule. Throughout this process with Rachel, he was coming to see that it was a much bigger proposition and undertaking than he'd originally thought. Was it worth it if it was going to be the same old thing, just with his name on the front door? How would it be any different from his current work situation, except with added risk and more responsibilities? He liked his work fine, but he couldn't quite put his finger on what was missing.

It felt a bit self-indulgent and the epitome of first-world problems, but he wished he could figure out that magic ingredient. Rachel obviously had a passion for her job and loved what she did. He thought back to Aimee and how emotional and grateful her client was because of what Aimee had done for her. He wanted that. Not that exactly of course. The idea of those life-or-death stakes scared the hell out of him. But a feeling of satisfaction that the work you were doing mattered, was making an impact.

Luke gave himself a shake. This wasn't the time to wallow. Maybe he was feeling a bit disenchanted at work, but Rachel was right. No need to throw the baby out with the bathwater. He just needed to find his groove again and it'd be fine.

"WELL, LUKE, IT'S nice to finally meet you," Claudia said in a voice that was just a shade too bright and cheery. "Ma and I were partly convinced that Rachel was just making you up. Glad to know she wasn't lying."

Rachel gritted her teeth and tried to stay calm. They had landed in New York that afternoon and already had to put in a command performance. Her parents had insisted Luke come over for dinner. According to Ma, Thursday night dinner was the only time that would work. The next day was the rehearsal dinner and last-minute wedding prep, Saturday was the wedding. So far, things had been going well. Her parents had been polite, if a bit reserved.

Rachel turned to her sister and frowned. "Since when have you ever known me to lie? I'm almost honest to a fault. And besides, why would I make Luke up? That makes no sense."

"This is a first for me—I've never been a figment of anyone's imagination before," Luke quipped in an attempt to lower the temperature.

"Don't be like that, sis," Claudia said in a placating tone while rolling her eyes. "I know I was giving you a bit of grief about not having a plus-one for the wedding, so I thought you might have gotten a little desperate."

"I don't have the time, imagination, or energy to make someone up," Rachel insisted. "If you knew me at all, you'd realize that."

"All right, everyone, let's eat." Her mother came into the dining room holding a big platter of chicken curry stir-fry rice noodles. Her specialty. It joined a platter of sautéed cabbage with garlic, Chinese sausages, and some tofu with pork floss and soy sauce.

"This looks delicious, Mrs. Bai," Luke said, beaming. "I've never had an authentic home-cooked meal like this."

That was obviously the right thing to say because her mother puffed up with pride. But in the way only Asian mothers could. "I hope you won't be disappointed. They only had chicken breasts at the market today, not thighs. Thighs are so much more flavorful and moist. It may be too dry but please eat it anyway." Rachel refrained from rolling her eyes. She had no doubt that Rose had spent all afternoon in the kitchen pulling out all the stops for their "guest of honor" tonight. She'd bet any amount of money that everything was perfect.

"I'm going to love it, I'm sure." Accepting the invitation, Luke took the platter of noodles and started to serve himself a large helping.

Uh-oh. "Just take a bit. Let everyone serve themselves first, then you can go for seconds," she hissed in his ear.

With a sheepish grin, Luke put back some of the noodles then passed the platter to her.

There was blessed silence for a few moments as everyone focused on eating their food. Then there was a thud as Luke knocked over his water glass and sent a piece of sausage flying due to a chopstick malfunction.

"Whoops, sorry about that," he said with a chagrined look. "Guess I need more practice with chopsticks."

"Maybe he needs some kids chopsticks," Claudia snickered. Rachel threw her sister a death glare to no avail. But a look from Rose did the trick.

"Would you like a fork? Would that be easier for you?" her mother asked politely.

"I think that would be best for everyone." Luke's tone was rueful. "I'd hate to break anything or get anything dirty."

Desperate to get away from the table, Rachel popped up. "I'll go grab one from the kitchen."

Counting to a hundred under her breath, she made her way to the kitchen, plucked a fork from the utensil drawer and walked back to the dining room.

Sitting back down, she passed the fork over to Luke.

And that was when she realized everyone had stopped talking once she'd come back in.

"What?" she'd asked defensively.

"Luke was just telling us about his work, and how helpful you have been," her father replied.

Oh.

"Rachel's been great. I definitely got the better end of this deal—the work she's done and helped me with has been incredible."

"Considering how much we spent to send her to Dartmouth and Harvard, it better be," Ray mumbled.

Rachel saw Luke blink in surprise, and she almost envied him his innocence. Tiger parenting could be considered brutal by those who'd never seen it up close in person. She gave him a slight shake of her head. *It's fine. Don't worry about it.*

But Claudia wasn't done. "Maybe she didn't do such a good job, if she didn't even manage to teach you how to use chopsticks properly." After a pause, she gave Rachel a warning look. "You still have time. Make sure he learns by Saturday. I don't want any incidents at the banquet. I'll be damned if he screws up because of you and everyone ends up talking about it instead of focusing on me and Dennis."

With a clench of her jaw, Rachel decided to let that one slide. And naturally, her parents let it go too. Because of course they did.

Luke leaned over and whispered, "After dinner, let's go to Little Italy. I'll buy you all the cannolis you want."

Rachel shook her head and whispered back, "It'll take

too long and it's out of the way from your Airbnb. It's fine. I'll get over it—I always do."

"What are you two whispering about over there?" Claudia asked with a frown.

"Nothing," they chorused in unison.

"Aw that's so cute. You can read each other's minds. How did you find this guy, sis?"

"I told you, at a friend's birthday party." Rachel's voice was tight.

"Well, congrats. After all these years, who knew that flying across the country was the secret to you finally being able to find a guy. It's great that you're making the most of the opportunity." Then she turned to Luke and said in a mock whisper: "We were really starting to worry about her. So thanks for doing us a huge favor."

"Claudia, leave me alone, leave Luke alone, and just eat your food," Rachel said, voice clipped.

"Girls, we have guests," Rose warned, the steel in her voice unmistakable.

"It's not my fault," Claudia insisted. "Rachel is the one embarrassing herself in front of her date."

"No, I'm done. Claudia, you need to make up your mind." Rachel put down her chopsticks and looked at her sister straight in the eyes.

"About what?" Her sister looked at her confused, all innocence.

"Either I'm a pathetic dried-up old spinster who can't get a man's attention if her life depended on it, or am I the bitter jealous bitch who's trying to upstage your wedding.

Which one is it because I sure as hell can't be both." This outburst was so unlike her but months, maybe a lifetime of these offhand cutting remarks from her sister had taken their toll. Enough was enough.

Claudia's eyes widened in shock and her jaw dropped. Her parents were frozen in their seats, their faces blank and impassive as stones. Luke was giving her a supportive squeeze of the hand underneath the table. That small gesture was enough to calm and center her.

Hell, she'd gone too far to pull back now. "Well, which is it?"

Her sister shook her head and gave an irritated huff. "This is so typical of you. You really just can't let me have my moment, can you? You can't stand that for once, it's about me."

Rachel rolled her eyes and scoffed. "Since when is it not about you? But in this case, the solution to the problem is easy. I'm out."

"What are you talking about?" Claudia demanded.

"I'm not going to the wedding. That way all eyes will be on you like you want and your old, pathetic, bitter, jealous sister—or whatever you're thinking I am—won't be there to ruin it."

"You can't be serious," her sister wailed. "The bridesmaids and groomsmen won't be even. The photos will look horrible and everything will be ruined."

Fed up, Rachel got up and for once let her unfiltered self loose without a qualm. "Eff you and your wedding." Even in her state she didn't dare use the actual F-bomb in front of her parents. She was angry; she didn't have a death wish.

Now that the damage was done, she nodded for Luke to follow, and the two of them left her parents' house.

As they walked down the steps of the brownstone, Rachel took a deep gulp of fresh air and tried to process what had just happened. She wouldn't be surprised if her hands were as shaky as her heart.

"I can't believe that just happened," she murmured. She hunched over a bit, still trying to catch her breath.

Luke threw a supportive arm around her shoulders. "For what it's worth, I'm proud of you."

Rachel winced. "I'm sorry you had to see that. My parents may never forgive me for tonight."

He frowned. "First, dollar in the jar for the unnecessary apology. Second, what are you talking about? As far as I'm concerned the only person who was out of line was your sister."

"You don't understand. The worst cardinal sin an Asian kid can commit is to embarrass their parents by acting out and embarrassing them in public, making people think they didn't do their jobs to teach us to know better. I just embarrassed them."

"Sounds to me like you said some things that probably needed to be said a long time ago. It was good for you to get it out. Keeping things bottled up inside never helps."

"Still…"

After a long look, Luke took out his phone.

"What are you doing?"

"Looking up good cannoli places in Little Italy. Something tells me a couple hours away to take your mind off things may just be what the doctor ordered."

God knew he was right about that. Her current plan was to come back around eleven or midnight and sneak upstairs back to her old room while everyone was asleep. On the other hand, Claudia could still be carrying on and no one would notice if or when she came back.

Either way… "Lead the way. Let's get some cannolis."

Chapter Sixteen

JUST AS SHE was about to turn the bedroom light off, there was a knock on her door. Rachel gave an inward curse. It was eleven thirty and she'd been so close. She had turned off her phone to avoid the barrage of calls and texts, and she was in no mood to deal with anyone. She'd already listened to her father's voicemails berating her for her behavior and demanding she come home immediately—that was more than enough. Rachel crept away from the door.

"Rachel."

Crap. It was her mother.

"Open up," Rose demanded.

Reluctantly, Rachel opened the door.

Without missing a beat, her mother laid down the law. "You're going to the wedding."

"I said what I said. I'm not going"

"Yes you are. It's one day. And it's your sister's wedding. You know you'll regret it if you miss it."

"No, I'm not sure I will." With a turn, Rachel went downstairs and plopped down on the living room sofa. This was so typical. Of course Rose was taking Claudia's side.

"Fine. If you won't do it for Claudia, do it for me." Seeing the look on her daughter's face, Rose held up a hand.

"I saw and heard everything that happened. Claudia was wrong and out of line. I told her she deserved to be told off, and if I were you, I would have told her to fuck off too."

Holy shit. Hearing the F-bomb coming out of her mother's mouth was enough to almost make Rachel drop her glass of water.

"Be careful," her mother warned. "Glass is hard to clean up—you'll cut yourself." Then she handed Rachel a coaster.

"I know your sister has been miserable to deal with," Rose continued, "but give her a break. It's her wedding, and she's gone a little crazy, it happens. Besides, she's always had a hard time living up to you."

"What are you talking about?"

"Her whole life, she's been trying to live up to you."

"That's ridiculous. She was senior class president, got two prom invites, and she's five years younger than me and getting married before me. She wins."

Rose gave a stern look. "This is not a competition. But try looking at it from her point of view. You have an Ivy League education, and graduated top of your class. You got a job at a major Fortune 500 company; you're living a glamorous life in San Francisco. You know how the family talks about you."

"Yes, they're ecstatic about her wedding, and already

asking about when she's going to have her first baby. I'm the freak who can't find a man to marry her."

"Stop being stubborn."

Rachel pouted, but kept her mouth shut.

"This is her moment to shine, so she's taking advantage of it."

"Claudia always loved being the center of attention."

"She never did as well in school, her design business is struggling, so she's grabbing on to anything she can," Rose persisted. "You need to give her a pass and let this go."

"Because it's her day and I'll be the mega-bitch who ruined her sister's wedding. It'll be all my fault. So really what choice do I have?" Honest to God she was tired of always being the one who had to be the bigger person, while Claudia got away with murder.

"Grow up," Rose snapped.

"You always take her side. It's not fair." Even as the words tumbled out of her mouth, Rachel knew how immature she sounded, but she couldn't help it. It really wasn't fair.

Her mother just raised a brow. "I have always treated you girls equally, and you know it. Trust me, if you ask Claudia, she would say the same about you."

"Since when have you ever defended me or been on my side?"

Even as the rational part of her brain knew she had crossed the line and lost some objectivity, Rachel couldn't bring herself to regret what she'd said. At that moment, she meant every word, from the depths of her soul.

But that changed the instant she saw the look on her mother's face. The sheer hurt, pain, and disappointment cut her off at the knees and made her heart sink. In classic Rose Bai fashion though, she gained her equanimity immediately and the usual poise and control returned as if Rachel had just imagined she saw that hint of emotion crack her mother's impeccable facade.

"I'm sorry you feel that way," Rose said, stiff, proper, and regal. "All I can say is I'm not perfect and I never claimed to be. I did my best."

"I know you did. I'm sorry I said that. I didn't mean it."

"Yes you did. Some part of you meant it, or it wouldn't have come out of your mouth. At least give me the respect of being honest with me."

Rachel hung her head, ashamed. "You're right. I'm sorry. I really am. It wasn't just today. She has been doing this for months, making me feel like garbage. And she embarrassed me in front of Luke. It hurts." The confession stung, but at the same time, it was freeing.

Rose's face immediately softened, and she scooted over to sit next to Rachel. She gently stroked Rachel's hair and her tone was calm and soothing.

"I know it hasn't been easy, and you're right—it isn't fair. You're so strong and always take things in stride, sometimes it's easy to take it for granted. I promise I'll try to do better. Claudia has been a lot, but I still want you at the wedding."

Rose held up a hand as she continued. "And look. I

promise, if she acts like a brat again, you can tell her to fuck off. But try not to say fuck. I don't like that word. I taught you better than that—I don't know where you got your filthy mouth from."

Should she be concerned about how comfortable her mother was with using the word fuck?

"Okay. I'll be there."

Rose gave a relieved smile. "Good. And just between you and me, I think the yellow is awful too. Don't tell Claudia I said that," she added with a conspiratorial whisper.

"Right??!!"

Her mother just shook her head. "No idea what she was thinking. I'm glad we got that settled. But I need to talk to you about something else."

Uh-oh. She should have known her mother had something else up her sleeve.

With a look, Rose drilled her to the back of the sofa.

"Now about Luke."

"What about him?" She couldn't deny that she'd been dreading and hoping to avoid this conversation. It wouldn't have mattered if Luke was just a friend. But now that stupid feelings were involved, the stakes were a lot higher.

"It's obvious you like him. And I think he likes you too. So what's going on? It must be serious if he's here meeting the family."

Rachel grimaced. "Sorry, it's more complicated than that."

"What's complicated? Do you like the boy or no?"

"That isn't the point."

Rose raised a brow. "That's the only thing that matters."

Rachel gave a snort. "Please. You can't tell me you think I should be with Luke instead of someone like Brandon." Or any other proper, respectable Asian boy.

Her mother paused and chose her words carefully. "We know Brandon, and yes it would be easier. Your father and I wouldn't have to worry about translating what we're saying, or worrying what he thinks about us behind our backs. We won't have to explain things to Brandon. We won't have to make turkey at Thanksgiving." At that, Rachel gave a small laugh.

"But you are not interested in Brandon are you?" Reluctantly Rachel shook her head.

"Then that's settled. If Luke's the one, then go after him."

"I didn't think you even liked him."

His mother rolled her eyes. "I just had to make sure he was good enough for you. You're my child. I want you to have every chance to chase your dreams and pursue your happiness. That's why we're here after all. We want you to build the future you want. And you deserve everything."

Moved beyond words, Rachel gave her mother an impromptu hug. Rose held tight for a brief moment then gave an awkward pat on her shoulder.

"Okay, that's enough of that."

"Are you sure you're okay with me and Luke?"

"I'm never going to understand why the white people

insist on eating turkey on Thanksgiving. But it's okay. And well, he's pretty. Very pretty."

"Ma!"

"I'm old, not blind. Or dead."

"Oh my God."

"But don't tell your father I said that," Rose said, patting her hair.

"You'll never be too old." Unless she was mistaken, her mother preened slightly at the words.

Rose looked at her watch. "It's time for me to go to bed. We have a big day tomorrow, and you need your rest." Then she gave Rachel a look. "Just so we're clear, if you have to, you're only allowed to say fuck once. Any more than that, you answer to me."

"Ma, you say you don't like the word fuck, but you keep using it."

"I don't know what you're talking about." All dignity, Rose got up from the couch, and smoothed her pajamas. "Do you feel better now?"

Rachel nodded.

"Okay, baby," she said with affection. She patted Rachel on the cheek and got ready to head upstairs. "I'll have Claudia call you to apologize."

"She has to mean it!"

Rose shook her head and pursed her lips. "I don't how I ended up with two daughters who are so stubborn, and stupid competitive. Where did I go wrong? How could I have failed so badly as a parent?"

Rachel gave an innocent shrug. With an exasperated

sigh, Rose turned and went up the stairs. Rachel couldn't help but grin, her heart a thousand times lighter.

It was going to be okay.

Bright and early the next day, Ray knocked on her door and came into her room. With a sheepish look, he pointed at his tie.

"I heard you and your mother had a talk last night." As promised, Claudia had issued the requested apology, though it was clearly scripted. And her father had pulled her aside and mumbled an "I'm sorry." for yelling at her via voicemail.

"Yes," she replied, cautiously.

"Can you tell her we made up? I don't want to have to spend another night on the couch."

Rachel was astounded. "Mom sent you to the couch?" She got up and helped him with the tie.

Squirming, Ray shuffled his feet and avoided her gaze.

"What happened to the man is the head of the family?"

"You all know your mother is really the one in charge."

"Please. Growing up, all I ever heard was 'Listen to your father.' 'Wait until your father comes home.' 'Your baba's decision is final.'"

"Your mother tells me what to do—you never see it because she waits until we're in our bedroom. She read me the riot act when I tried to stop you from applying to Harvard. And why do you think I changed my mind and paid for you to do that summer program at the London School of Economics?"

Rachel's head was spinning. This new view of her

mother was disorienting. Clearly, she had underestimated her. Big time. Rose Bai was a woman with hidden depths.

Just then her mother walked into the room. Impeccably dressed as always, she was ready for the wedding rehearsal and meal afterwards.

"Why did you never tell me?" Rachel demanded.

Rose's brow rose in warning. "Who do you think you're talking to in that tone?" Her voice was dangerously low, calm, and even.

"Sorry, Ma," Rachel mumbled. But then she rallied. "Why did you never tell me you were the reason I got to go to Harvard and London?"

"Would it have made a difference? Why does it matter why? The point is you wanted to go and you went."

"Of course it matters!" Rachel blurted. "I spent my whole life thinking you were the stereotypical obedient Asian wife and the whole time you were the power behind the throne. This is amazing. It changes everything!" Her mother was downright Machiavellian. Now she was going to have to re-examine her entire childhood.

Rose gave a small smile and sat down beside her husband, her hands primly in her lap. "Sometimes it helps to use preconceived notions and perceptions to your advantage." Totally Machiavellian. She gave Ray a look. "Did you apologize?"

"Yes," he muttered.

With a satisfied nod, Rose turned her attention back to her daughter. "I believe in letting results speak for themselves. If you have power and influence, no need to yell and brag about it. Have you ever noticed how the people who go on the loudest about how smart, rich, powerful, and successful they are, are never any of those things? Better to speak softly and carry a big stick." And now her mother was quoting Teddy Roosevelt. She really wasn't equipped to handle all this.

"You may be a Bai, but you're also *my* daughter which means you're part Hu. And Hu women know what they want and go for it. And get it. You understand?" Rose locked eyes with her daughter and raised an eloquent brow that spoke volumes. In response, Rachel could only nod.

"Hu men on the other hand are a different story. But I'm not worried about you." She brushed away a strand of Rachel's hair and gave a small smile.

"Thank you, Ma," was all Rachel could manage.

"A wai guo ren for a son-in-law," Ray muttered, shaking his head. It was on the tip of Rachel's tongue to tell her father he was jumping the gun but her mother beat her to it.

"Hush," Rose admonished. "It's Rachel's choice. As long as he's good enough for her, that's all that matters." She got up and tugged at her sleeve. "Rachel grab your things so you can meet up with the other bridesmaids and get ready—and thank you for helping straighten your father's tie. Ray, you better not spill or get anything on your clothes. We're going to be late. Hurry up, you two." With that, Rose got up and sailed out of the room.

Her father just got up and followed suit. But not before throwing Rachel a look that said, "See what I mean?" and closing the door behind him.

Rachel just sat here, shaking her head. She was going to need a minute.

DESPITE WHAT RACHEL had told Luke about the ways of a traditional Asian wedding, it seemed like Claudia and Dennis wanted to have the best of both worlds. A formal banquet dinner and a huge-ass dance party of a reception. Because Claudia was Claudia, she'd even changed into a different dress for the reception. The start of the day had her in the white fairy-tale princess ball gown with the lace-up corset-like back for the wedding ceremony, which then transitioned to the traditional qipao for the banquet where she and Dennis made the rounds and visited every table. Now for the reception she was wearing an off-the-shoulder ivory silk fit and flare with an aggressive amount of sparkle.

Rachel really didn't want to think about how much this whole spectacle was costing her parents. But the bride was happy, and that was all that mattered, she supposed. As long as her parents weren't going to go broke and declare bankruptcy over it and making the situation a Rachel problem, it was none of her business.

The ballroom at the Hayes Spencer Hotel was pumping and everyone was currently getting down to The Black Eyed Peas, who weren't the only ones getting feelings. Not necessarily her taste but she couldn't fault the song choice. Rachel's eyes widened in horror as she watched Aunt

Wendy and Uncle Charlie busting a move. Or the Asian auntie and uncle version of busting a move. Limbs were flinging everywhere and the awkwardness was palpable.

Some things, once seen, could not be unseen. The important thing was everyone was having fun, Rachel reminded herself. At least her parents were too busy with guests to attempt any dance maneuvers. Thank God.

Just as she was calculating how much mind bleach she'd need, she felt someone plop down beside her.

"Why aren't you dancing?" Luke asked slightly out of breath.

"Taking a break," she murmured. To be honest, the day had involved a lot of people-ing and she was reaching her max. She was dying to slip away for some much-needed peace and quiet but the reception was scheduled to last at least another two hours, so she was stuck.

"But you look like you're having the time of your life out there," she added.

"This is my natural milieu," he replied with a shrug. Then he gave her a look. "You okay? Today's been a long day."

She let out a sigh. "Just gotta ride it out. It'll be over soon. Though I'm glad the day went well and that everyone's happy."

"I slipped the DJ twenty bucks to play a request. It should be coming up soon. Save me a spot on your dance card," he said.

Rachel gave an indelicate snort. As if she were some debutante type, the sort of person who had men lined up around the block, dying to dance with her. "Deal," she promised.

"Don't start. You can't fool me. I saw you wiping a tear when your sister and dad were dancing to 'My Girl.' It was cute."

"I had something in my eye," she muttered.

"Rachel Bai, a sappy romantic underneath that cool analytical exterior. Who would've thought?"

Before she could think better of it, she gave him a slight punch in the arm. "Shut up," she mumbled. But it was true. The father-daughter dance had been incredibly sweet, and the sentiment of the moment had tugged on heart-strings she didn't even know she'd had. Claudia looked beautiful, the epitome of Daddy's little princess during the song, radiating joy and happiness. And her non-sentimental father had a bittersweet smile on his face, and his eyes glowed with pride as they danced.

Hell. You had to have a heart of stone not to be touched. And she never claimed to be a robot.

Luke began to play absently with her hair as they sat, silently observing the crowd, and her heart skipped a beat. But she didn't stop him.

Cecily was right. Feelings were so damn stupid.

"Thanks for coming and dealing with all this," she managed.

"My pleasure. I'm having a blast," he assured her. Then he perked up as the DJ started playing the macarena. "I'm going to see if your mom will dance with me."

"Yeah good luck with that," she scoffed. There was no

way. Luke ignored her as usual and strode across the ballroom to find Rose. Then she watched gobsmacked as he bent down, gave a charming smile, spoke to her mother, and ten seconds later, was leading Rose to the middle of the dance floor. He even managed to catch her eye and throw her a wink.

She should've known to never underestimate Luke. Of course he could get Rose Bai to do the macarena with a smile. She'd be damned if her mother didn't look like she was having the time of her life right now. Shit. Did her mother just wiggle her hips? This was too much.

The next thing she knew, she heard a swoosh of satin and her sister was sitting down next to her with a flute of champagne in her hands.

"Is that Ma doing the macarena? Or did I not have enough food and too much champagne today? Because I swear my eyes are playing tricks on me." Claudia's voice was a mixture of shock and awe.

"Yep. Either that's her dancing away or we're all under some sort of mass hypnosis or psychosis," Rachel agreed with a shake of her head.

"God I hope the photographer and videographer got footage of that." Then Claudia turned to her with a frown. "Why aren't you dancing?"

"Taking a break," Rachel repeated. "The heels were killing me."

Her sister rolled her eyes. "If you didn't insist on wearing flats all the time, you'd be used to it." Then she held up hand. "It's my wedding day. Let's not fight, okay?"

With an inward sigh, Rachel acquiesced.

"If you want, you can leave a little early," Claudia offered. "I know you have a flight back to California tomorrow so it's okay if you need to cut out. I won't be offended."

Rachel clung on to the excuse like the lifeline it was. "Thanks. I may leave in a half hour or so, depending."

"If you can drag him off the dance floor," Claudia snickered, tilting her head at Luke. The macarena was over, and now everyone was at the Love Shack with the B-52s, but Luke was still going strong. The DJ clearly had very eclectic tastes. In response, Rachel just gave a shrug.

"He's a grown man. He can find his way back to his Airbnb if he needs to. We can meet up at the airport."

"You know I've been getting questions about him all day. Trust you to hijack my wedding."

Rachel's stomach dropped. Just when she thought she and Claudia were making progress, now they were back to this again.

Seeing the look on her face, Claudia relented. "Relax, I'm just kidding."

Oh. "Were you really getting a lot of questions about him?"

"You know how these things are. The aunties and uncles can't help but gossip. But whatever. I'm the bride; no one can take that away from me. It's all about me today, and I intend to take advantage of it for as long as I can."

How the hell was she supposed to respond to that? "Whatever makes you happy, sis," was the best she could come up with.

At that, Claudia rolled her eyes and huffed out a breath. "For God's sake, I was only kidding. I know I've been hard to deal with because of the wedding but I wasn't that bad, was I? Don't answer that," she added when Rachel continued to stay quiet.

The two of them sat in companionable silence for a moment or two before Claudia spoke again. "Listen, I still don't know how you managed to land someone like him but I'm happy for you, sis. I wouldn't mind having him for a brother-in-law someday. It looks like he already won our parents over, so you got a good thing going. Just don't ruin it, it can't be that easy to find someone who can put up with you and find your quirks endearing and not irritating." With that, her sister got up and disappeared back into the throngs of the crowd.

Rachel decided to stay put for another few minutes. As far as she was concerned, she'd earned it. She also had to admit she was a bit proud of herself. In another time and place, Claudia's words would have hurt. But this time, she was letting them roll off her back. Claudia was her sister and deep down they loved each other. The two of them were very different and were never going to see eye to eye, and that was okay. Claudia was who she was, and she was who she was. Sometimes, despite blood ties, two people just didn't mesh and there was nothing wrong with that, and it didn't mean one person was "bad" or "wrong." All it meant was the two people weren't a match. Rachel and her sister were never going to be close friends. There was a freedom in finally understanding and accepting that, and letting go of the weight of those expectations.

Just then the DJ switched gears again, and when she heard the familiar drum riff she threw her head back and laughed. Katrina and the Waves. Sure enough, Luke was walking to her, hands outstretched with a mischievous twinkle in his eyes.

"I believe they're playing our song," he said with a huge grin.

"You are unbelievable," she muttered, unable to stop her lips from twitching.

"Best twenty bucks I ever spent. Come on, time's a wastin'." He lifted her to her feet.

Oh what the hell. Giving in to impulse, Rachel slipped off her heels and made her way onto the dance floor, ready to get her groove on.

She was going to use Claudia's out and escape after the song, but right now in this moment, she couldn't imagine a better way to cap off this insane roller coaster of a weekend. It was time to walk on some sunshine and feel good.

Bring it.

Chapter Seventeen

"THANKS FOR HELPING me clean up," Aimee said. It was her turn to host the monthly poker night and he'd volunteered to stay behind. It had been a week since he and Rachel had come back from their trip to Brooklyn, and he was looking forward to getting back into the swing of his normal routine.

"Happy to help," he assured Aimee. He turned his attention back to clearing the kitchen table with all the paper plates and pizza stains and crumbs.

"I'd think you'd be eager to go home and lick your wounds. You lost three hundred dollars tonight." Aimee, tongue tucked firmly in her cheek, was putting the leftovers back into the fridge.

Luke just shrugged philosophically at the reminder.

"Honestly, I don't remember you ever suffering such a bad beat since the night your girlfriend cleaned all of us out." At Luke's glare, she waved a dish towel as a white flag and backed off.

"You want to take the rest of the wings home? You can take the celery and carrot sticks too."

"Nah, I'm good," he said absently as he began to wipe down the table.

With a snap, Aimee closed the fridge and stood in front of him, hands on hips.

"Okay, what's going on? You haven't been yourself all night. It's weird. I'm starting to get worried about you."

Luke didn't even bother to deny his attitude. He gave a deep sigh and shrugged his shoulders. "Trying to figure some things out."

Aimee raised a brow, sat down at the table, and gestured for him to do the same, which he did.

"Anything I can help with? Women trouble? Did you have a fight with your girlfriend?"

"Her name is Rachel and no. But you're right. I do like her and I plan to ask her out soon." He was counting down the days until Rachel got word about her promotion being made official. Seeing Aimee about to gloat, he held up a hand. "You can spare me the I told you so."

The two of them sat there in silence for a few moments as Luke tried to gather his thoughts. When that didn't work he just blurted out the first thing that came into his head. "How do you do it?"

"Do what?" Aimee's brows furrowed in confusion.

"Your job. How do you handle the impossible pressure?"

"What the hell are you talking about? We're both lawyers—it's literally what we get paid to do."

Luke shook his head. "Not what I'm talking about. I deal with employment discrimination defense. It can feel high stakes, but it's mostly about the amount of money involved. But you deal with family law, which totally blows that out of the water. Like when I saw you with your client after the custody hearing. How do you handle it? The fact that literal lives are on the line, and the future of a family depends on you? I could never do it."

"Don't tell me you're thinking of trying to change fields." Aimee's eyes widened in surprise.

"Of course not," Luke scoffed. "I don't have the chops for it—I know that. It's just that I've been thinking about how I've been going through the motions at work lately. Like two weeks ago, I reached a settlement for my client and they were thrilled. And opposing counsel and their client were staring daggers at me, but I almost didn't care. Meanwhile your client was crying and so utterly grateful."

"You want your work to be more fulfilling and meaningful?"

"Yes," he said, relieved. "But I have no idea how to go about it. And what if it doesn't work out?" For the past six months or so he had seen Rachel put her heart and soul into nailing her promotion. It clearly meant a lot to her. He couldn't remember the last time his work had gotten him so pumped and raring to go. He needed to find something that sparked that same fire in him, find purpose and meaning, instead of just coasting through. That was no way to live; he saw that now. Besides, Rachel deserved someone who was as dedicated and hardworking as she was.

Aimee took a deep breath. "I won't lie to you. My work is hard. How can it not be when you look at the face of that little six-year-old kid, knowing the whole trajectory of their future can hinge on whether or not you win this custody hearing?"

"That sounds terrifying," Luke murmured.

"Scares me to the bone every time," Aimee agreed. "But the way I see it, that may be a good thing. The day I start not giving a damn? That's when I know I've burned out and need to get out. I'd rather care and get burnt every now and again than the alternative. There are days when I lose a case and it eats me up inside, but the days like the one you saw last time make up for it a hundredfold. I don't want to lose my soul. It's hard but worth it. I love what I do, and I wouldn't have it any other way."

That made total sense. "You've given me a lot to think about," he said with a lopsided smile.

"Now, in the interest of full disclosure, not all of family law is like that. Sometimes I'm dealing with a divorcing couple where both spouses are assholes, and they're arguing over country club fees and the equitable division of assets. I once had a conference meeting where the husband and wife were screaming about the Tiffany candlesticks that Great-Aunt Peg gave them as a wedding gift and the husband's precious coin collection. It helps bring some balance and perspective to the proceedings."

Luke winced a bit. "That sounds like a total night-mare."

"It can be. You get the best and worst of humanity in my line of work. Comes with the territory." Aimee shrugged.

"I think I need a career pivot but that doesn't seem to be the solution. I have no idea how to go about it." Luke shook his head in frustration. Knowing you needed change didn't mean you automatically knew what change was needed and how to put it into action.

His friend rolled her eyes again, then crossed her arms. "Permission to be brutally honest?"

He nodded. "Permission granted."

"This attitude of yours needs to stop. There's no reason for you to be all 'woe is me.' You have plenty of opportunities to do what you want with your life. What's stopping you? Nothing. Quit acting like you have no agency. If you're unsatisfied with your job, do something about it. You're trying to figure out a career shift, not starting from scratch. Just get off the fence and do it."

Luke almost felt like he'd been struck like lightning. Why the hell hadn't he thought of it before. Inspired, he now had so many ideas rolling in his head. He leaned over and gave Aimee a peck on the cheek.

"You're brilliant," he told her, beaming.

Aimee gave a little shrug. "Happy to help. So, do you want a tote to take home the rest of the leftovers?"

"I'll take the rest of the pizza and wings too," Luke agreed. Now that he had a plan to fix his work problem, his appetite had returned. He was ready to tackle this thing head on.

Everything was going his way and he couldn't be happier.

AFTER TAKING FIFTEEN minutes in her office to get herself back together, Rachel took a deep breath and did one of the hardest things she'd ever had to do. She called a meeting and met up with her team in one of the open conference rooms.

The big meeting with the partners had just ended and it'd been a total disaster. Despite all of the overtime she and the team had put into the project, and all the pressure from Amanda and the higher-ups about how important this meeting was, they had dropped the ball, badly. She had thought there would have been plenty of time to double- and triple-check everything after her weekend back in Brooklyn for the wedding, but she'd been wrong. Dead wrong.

Her first clue that things were going awry was when they had started asking pointed questions.

"You're recommending we buy Whitford Pharmaceutical stocks. Didn't the CEO just get indicted this morning?"

"About this French telecommunications company in this portfolio. Their workers have been on strike for almost a month now. How will that affect prices?"

"I don't understand why you included Burkett. Didn't they have a product recall a few months back? Something about contaminated lettuce?"

And the hits kept coming. Rachel kept her composure and did the best she could but there was no denying that the impression she and her team had made wasn't the one they were hoping for. When they left with the requisite handshakes, she'd had a boulder sitting in her stomach and she could barely breathe. Amanda didn't even make eye contact with her, and her lips were pursed as she left for her next meeting.

This was bad. So bad.

It was probably in her head, but she felt like Hester Prynne as she walked down the hallway, except with a scarlet F for failure instead of an A. Then again, it couldn't be all in her imagination that she was getting surreptitious looks and causing a firestorm of hushed, whispered conversations. Nevertheless, she kept her calm and her eyes straight in front of her as she walked to the conference room and shut the door behind her.

The mood of the room was as dark and somber as she felt. All she saw were grim faces and tight lips. And she couldn't blame them a bit.

Brian was the first one to speak and break the silence. "I'm sorry. I should have caught the indictment—I don't know how I missed that."

"It was my job to check the news for anything relevant," Contessina countered. "The stuff about the French on strike didn't even register on my radar."

A mini argument broke out amongst the group where it seemed everyone was trying to take the lion's share of the blame. It was as if they were having a Spartacus moment, seeing who would be the one to volunteer as tribute.

That had to stop. Now. Rachel put two fingers in her mouth and gave a loud piercing whistle, which immediately shut everyone up.

"This isn't helpful, guys. And there is only one person

who screwed up here. Me."

The silence in the room was deafening but Rachel was pretty sure she could hear everyone's jaws drop.

"They put me in charge of overseeing things and that means it's up to me to make sure we didn't miss any angles. I let you all down and I'm sorry," she said, her voice low but firm.

No one moved or said a word.

"The way I see it, we have a two-prong problem here. The first and more immediate one is how to fix this mess, and I have some ideas to do that. But the second is to figure out how we can make sure something like this doesn't happen again. And I'm asking for your help with that. I'm open to any and all feedback and suggestions to help me improve. To help us improve."

She was still getting the same blank stares.

"Someone please say something."

Contessina raised her hand.

"We're not in a classroom—you don't need to do that." She could've sworn she already told them that.

After clearing her throat and putting down her hand, Contessina spoke. "I think I speak for all of us when I say this is not how we expected the meeting to go."

Rachel frowned. "What did you expect to happen?"

"We thought you were going to fire all of us after reaming us out," Brian piped up. There were nods and murmurs of agreement.

"That's silly. And wouldn't solve the problem at all." Rachel looked around and she saw her team's facial expressions relax and their shoulders loosen up.

Her tone was earnest. "I think we can still salvage this deal. I'm going to get the partners on the phone to see if they'll give us at least forty-eight to seventy-two hours to turn this around. But only if you guys are on board—I can't do it alone. That means the next few days are going to be long and miserable, but if we pull together we can make it work. So what do you say?" Rachel held her breath as she waited for the team's response.

Annika was the first to speak up. "I'm in. Let's do this." She held out her hand. Brian put his on top of hers. One by one, the rest of the team followed suit, with Rachel putting hers on top.

"Go team on three?" With a nod from everyone, she started the count down.

"Three, two, one. GO TEAM!"

When she'd walked into the room, her spirits had been core-of-the-earth low. But as Rachel looked at her team now, she felt energized and ready to go, and saw it reflected on their faces too. She could do this. They could do this.

"Okay, let's meet back in thirty. Dinner's on me tonight. Go do what you need to do to clear your calendars for the next few days."

As everyone dispersed, Rachel took a deep breath and started to figure out her plan of attack. This time, instead of faking confidence, she walked out of that conference room with her head held high.

AMANDA HURRIED OUT of her office to meet her. "Hey, Rachel, come on in. Sorry, had a phone call run long." Rachel bit her lip, trying to avoid her boss's gaze. It had been a week since the disastrous meeting and she was still trying to fly under the radar.

"Not a problem," she replied. Because really, what else could she say?

She walked into the nicely appointed office and took a seat. Amanda sat behind the huge mahogany desk and steepled her hands.

"I'm not going to beat around the bush," she began. "I'm just going to come out and say it. The partners and I met, and we are extremely happy with the work you've produced and how you managed this project."

"Despite the massive screw-up?"

Amanda raised a brow. "Yes, that meeting was bad. But the fact that you owned the mistake, went back to your team and recovered is the important thing. That was an impressive display of leadership. I talked to Brian, Annika, Contessina, and the rest of your team. They're ready to take a bullet for you at this point," Amanda said, slightly amused.

Oh.

"That, along with everything else tells me you've earned this promotion. It won't be absolutely official until the paperwork is put through, but let me be the first to congratulate you."

With a bit of shock, Rachel shook Amanda's hands.

"I've talked to your old manager Jake, so I know how

far you've come. You should be proud of yourself."

"Thank you," Rachel managed.

"You'll have to talk to HR and they'll go over your new salary and compensation package with you."

"Okay." Then a thought struck her.

"Do I still get to keep the team and office I have now?" She liked the way things were currently, and didn't want to change if she didn't have to.

"Actually it will just be an extension of the arrangement you have now. Except you'll be able to appoint your own team and you'll have more managerial responsibilities."

"I like the people I'm working with." Thank God she wouldn't have to start from scratch with a whole new group of people. What a nightmare.

"Good to know, and you'll still report to me."

That suited her fine. Amanda had a hands-off policy, happy to let Rachel do her own thing, and she was more than willing to keep that going.

"Well that sounds good. I'm happy to accept and excited to stay."

"Great." Amanda smiled. "I have to admit, I'm glad you aren't too disappointed not to be heading back to New York."

"What can I say? This place has grown on me I guess."

"Congratulations, and welcome aboard. Again. For good."

"Thank you, Amanda." With that, she left the office, practically floating on air.

She couldn't wait to tell the girls the news. And Luke.

Maybe they could all get together this weekend and celebrate. But first she had to go back to her team and thank them. Take them out for a round of drinks or whatever. What an amazing turn of events. She had great news to share and people she was excited about sharing it with.

Life was good.

Chapter Eighteen

MORE CURIOUS THAN he'd care to admit, Luke paced his living room as he waited for Rachel to arrive. Two hours ago, he'd gotten an excited text from her saying she had news and wanted to see him right away. He knew she'd been anxious the past week, worrying about the fallout from the disastrous meeting and how that'd affect her future prospects at the company. For her sake, he hoped it was good news.

In the meantime, he'd been busy putting his new plan into action. He'd set up an appointment with Terry to look over the potential new lease (in exchange for swapping poker night hosting duties twice), and had set up interviews with potential assistants and paralegals. Everything was falling into place. As for his plans to win Rachel over and convince her to go on a proper date, he'd been toying with luring her back to the original scene of the crime, the Wild Saguaro. That would be fitting and romantic, to bring her back to the place where everything began when he asked her to embark on a new relationship with him. Surely Rachel would appreciate the symbolism of it and whatnot. What woman wouldn't?

With a shake of his head, Luke reminded himself that

tonight was about Rachel. No matter what, he was there for her. Only if the news was good could he proceed with his master plan. When he heard her distinctive knock, he raced to the door and opened it, pasting on his most reassuring smile. When he saw Rachel, he couldn't help but notice the bright, slightly goofy smile on her face. She was practically giddy.

"Hi," she said, slightly out of breath. "I got here as fast as I could." She held up a bag. "I brought provisions." She handed him the bag and he peeked inside.

"Two bottles of champagne?" he asked, with a raised brow.

"One for now, one for later," she said happily.

"I take it the news you have to share is good."

"Oh more than good." She beamed.

"Well don't leave me hanging," he said, as he closed the door behind them and led the way back into the living room.

"Okay," she said, practically bouncing.

"You're making me dizzy."

She frowned, and he felt like a complete ass for taking away her glow. "I mean I'm just really anxious to hear your news."

"I officially got the promotion!" She grinned, throwing her arms wide. Without a word he gathered her in his arms and held on tight.

"Congratulations," he exclaimed. This was fantastic.

She'd done it. Of course she had. And he couldn't be happier or prouder of her. Rachel had worked so hard, and she deserved the chance to bask in the glow of her success. Now all he had to do was get his plans in order and everything would be perfect.

"I was so relieved and so surprised. But mostly I am so glad I got to tell you in person. I wanted you to be one of the first to know." She beamed at him, and his heart squeezed just a little bit more.

"I appreciate that."

"I mean, I couldn't have done it without you," Rachel babbled. "Your methods were unconventional, but you can't argue with the results. Even if I did complain a bit. You helped me gain the confidence I needed, and I am so grateful."

"Happy to help."

"We need to celebrate! But that second bottle is for this weekend."

"This weekend?"

"Yes, with the squad." Rachel grinned. "Cecily said she'll make the reservation. So you know the food will be good. You don't have any plans this weekend right?" she asked with a worried frown.

"No," he assured her. And even if that wasn't true, he would have canceled whatever it was without a qualm. Anything for Rachel.

"I'm actually looking forward to it," Rachel said with a small laugh.

"You deserve it," he said again, sincerely.

Rachel shook her head. "Not without you. I could never have done this without you. I owe you." Her voice was thick with emotion.

"None of that," he said firmly. "This was all you and the hard work you put in."

"But the best part is that now we can focus one hundred percent on you," Rachel went on enthusiastically. "I'm sure we'll be having a grand opening for you in no time."

He dismissed that with a wave. "Don't worry about it. Tonight's about celebrating you." Besides, he had everything under control.

Rachel frowned. "But there's still so much I can help with," she insisted. "I definitely feel like I got way more out of this arrangement than you did. Besides, I've really enjoyed the time we spent together the past few months. I was hoping that could continue." Her voice turned suddenly shy, and Luke frowned in confusion.

Then Rachel took a deep breath and clenched her fists, as if she was trying to screw up her courage.

"You okay? What's going on?" He'd never seen her so hesitant before.

"Do you want to go to the Palo Alto music festival with me next week?"

At those words Luke froze. Under other circumstances he'd be thrilled at this turn of events. He and Rachel were on the same page and now he knew that if he'd asked, the answer would have been a resounding yes. But. And there was always a but. He had a plan and he meant to follow through on it. He was determined to get his business and affairs in order so that he could do this properly. That's what Rachel deserved. He needed a little more time.

"I'd love to," he said sincerely. "But I don't think this is the right time. And I'm flattered, truly. There are things I need to sort out in my life before I can say yes," he said, hoping Rachel would get the hint. At the look on her face, it was evident that she hadn't.

"Wow, don't I feel like an idiot," she said, her voice tight.

"This isn't about you, it's me," he assured her. In time, she'd see that he was doing the right thing for the both of them.

Despite it all, Rachel managed to maintain her poise and she still faced him straight on. "Don't. I was going to tell you that even though we agreed to keep our relationship business only and platonic, I've developed feelings for you. Your mother, Cecily, and others were all convinced and told me you did too. The way you came to Claudia's wedding, looking after me when I was sick, and everything. I was hoping they were right and that we could maybe explore where this was going. But clearly, you aren't interested."

"No, that's not it," he protested, trying desperately to fix the situation. How could he have so thoroughly screwed this up? "I told you, this isn't you. It's me."

Rachel gave a hollow laugh. "I feel like I should be insulted that you're using such a clichéd and bullshit excuse. Why not just go with the truth? I was good enough for a one-night stand but not a potential relationship. And just when I thought that this time may be different. That you're different. That someone finally may accept me and be interested in me as I am. That for once I was enough… What a fool I was. Duly noted," she said, her tone bitter and self-deprecating.

"That's not what I meant at all," he protested. Where was this coming from? All he was asking for was a little more time. Rachel seemed to be taking it way out of proportion.

"I need to leave," Rachel said heading to the door.

Instinctively, his arm shot out to stop her. "Please stay. Let's talk this through and figure this out. This is just a big misunderstanding, I swear."

She tilted her head. "What exactly did I misunderstand?"

"I should have chosen my words more carefully," he admitted. "This has absolutely no reflection on you. I think you're amazing, and you're more than good enough for a relationship." If she'd just given him some more time, he could've shown her that in spades.

After studying him for a moment, she spoke again. "That's what I thought. Thanks but no thanks." Rachel shook her head and pressed her lips together.

"What are you talking about?"

"There is no way anyone can do a one-eighty like you did just then. It makes no sense. The only explanation is you're taking pity on me and trying to spare my feelings. Screw that. You can take your pity and shove it where the sun don't shine."

"This isn't pity. Please don't go," he whispered.

She gave him a look. "I poured my heart out to you

and you've made me feel like an utter fool. The least you can do is let me leave with whatever dignity I have left intact. You owe me that much, if nothing else." Then after a devastating pause she spoke again. "How ironic. Before I would have just left without saying that. Now, I'm glad I said what I did, and I have you to thank for teaching me how to best express myself."

With that, Rachel turned and left without a look back or another word. As the door clicked shut behind her, all Luke could do was sit down on his couch and shake his head.

His master plan had suffered a bit of a setback tonight, to say the least. He was sorry that Rachel was so upset, but after a few days, surely she'd come around. And once he sprung his surprise on her, all would be well. Rachel would understand why he did what he did and they could absolutely go to the concert. Though now he wondered if he should include some musical element when he did his big reveal and asked her out. He was working hard on this surprise and it was about to pay off soon. He was so close he could taste it. Everything would be perfect.

SHE DIDN'T KNOW what to do, and didn't know where to go. The world had collapsed around her, and she was totally lost.

It was lowering to admit a man had reduced her to this condition, but it was the truth. This was what she got for thinking she had figured out the knack for dealing with people.

Ha. What a joke. She was as clueless as ever, if not even more so.

Rachel knew what she must look like—blotchy, red-eyed, frayed sweatshirt and jeans, mismatched socks, raggedy sneakers, and her glasses were crooked. But at the moment she couldn't have given less of a damn.

There was no way she was going to talk to any of her co-workers about this, so that left only one option of where to go in her time of need.

God she hoped this wasn't a mistake. She was standing outside Cecily's door right now, debating whether to knock.

Surely CeeCee had better things to do with her time than deal with her friend who had devolved into the Bad Place and was the very definition of a Hot Mess. Cecily had a busy career and was planning a wedding. She didn't need this on top of everything else. In fact, Rachel wouldn't blame her for being annoyed at being interrupted for something as stupid as emotional drama.

She should go. She should go back to her apartment, get in bed, pull the covers over her head, and stay there for a few days.

Rachel had turned and was about to walk down the hallway when the door opened. Jeffrey's look of surprise at seeing her quickly turned to welcome, then concern.

Of course. She couldn't even pull off a successful escape. This was the kind of luck she was having.

Fucking hell.

"Rachel? What are you doing here?"

See, she knew it was a mistake coming here.

"I'm sorry, I didn't mean to impose. I was just about to leave when you opened the door, I swear. I don't even know why I'm here. Please pretend you didn't see me."

Jeffrey's expression turned chagrined and sympathetic. "No, I'm sorry. That's not what I meant, at all. I was just getting the mail, and you took me by surprise. You're welcome here anytime, obviously. Come in—you're soaking wet for God's sake!"

Brooking no protest, Jeffrey reached out and practically pulled her into the apartment.

"I'm gonna get you a towel," he said with a soothing smile. Then he turned and yelled down the hallway. "CeeCee! You have a visitor!" He then disappeared to find the towel.

"What are you still doing here? The mail," Cecily scolded as she walked over from the kitchen. Just then she saw Rachel.

The look on her face must have said it all because without missing a beat, Cecily rushed over and enveloped Rachel in a huge hug.

"What's wrong?" she demanded when she pulled back.

"I just ruined your clothes."

"Screw my clothes. What happened? What's wrong?"

"I'm sorry, I shouldn't be here bothering you."

"I swear to God if you keep up with that, you're going to piss me off."

Somehow Cecily's impatient reply was a thousand times more comforting than any soft, soothing words.

Jeffrey came back into the room with a towel and large soft terrycloth bathrobe. He offered them up to Rachel. "Why don't you go change and dry off. You know where the bathroom is." His tone was almost unbearably kind.

She really didn't know how much more of this she could take. Without a word, she went down the hall, disappeared into the bathroom. The harshness of the bathroom lights highlighted how raggedy she looked and felt. Puffy eyes, blotchy face, red nose, every bit of evidence of her misery was on display. Partly out of self-defense, she turned away. As quick as she could, she toweled off and got dry and warm in the robe. She grimaced at the pile of wet clothes on the floor. With a sigh, she tried to wring the water out of them as best she could and wipe up the water. Leaving the clothes on the edge of the bathtub, Rachel summoned the courage to go back outside.

Cecily gave her a considering expression as she looked up from her phone. "That's better," she said with a nod. Then she frowned. "Where are your clothes? We need to get them in the dryer ASAP."

Rachel opened her mouth to protest that it really wasn't necessary, but Cecily must have read her mind. The look on her friend's face had her shutting up. Fast. She gave Jeffrey a look, who just shrugged. The look on *his* face said: *Just do what she says. Life is easier that way.* Slightly chastened, she went back to the bathroom and came back with the clothes.

With a satisfied nod, Cecily took them from her. "This will just take a second." Indeed, not even thirty seconds later, the low hum of the dryer could be heard.

"So that's done. The bathrobe will do for now, but we can find you something else to wear tonight. And the guest room should be all ready."

Wait, she was staying the night?

In problem-solving mode, Cecily seemed to not realize she was steamrolling. "You're too tall for any of my stuff to fit. My bathrobe barely hits your knees. We can grab you one of Jeffrey's T-shirts and some sweats. You'll probably be swimming in them, but that may not be a bad thing."

"Mi closet es su closet," Jeffrey quipped.

"Don't you have somewhere to be?" Cecily asked pointedly.

"I do? Oh I do," he replied in response to the look on her face. "I'll swing by Greg's, help him out with some budget and production stuff, play with Sabrina."

"Make yourself scarce when you get back," Cecily ordered. "You're on deadline so this works out. Just go write in your office. Tomorrow."

"Will you at least leave me a tray of food outside the door?" he asked drily.

"I'll heat up some leftovers for you. We also got plenty of chips and salsa. You'll be fine." At the look on his face, she sighed. "Yes, I'll give you a brownie too. A big piece." Then she gave a roll of her eyes as he raised a brow. "Fine. Two brownies."

"That's all I ask."

Now she felt awful. Not only was she responsible for kicking the man out of his own house, she'd also had him banished to his office.

"Have fun," Cecily chirped, obviously eager to get rid of him.

"I'm leaving, I'm leaving. I know when I'm not wanted." With a roll of his eyes, Jeffrey got his things and prepared to go.

"That's one of the things I love most about you. How smart and perceptive you are." Cecily gave him a smacking kiss, a light tap on the butt, and got him out the door.

With that done, she turned her attention back to Rachel.

"Luke?" she asked, getting straight to the heart of the matter.

Rachel gave a nod. "Needless to say, the celebration dinner may have to be postponed."

"Thought so. Let me get some blankets and we can get cozy on the couch." A ding from her phone had her checking her messages. She looked back up at Rachel. "What's your favorite flavor of ice cream?"

"What?"

"Adrienne is picking up ice cream for us on the way, plus extra tissues and a couple bottles of wine. So, what flavor do you want?"

Utterly confused, Rachel just stared. "Adrienne's coming?"

"Yeah she'll be here in about forty-five minutes. I texted her while you were getting changed." As Rachel continued to look baffled, Cecily pressed on. "What? Just following protocol here. All this is Girl Code SOP."

"I didn't want to bother you all." Now she was everyone's pity case?

"I really do need to make you start putting a dollar in a jar every time you say something stupid and asinine like that." Cecily unwittingly echoing Luke's words was a painful reminder and jab to the heart.

At Rachel's hurt look, Cecily relented. "Look, when I was having a rough patch with Jeffrey, Adrienne came to my rescue. We had ice cream, watched Netflix, and vented about stupid idiot men. She got me through it, and whatever this is, we're going to get you through it too. Let us be there for you. It's what friends do. So, what ice cream do you want?"

"Strawberry," Rachel said, struggling with the lump in her throat.

"You got it. Now, go get settled on the couch. I'll be back with the blankets and sweats."

True to her word, Adrienne showed up forty-five minutes later. Without ceremony, she came in, dumped the wine on the kitchen counter and passed three tubs of the ice cream over to Cecily who stored it in the freezer.

"Okay, so what did that jackass do?" she demanded, hands on hips.

"Thanks for coming," Rachel said timidly from the couch.

At that Adrienne's face softened in sympathy. She plopped down on the couch beside her and gave Rachel a fierce hug.

"Of course. The Bat Signal goes up, I answer the call. But it wasn't that long ago when I had to do the same thing for CeeCee. You two are exhausting. You're both lucky I love you."

She heard a snort. Cecily had come back to the living room with three bowls of ice cream. "Just wait until it happens to you. You're up next."

"Highly doubtful." But there was a flash of emotion on Adrienne's face that Rachel couldn't quite place. A mixture of regret and pain. Typical Adrienne though, it disappeared as soon as it appeared.

Adrienne then pointed a finger at Cecily as she opened her mouth. "Don't," she warned.

"Whatever you say. But you're right. It's about Rachel right now." Without missing a beat, Cecily laid out the snacks and passed over the box of tissues.

"Okay, time to tell us everything. Spill your guts, don't leave out any details. Once you're done getting it out of your system, we'll find something mindless to watch. Pizza will be here shortly. We're all set."

As it turned out, Rachel was wrong. The Girl Code definitely had provisions for handling a girlfriend's emotional and mental SOS Bat Signals. And thank God for it.

WITH THE MORNING light streaming through the windows, Rachel gave a groan and opened her eyes. Then gave a start at the unfamiliar surroundings. And why the hell was she sprawled on some stranger's floor on an air mattress with a bunch of blankets and a pillow? Then she remembered she was at Cecily's, who was curled up on the couch, and Adrienne was on the futon.

She really needed to stop making a habit of waking up in strange places. Which never happened when she was in New York. After a quick stretch, Rachel stood up and surveyed the damage. Pizza boxes, brownie crumbs, wine glasses. A half-empty bottle of both cabernet sauvignon and one of rosé gave her a hint as to why her head was pounding.

With a slight whimper, she started trying to clean up the mess. She was in the middle of putting the rosé back in the fridge when she heard a groggy voice.

"I was going to do that. What are you doing up so early anyway?" Cecily rubbed her eyes and yawned. She walked by Rachel and grabbed a glass of water.

"Shh you'll wake up Adrienne." Rachel gave a glance back toward the living room, where Adrienne was still sleeping.

"No, she sleeps like the dead. Not even a nuclear apocalypse would wake her up."

"I heard that," Adrienne mumbled, her voice heavy with sleep.

Great. Some friend she was. First, she'd inconvenienced them by taking up their weekend. Now she was trying to do a nice thing and ended up waking them instead.

Adrienne pushed herself up and made her way to the

kitchen to join them. She gave Rachel a look. "How are you doing? Feeling a little better?"

"I don't know," Rachel confessed. If she were honest, this was the first time she'd suffered anything resembling heartbreak and she didn't like this process one little bit. "But you two did an amazing job trying to help take my mind off things," she added quickly, not wanting to sound ungrateful.

"Well, these things take time," Cecily said, sounding more alert. She draped a supportive arm across Rachel's shoulder. "Seriously, put that stuff down. It'll take me five minutes. I have a system. Go sit on the couch."

Neurotic and anal, Adrienne mouthed at Rachel, who stifled a giggle.

"I saw that."

"But CeeCee is right," Adrienne said, ignoring Cecily completely. "It's almost breakfast time. I could go for some eggs and bacon."

That sounded delicious.

"I can fold the blankets while Cecily makes breakfast."

"I could help with the tidying up," Rachel offered. Seriously, she'd spent most of the past twenty-four hours sitting and she hadn't even removed the borrowed pajamas.

"You can lay them on the corner of the couch. I'll put them away later. I have a system."

Adrienne quirked a brow, but the two of them dutifully straightened up the living room a bit and went to the bathroom to wash their faces and brush their teeth while Cecily dealt with breakfast.

In no time at all the three of them were sitting in the kitchen, digging into the crisp bacon and soft scrambled eggs. There wasn't much conversation, but the silence felt comfortable, instead of stilted and awkward.

Just then Adrienne's phone pinged.

"Ignore it," Cecily commanded.

"You know I can't. I have that trial next week. It's DefCon One, all hands on deck. Sorry," she said to Rachel with an apologetic glance.

"Don't worry about it," she replied around a mouthful of bacon. "You guys are saints to be doing this anyway."

Adrienne looked at the message and let out a soft curse. "Looks like I gotta get the rest of my breakfast to go. I'm needed back at the office. God save me from incompetent opposing counsel and skittish first-years," she said with a sigh.

"All right, I'll see you at the office tomorrow," Cecily said, getting up to get to-go containers.

"I'm really sorry to be bailing on you," Adrienne said with a quick hug. "But I'll make it up to you, promise. Happy hour next Friday. No men."

"Count me in," Cecily cheered.

"Should I be concerned that so much of our time spent together involves alcohol?" Rachel asked. Which was apparently the wrong thing to say, if the blank looks she got in response were any indication.

"But really, thank you for being there for me. It means a lot."

"Of course, anytime! Girl Code is sacred," Adrienne

said with a fist bump.

"And despite your protests, when it's your turn, Rachel and I will return the favor," Cecily added with a cheeky grin.

Adrienne just narrowed her eyes, clenched her jaw and let out a stream of rapid-fire Spanish. Rachel didn't understand a word of it, but considering the tone, it didn't sound good.

Quick as a whirlwind, Adrienne got herself together and left, blowing a kiss to the other two. With another death glare for Cecily.

"What was it she said to you in Spanish?" Rachel asked, curious.

"Oh I have no idea," Cecily responded with a shrug.

"Well, it didn't sound good."

"Eh, I'm not worried. We go back too long—her threats have no power over me."

Cecily took a look around, as if trying to ascertain if someone else was in the room listening.

"What?" Curious, Rachel craned her neck and looked around too.

"I wanted to talk to you about this, but wasn't sure about doing it with Adrienne around, so I'm glad we have the time now." Cecily reached out and put her hands over Rachel's.

"What did you want to talk about?" Rachel croaked. The show of support and solidarity had her trying to swallow hard past the lump in her throat.

"I'm not trying to be rude or insensitive. But I have to

ask. We know Luke was a stupid ass, and you know he's a guy—he can't help it to some extent. I'm also wondering if part of the issue is because well, he's a little…melanin challenged."

"Huh?"

Cecily rolled her eyes. "White. Because he's Caucasian. No matter how hard they try, there are some things that they may never be fully able to understand. And that's hard."

Rachel relaxed and gave a small chuckle. "No, nothing like that. That being said, he won my parents over at the wedding."

"I heard about the macarena." The two of them looked at each other and shook their heads.

"I just wish I was more normal." The words slipped out before Rachel realized it. She gave a blink as the implication of what she'd said sunk in.

"What the hell?" Cecily's tone was sharp as a whip and carried the same amount of sting.

"Claudia's married, and probably going to pop out half a dozen grandkids. My parents will be thrilled. While I get all the worried glances about me being a workaholic who can't find a man and who'll die alone a shriveled-up old maid." Maybe not so much her parents anymore, but the rest of the family and neighborhood were still talking about her.

"Well, they met Luke, so at least your parents know you are no shriveled-up old maid," Cecily cracked with an arch of her brow.

"I'm serious. I've come to terms and accept that, for better or worse, I am who I am. I just wish that was good enough. I hate always feeling like I never measure up. Like Claudia said, I'd be lucky to find anyone who'd be willing to put up with me. I thought I had, but apparently not. Even though Luke supported me when I went off on her. He told me I did the right thing. Guess he was just being a friend after all, nothing more." Part of Rachel was astonished that she'd said all that in front of another human being. But perhaps suffering heartbreak meant you were more open to spilling your guts.

Cecily took a deep breath and then looked Rachel dead in the eyes and said five words in a crisp, low, and firm tone. "What complete and utter bullshit." The switch from her cracking a joke to the deadly serious look on her face was almost enough to give Rachel whiplash.

"I know you're a friend and that's what you're supposed to say but it's okay." Truth was truth, after all.

"You know, for someone who's so brilliant you can be really dumb," Cecily muttered.

"Look, facts are facts," she replied, her shoulders hunched defensively.

"You are smart, fun, loyal, and a good friend. You're good enough and then some. Stop belittling yourself," her friend snapped.

Rachel blinked in surprise.

"If you're not going to think well of yourself at least give me some credit," Cecily ranted. "If you think you're such a defective person, what does it say about me that I think you're a great friend and like spending time with you? That must make me an idiot with the worst judgment. After all, only someone dumb wouldn't realize that someone she cares about is a total loser. Is that what you're trying to say about me? After all the time we've spent together? And the time you spent on my couch yesterday?" Her friend's eyes flashed, hands firmly on hips.

The indisputable logic of what Cecily said was staggering. "I guess I never thought of it that way," Rachel said in a small voice.

"Remember that the next time you're tempted to beat yourself up," Cecily said, her tone softening a tad. The frown lines smoothed out and she sat down next to Rachel. "And remember that comparison is the thief of joy."

"I'll try."

"To quote Jeffrey, do or do not. There is no try."

"I think that's Yoda."

"Of course it is," Cecily grumbled. "That man and his film references."

Relieved that the crisis had passed, Rachel gave a small smile. "I can't believe you just yelled at me."

Cecily shrugged. "Girl Code. The squad is a full-service operation. We support you and got your back, and will coddle and let you cry and vent. We will also tell you what you need to hear, not what you want to hear, and give you a kick in the ass if that's what you need. Whatever the moment requires." She paused. "And yeah, we will show up no questions asked with shovels and tarps in the middle of the night if you need help burying the body. All in a day's work. All in the code." In other words, true friendship.

"Good to know, CeeCee." Rachel laughed.

"And I meant what I said earlier. If Luke is too stupid to recognize what a prize you are, that's his loss. Even if he did come to your defense," Cecily added with a thoughtful frown.

"Ba did say I had to be the one who picked a wai guo ren," Rachel admitted.

"We can just call that a latent teen rebellion phase thing."

"Maybe I am a problem child, just a little bit."

"Fine, if you want to be that way." Cecily cocked her head and considered. "Speaking of which…"

Oh boy. "There's nothing to discuss, it's over."

Cecily held up her hand. "Understood. I'm sorry things didn't work out. I really thought you two had something. I do think he meant what he said—he wasn't pitying you, Rachel."

That was what hurt. That she'd thought that too. For a moment, Rachel had been foolish enough to indulge in the fantasy of finding someone who wanted and accepted her just as she was. What a joke.

"It was bound to end badly. At the end of the day, we were probably too different. And even if he wasn't agreeing to go out with me out of pity, who's to say it would have worked out anyway? Maybe he was doing me a favor because we would've ended up in the same place six months from now. It's my stupid fault for developing stupid feelings when my relationship with him was probably never destined to be more than it was."

"Are you sure about that?"

"I know you just yelled at me about this, but the fact is there are over seven billion people on this planet. Statistically speaking it's got to be a miracle if anyone can say they found the one," Rachel said, putting air quotes over the last two words.

CeeCee shrugged. "I found mine."

"It's easy for you to say. You and Jeffrey didn't have those problems. You grew up together; your families know each other. You two are perfect together."

Her friend raised a brow. "No but we had plenty of other issues to confront. And neither of us are perfect. I fully acknowledge that I can sometimes be a stubborn pain in the ass. But Jeffrey is also a major pain in the ass. The point is he's my pain in the ass and vice versa. We wouldn't have it any other way."

Touché.

"What's your point?"

"My point is the road to true love never runs smooth, but when you find the right one, it makes all the difference."

"What? When it's true love, it'll all magically work out?" Rachel couldn't help the derisive laugh or tone.

"No," Cecily said softly. "When you find the right one, the work and sacrifice is worth it, and you come out the other end better and stronger because you're doing it together. And you can't fathom facing the storms life tosses at you with anyone else." Cecily laid her hands over

Rachel's again. "So my question to you is, is Luke the one? Despite his current unfortunate case of head-up-his-ass-itis, is he worth it? If so, consider giving yourself some time to lick your wounds, then go knock him upside his head if you need to. If not, the hell with him. You'll find someone else who loves and accepts you as you are because you deserve it. Someone who wants to be with you because of your quirks, not despite them. When you're ninety, who do you picture sitting next to you in that rocking chair? The one you can't have imagined going through the past fifty or sixty years without, even on the days they piss you off so badly you want to throw them out the window? You need to figure that out for yourself because that's what I found with Jeffrey, and I want nothing less for you."

With that, Cecily got up and left Rachel to stew on those thoughts.

Chapter Nineteen

MUNCHING SOME PEANUTS, Luke kept half an eye on the Warriors game on the big screen at the bar while going over his checklist. It had been a week since he'd last talked to Rachel, and he missed her. But he had been so busy putting the final touches on his plan he'd barely had time to come up for air. He was browsing various websites so he could comparison-shop for office supplies and he was also reviewing the malpractice insurance policy he needed to sign. And because it wouldn't be him otherwise, he was also toying with having a huge open house/grand opening celebration where he wanted him and Rachel to be front and center. He just knew she'd love this.

"Oh you've got to be fucking kidding me." The voice was sharp and distressingly familiar. Luke looked up.

Yep. It was Jeffrey Lee. Despite the tone, Luke perked up a bit. Someone with a connection to Rachel.

Great.

Without wasting time, Jeffrey turned to his friend who'd come in behind him. "Go grab us some seats. I'll be there in a second. I have some unfinished business to take care of."

With a nod, the other man walked away, and Jeffrey sat

down beside Luke.

"How are you?" Luke asked, putting his work aside and giving the other man his full attention. "How's Rachel?"

"How's Rachel?" While Jeffrey sounded a little aggressive at the beginning, now he was just bewildered.

"Yeah," Luke said eagerly. "I've been busy and haven't seen or talked to her in a few days. I hope she's okay." He frowned. Now that he thought about it, and the fog of work was lifting a bit, it started to not sit well with him that Rachel had been incommunicado for so long. Despite how things ended at their last meeting.

"Given what you've done, I'm surprised you're asking. As if you cared."

Luke frowned. Where was this coming from? Of course he cared. "If you don't want to answer, fine. I'll call her and ask myself. Like I said, I haven't heard from her."

"Can you blame her?" Jeffrey retorted. "You seriously wonder why she hasn't been talking to you?"

Dread began to settle in his stomach. "I know she was upset the last time we spoke, but I already told her it was me, not her. I just needed a little time. Don't tell me she's still holding that against me?" That seemed a tad unreasonable.

Jeffrey shook his head. "Wow you really are an idiot. I can't believe you are that clueless. You don't know what you've done, have you?"

"I have my reasons," Luke protested. "And it's for the best. Surely she'll see that."

"Breaking her heart was for the best?" The scoff from

Jeffrey only raised the red flags further. But still.

"Breaking her heart? What are you talking about?"

Jeffrey gave a derisive snort. "Rachel came to my place last weekend a total mess. When I was finally allowed back home, she was still there. There were multiple containers of ice cream, pizza, and wine. It didn't take a genius to put two and two together."

Oh hell. Now he felt lower than dirt.

"The squad assembled and I got kicked out of my own house. My. Own. House. And you think you did nothing wrong." Jeffrey's voice got more menacing with every word.

At that, Luke couldn't help but cringe. "I'm sorry." But how the hell was he supposed to know Jeffrey would end up being collateral damage? "I didn't mean to hurt Rachel, but all I did was tell her I needed some time. She's taking this way too hard."

"Way too hard? And that's what you told her? You needed some time?"

"Yes."

"And you didn't think she would interpret that as a brush-off?"

"No, because it wasn't! I had a plan, I have a plan," Luke corrected himself, "and I needed time to put it into action. How is that possibly a brush-off?" Now he was baffled.

"Think about who we're talking about here. Rachel Bai. Who grew up with tough, strict parents, always being made to feel she can't measure up. Someone who has a hard time feeling like she fits in and belongs. But she finally takes the plunge, puts her heart on the line, only for the guy to tell her, 'Sorry not now. It's not you it's me.'" Jeffrey shook his head. "Look, far be it from me to wade in as an outsider, and I don't know all the details, thank God, but my diagnosis is you screwed up big time. I agree with my fiancée. Rachel can do better and she deserves better than you if you're such a clueless idiot." Jeffrey crossed his arms and gave a disapproving glare.

As the other man's words hit him like a ton of bricks, and Luke began to understand the magnitude of his mistake, he grabbed his beer and took a huge gulp.

Wow. He had totally misread and misjudged the situation. Thinking about the pain he'd unwittingly caused Rachel made him sick to his stomach. As much as he hated to admit it, the other man was right. He'd messed up—royally. Luke gave himself a mental shake. He could beat himself up later. Now he had to figure out how to fix it. Because he could totally fix this. He refused to think or believe otherwise.

"Do you have any idea of the hell that's about to be unleashed on you?"

Trying to clear the fog from his head, Luke just gave a blank stare.

With a heavy roll of his eyes, and a deep sigh, Jeffrey signaled for a beer then explained. "Let me lay it out for you. All I *do* know is…Rachel spent the weekend with my fiancée and her best friend. Both of whom are lawyers. They have heard in excruciating detail all the ways you screwed up, and now probably consider you lower than pond scum. They are going to be highly motivated to exact revenge and cause you an extraordinary amount of pain because you hurt their friend. You mess with Rachel, you mess with them. Dude, you're beyond fucked."

Jeffrey gave a satisfied nod as all color drained from Luke's face. "Now you're getting it."

"Oh God."

"Oh, even He can't help you now," Jeffrey replied with earnest, malevolent cheer. "You should've known better than to mess with other lawyers. They're probably going to be ruthless. You know Ivana in *First Wives Club*? 'Don't get mad, get everything.' You're lucky if that's all they do to you."

Honestly, that would probably be more than he deserved. Luke just poured another shot and threw it back.

"Okay, I realize where I went wrong," Luke admitted. "Now it's up to me to fix it."

"Oh, just like that?"

Luke's brows furrowed. What was with the skeptical tone? "I'll apologize and explain the misunderstanding. Once I clear things up, it'll be fine. I had planned to ask her out after she got her promotion," he explained. "But I also wanted to get my work life in order. She's inspired me to reprioritize some things and get my ass in gear, and I wanted to show her that. It was supposed to be this whole romantic thing."

With a roll of his eyes, Jeffrey waved away the explanation. "This is so typical."

"Typical what?"

"This was all about you. What you wanted to do for her. How you were going to impress her, instead of thinking about Rachel and what she wants and needs. And instead of being honest, you play verbal sleight of hand and mess with her head and heart. Some prize you are."

The accusations stung, and they seemed a bit unfair. "But I didn't mean for that to happen."

"Just more excuses. It's so cliché coming from a guy like you. A privileged white guy getting by on good looks and charm, and who probably never faced any real obstacles or consequences for his actions, and is stunned when things don't go his way like they do 99.99 percent of the time. Who has no real concept of taking responsibility. The kind of guy who was born on third base and thinks he hit a home run and really did something. Stop making excuses. You made this mess, now step up and fix it!"

The hell of it was, he couldn't deny anything that had just been said. If he hadn't been so tunnel-visioned and focused on what he was doing, and had stopped to consider Rachel's feelings and expressed himself more clearly, he wouldn't be in this mess. And the fact he hadn't even realized the extent of the damage he'd done was beyond damning.

Luke also then remembered Aimee's admonition to him when he'd complained about having trouble figuring out his new career path and how she had told him to grow up and figure it out. Now here was Jeffrey, a virtual stranger, telling him the same thing. Time to roll up his sleeves, take responsibility, and step up.

"Okay, I need to make this up to her," he muttered to himself.

At that, Jeffrey nodded in satisfaction. "Finally, the light dawns."

"I think I need a big overture. That's the only way to get her to talk to me again." His palms began to sweat at the prospect of messing it up and potentially losing the best thing that ever happened to him. His original plan was all well and good, but he needed to take it a step further now if he had any hope of ever winning Rachel back.

"Look. You and I barely know each other, and I'd probably catch all sorts of hell if the squad knows I'm talking to you. Against my better judgment, I'm rooting for you. Besides, if by some chance you do somehow convince her to take you back, you and I are going to have to spend time together so we may as well try to get along. But my two cents, for what it's worth?"

Luke gave a nod. What the hell? At this point, what did he have to lose?

"Having been where you are, my best piece of advice is to get your head out of your ass."

"Excuse me?"

"You heard what I said. I've found that when you get over yourself, things become clearer and the quicker you realize and acknowledge what an utter ass you've been, the better."

"Thanks...I guess."

Jeffrey gave him a hearty slap on the back. "You bet. We've all been there. Now I really gotta go. My friend is probably wondering what the hell is going on. Just remember what I said. And oh, just so we're clear, if you breathe a word of this to anyone, I'll deny it to the grave. You're on your own, buddy. Vaya con Dios."

With that, Jeffrey grabbed his beer and disappeared into the depths of the bar.

Luke took his seat back at the bar, the previous plans and to-do lists forgotten. He had a gesture to plan and the stakes couldn't be higher. The hell with a multimillion-dollar settlement for a client—that had nothing on this. All his life, he'd managed to achieve just about anything he'd set his sights on. Due to hard work on his part, but yes, as was brutally pointed out to him this evening, a huge dose of luck and privilege. Luke just had to make sure it'd see him through one more time.

THERE WAS A note on her door. An envelope with her name scrawled on it, taped to her door. Rachel eyed it with deep suspicion. This was not normal. For all the strides she'd made to be more of a people person, she still hadn't made friends with her neighbors, and she intended to keep it that way. She had no idea who'd left her this note. She tried to do the math on how many people had access to the floor and who knew her exact address and became even more concerned.

While she contemplated whether to call the police, she heard someone walk up behind her. Rachel whirled around and nearly had a heart attack as she saw Cecily, who was about to tap her on the shoulder.

"God, don't scare me like that!"

Cecily raised a brow. "Did you forget lunch? Jeffrey's joining us because he's still a bit bent out of shape after his tux fitting, and I promised him all the dumplings he can eat." Oh great. She was now having lunch where she'd be the third wheel and enduring the lovey-dovey schmoopy couple. Damn it.

Wait.

"I don't remember us having lunch plans," Rachel frowned in confusion. It had been two weeks since that fateful weekend when she'd shown up at Cecily's doorstep in shambles. Meanwhile, despite how busy she was with work, Rachel had done some soul-searching. Cecily was right, as much as hated to admit it. She did still see Luke beside her in the rocking chair in fifty years. But being the pragmatic person she was, Rachel refused to keep moping. She'd licked her wounds, and it was time to move forward, whatever that meant. While she'd hoped Luke would be part of her new life in San Francisco, she'd learn to be happy and content without him. Even if it was proving harder than she'd expected.

"Well I have it written down so you must have forgotten." Then Cecily's gaze landed on her door. "Hey, what's this?"

"I have no idea."

"Aren't you going to open it?"

"No, it may have anthrax on it. I was about to call the

police." Rachel crossed her arms and set her jaw.

Cecily shook her head. "You really need to cut back on those murder podcasts." At the mulish look on Rachel's face she sighed. "Never mind. I'll open it."

Before Rachel could protest, Cecily snatched the envelope and ripped it open. She peeked inside. "Huh."

Dying of curiosity, Rachel blurted out a "What!?" before she could help herself.

Pulling out the contents, Cecily brandished a key and a Post-it note. "There's an address on the Post-it. I assume the key opens the door to wherever this is." She glanced at her watch. "It's not too far from here. We should have time to swing by before lunch."

"What? No. Let's just go to lunch. I don't trust whatever this is." Rachel was horrified she was a heartbeat away from pouting and stomping her foot, but damn it she couldn't help it. She didn't need more surprises and unexpected curveballs thrown her way. All she wanted was to have some lunch and go back to her normal routine.

No matter how boring and dismal it now felt. At least she had the comfort of the familiar.

"No, now it's got me curious. We're going," Cecily said, her tone determined. She grabbed Rachel by the shoulder and directed them toward the elevators.

Puzzled, all Rachel could do was shrug. This was not how she imagined the day going. At all. It made no sense. Surely she would have remembered making plans with her friends. It wasn't like her to forget an appointment. But then again, this was the first time she was dealing with heartbreak. These were uncharted, unprecedented waters she was wading into here. Maybe when recovering from a broken heart, one developed cognitive issues and started to forget things.

In which case, breakups really freaking sucked ass and could go to hell. She was so not a fan.

"I want carbs," she mumbled.

"I promise you can stuff yourself with all the fried rice and noodles," Cecily assured her. "After we take care of this."

At least there was that.

Chapter Twenty

WHERE WAS SHE? The longer the wait dragged on, the more nervous he got. For perhaps the first time in his life, Luke wasn't quite sure of his footing here. Despite all his work, he couldn't be sure he'd be able to pull it off. But Cecily promised she'd deliver Rachel. She'd be here. She had to be.

Just then he heard a key turn in the lock and the relief he felt was overwhelming. Thank God this had worked. She was here. He hurried out to the front to meet them.

The scowl on Rachel's face when she saw him wasn't the least bit reassuring. But at least she was here now.

"What the hell are you doing here?" she demanded.

"I've told you, you ask that question all too often," he joked weakly, trying to break the ice.

Without another word, she turned on her heels to leave. But Cecily, God bless her, blocked the door.

"I want to go," Rachel insisted.

"Hear him out first."

"Wait. You knew about this?" There was hurt in her voice, and confusion.

"The idiot made me promise to make sure you got here so you can hear him out. Just five minutes. Then we can leave, I swear."

"What about the Girl Code?" Rachel demanded.

Cecily jerked her head in his direction. "This man came to my office when Jeffrey and I were about to leave for dinner, and asked me for help. My fiancé is too persuasive for his own good and convinced me to take pity on him. So I agreed to bring you here."

Thinking back to that meeting, Luke could only be grateful he'd escaped intact. Jeffrey hadn't exaggerated when he described how upset Cecily and Adrienne were on Rachel's behalf. But once he'd explained what he wanted to do, and asked for their feedback to make sure it'd be something Rachel would go for, she'd reluctantly gotten on board. At least Jeffrey had given him a small nod of approval as he left her office.

Rachel turned to him and glared. "So now you've turned my friends on me too?" she said with a roll of her eyes, her arms still crossed. "Typical."

Cecily shook her head. "You know that's not true. I'm only trying to help you, the way Adrienne helped me. And I freely admit this may not go according to plan. In which case, the shovels and tarps clause of the Girl Code kicks in."

He had no idea what the shovels and tarps bit was about (women were way too confusing), but it at least seemed to have satisfied Rachel. She gave a reluctant nod and turned back around.

"She is totally on your side," Luke said. "She nearly called security to throw me out when I went to see her." At that, Rachel looked slightly mollified, a smile twitching at her lips.

Taking charge, Cecily dragged them both into the middle of the room.

"Talk," she ordered them both. Then she turned to Luke and poked him in the chest. "Don't make me regret doing this," she said, her eyes full of warning, and her tone low and deadly.

"I'll do my best." He swallowed.

Then she turned to Rachel, hands on her shoulder, whispered in her ear, and gave her a fierce hug. "I'll be right outside, and you can leave anytime," she reminded Rachel. She made her way out the door and quietly closed it behind her.

"I don't know how you convinced her to do this, but it must have been quite a show," Rachel muttered.

"She drove a tough bargain." And made some very specific and terrifying threats as well.

Ignoring him, Rachel just looked around. "So, you got me here. What do you want?"

"I really thought about what you said the last time we saw each other."

"About what?"

"Everything," he admitted.

She frowned. "You're going to have to be more specific. Everything is vague."

At that he couldn't help but chuckle. It was nice to see that some things hadn't changed.

"The point is everything you said was right. You deserve to be with someone who won't make you feel like a pity case. It wasn't my intention and I'm sorry that happened," he said sincerely.

"Oh."

"The truth was, I was planning to ask you out, and you took me by surprise when you invited me to go to the music festival. I had this whole plan in mind and I wanted to see it through. I was sure it'd be exactly what you wanted. Thanks to some of your friends, I realized how tunnel-visioned I was and ignored how it would affect you and make you feel. I'm sorry about that. But the main point is, I realized I needed to make some changes and get over myself. So thank you for giving me the kick in the ass I needed."

"Well, you're welcome, I guess." She blinked. "Is that it?"

"No." He waved a hand around the space. "So what do you think?"

"About what?"

"About this location. For my new office."

"What are you talking about?"

His lips quirked as he reached behind him for the file he was looking for. Gently, he placed it in her hands.

"I just signed a five-year lease for this place. So I guess you could say I took the plunge. Big time. This place checks all the boxes of the things you helped me realize I needed. It's public-transportation accessible, has plenty of parking, handicap-accessible, everything."

Her eyes wide as saucers, Rachel's jaw dropped. "You did what?" she croaked. She flipped through the pages with a dazed look.

"I talked to my realtor friend Dave, and he found me this spot. I signed the lease." He took a deep breath. "I also have interviews lined up for a receptionist, two paralegals, and a translator. I've already talked to one of the graphic designers you recommended. All the permits and tax paperwork is done, thanks to you. I'm basically ready to roll."

"A translator?" Rachel asked, confused.

He gave a small smile. "I really thought about what you said about standing out from the crowd and figuring out what I could bring to the table that was unique. And then it came to me."

Luke paused, trying to gauge Rachel's reaction. Her arms were still crossed, but her body language was softening. She was definitely listening. That gave him the push to keep going. "I decided to do a pivot. I'm going into a different area of law. Well slightly," he amended.

"What?" she asked, baffled.

"Our experience together made me think there are probably countless people who are trying to open their own businesses. And I thought I could help small business owners navigate the paperwork and licensing and zoning and all that. And you know, turn my people skills into an asset. It can't hurt to have a lawyer who is good at networking and has relationships with local elected officials and business leaders. As for the translator, I thought I could focus on the Hispanic and Latinx community, especially the ones in underserved neighborhoods. I'm going to hire someone who can speak Spanish and brush up on it myself. Took it in high school but I'm so rusty," he said ruefully.

"Fucking hell. You did it," she said in an awed whisper.

"I did. I'm not going to lie. Part of me is still scared as hell. But I'm not going to let that stand in the way of going after what I want anymore. For a long time I've just been going through the motions. It's finally time for me to put my money where my mouth is and do my part to help give back and help other people achieve their dreams." Luke shrugged. "I was trying to find a way to make my work have meaning and impact, and this is it. Why not use my powers for good, as it were?"

"Well you shouldn't be scared," she muttered. "I did those numbers and projections for you and I'm never wrong, even if they need to be adjusted to accommodate these changes you're making. You'll be fine."

"I should never have doubted you," he said with sham gravity.

Giving herself a shake, Rachel took a deep breath and took another good look around. "Well thank you for telling me this, and for showing me your new office. I'm glad my contributions helped make a difference. Congratulations, and best of luck. I wish you all the best." She turned around to leave.

His heart dropped as he saw her walking away again. Luke took a deep breath and pulled out the last card he had to play. "This was all because of you. I couldn't have done this without you."

Rachel froze then turned around. He gave a small sigh

of relief. At least she was still here.

"What the hell are you talking about?" she demanded. Her tone was still terse, but Luke saw her bite her lip and her voice wasn't quite steady.

Seeing the chink in her armor gave him a small measure of relief. He walked to her and led her toward a chair.

"I had this epiphany weeks ago. After we got back from the wedding, actually. I'd wanted to ask you out for ages, but I realized I needed to get my act together and figure my career out before I could do that. And besides, you had to secure your promotion first. I didn't want to do anything to interfere with that.

"And I meant what I said. This," Luke said, gesturing around the office space, "is a testament to you. Everything here is because of the work you put in, because you believed in me. You took a vague and nebulous plan I had and made it a reality. I owe you."

Rachel shook her head. "I was just holding up my end of the bargain."

"You know that's not what I meant. You inspired me to step up my game. That's what I wanted to show you. Originally I wanted to bring you here and show off everything that I'd done. I've checked off all the boxes. I wanted you to see what an amazing job I did. But I realized I'd gotten it all wrong. This wasn't about me. This is about showing the incredible influence you've been on me. Because it's true. Your suggestion that I focus on a specific community to stand out is what helped give me the idea. You are a phenomenal woman, Rachel. You never give up and you work hard to overcome challenges and emerge better and stronger for it. That's why I wanted to show you that I'm someone as dedicated and driven to accomplish their goals as you. You deserve someone like that."

"Oh." She blinked. Clearly this wasn't what she was expecting to hear. Though hopefully in a good way.

"Like you said, you do deserve better. But I'm asking for you to take pity on me. I need you back in my life, Rachel."

"You know my stance on pity." But her body language had softened even more. Thank God.

"I'm asking for it anyway. You are the best thing that ever happened to me. Not just because of your help with my new business but in my life. You've inspired me to get off the sidelines and go after what matters and that means you."

The spark of hope in her eyes at the words tightened his chest. It gave him the courage to go on.

"You're the only one who can make me laugh with your off-the-wall observations. I need someone who believes in me and isn't afraid to push me to be the best version of myself. Someone who will be worthy of her."

"I can do that," she whispered.

"You were the one for me when we first met. You were so not impressed with me," he said with a chuckle.

"I was still wondering why someone who looked like you was talking to me," Rachel admitted wryly.

"Please. Walking into that bar was the best decision I ever made. And don't sell yourself short. You're beautiful and you know it. Dollar in the jar."

Rachel rolled her eyes and laughed. "You're right. I'm glad I went there that night too."

"You always say numbers and data don't lie, but I'm hoping to show you I'm making a real commitment here. I'm going to do everything I can to make this new firm a success, and it's all thanks to you."

"I'm always happy to help and I'm excited for you. I'm proud of you for taking this next step and I have every confidence you'll be a smashing success."

"But none of it would mean a damn thing if I don't have you with me," he blurted out. "I'm done going through the motions and taking the easy road. The important things in life may be hard but they're worth the effort. Like you. You are absolutely worth the effort."

At that Rachel's eyes began to blur.

"I want another chance to show you that I'm making a real commitment to you too. And our relationship. That is if you can find it in your heart to forgive me and give me another chance."

For a long moment Rachel didn't respond, and his heart sank. Then she shook her head and said the most Rachel thing ever.

"How the hell do you do this? The way you're looking at me, and the things you're saying, how the hell am I supposed to say no? It's not fair."

Oh thank God. With a relieved laugh, he strode over to her in three steps and gathered her in his arms.

"Besides," she continued, with her voice muffled, "you

promised me we could go to an escape room if that's how I wanted to celebrate my promotion. I'm holding you to that."

At that he let out a hearty laugh. Leaning back, he framed her face gently and tenderly wiped away the tears.

"Absolutely. And just so you know you've also made Mama very happy. She was ready to kick my butt when I had to confess what happened. In fact I'm pretty sure she likes you a lot more than she likes me right now."

"Good to know."

"Mama's not the only one. You definitely have friends who adore you and will do anything for you. And who frankly scare the crap out of me."

"They're the best. Even when they're sneaky," Rachel agreed, throwing a look at the doorway Cecily had walked out of.

"And me. I love you." It was actually freeing to say it for the first time and genuinely mean it with all of his heart. It wasn't scary at all. Just felt right.

"That's the best thing of all. I love you too."

"Now that we're making this official, maybe this means you'll finally take it easy on me when we play poker. Or at least teach me all of your tricks."

"Never going to happen. I'm taking my poker skills to the grave." Rachel shook her head vehemently.

"I have ways of convincing you," he murmured as his lips descended on hers.

"Do your worst," she mumbled before he left her unable to speak.

They kept themselves busy for several minutes before they heard a loud pointed cough. Dazed, he pulled back and saw Cecily standing in front of them, with an amused smirk on her face. For her part, Rachel started to blush furiously.

"Not that I have any personal objection to what you two were doing, but I felt I should remind you that the front of this office is all glass, and people can see."

"Oh God," Rachel mumbled, unable to meet anyone's gaze.

"I don't blame you for being distracted, but now that my work here is done, I think it's time to move along," Cecily said with a brisk tone. "I meant it when I said Jeffrey is getting cranky and needs to be fed, pronto. But something tells me you two won't be joining me."

"I should be mad about you bringing me here on false pretenses," Rachel said, trying to rally.

Cecily cocked her head. "I suppose you have grounds. But the way I saw it, bringing you here would accomplish one of two things. One, you kill him and get some closure. In which case the tarp and shovel clause gets invoked." Rachel's lips started to quirk in amusement. He had no idea what Cecily was talking about, but clearly she did.

"Or two, this," Cecily said waving up and down toward them, "would happen. So either way you couldn't lose, could you?"

"Thank you," Rachel said, pulling him close to her. "I don't know how I can ever repay you."

"The Girl Code does not believe in ledgers. Seeing you

happy is all I wanted." Cecily smiled and when Rachel stepped out of his embrace, the two women hugged again.

"Okay. Enough of that," Cecily said as she dabbed at her eyes with a tissue. "Now I really gotta go. Have fun, you two, and don't do anything I wouldn't do." Cecily paused. "Wait. Yeah, I stand by that. Don't do anything I wouldn't do." She gave Luke one last warning glare. "Don't screw this up."

"I won't, ma'am."

Cecily's eyes narrowed.

"He's from Texas—he can't help it," Rachel explained.

With an eye roll and a huff, Cecily left.

Alone again, he couldn't seem to keep his hands off of her. He hugged her close and didn't let go. He kept playing with the strands of her hair. For her part, Rachel didn't seem to mind.

"I didn't have plans for the rest of the day except for work," Rachel mused. "Somehow I'm not in the mood for that anymore. You have any suggestions?"

With a wicked glint in his eyes, he murmured, "I have an idea. How about trying out a new experience?"

"Such as?" she asked, her face and tone wary.

"Make-up sex," he said with a wide smile. "I highly recommend it."

With an answering grin, Rachel laced her fingers with his. "I'm game. Lead the way."

Life was good.

Epilogue

A few months later

"ARE YOU SURE we have to do this?" Standing in front of Tokkaido, Rachel crossed her arms and gave Luke an uneasy look.

"Pretty sure we don't have a choice, I'm afraid," Luke said with a shrug.

"I have a bad feeling about this," she insisted as she tugged on her cardigan.

"You said that the last time we had dinner with my parents and it was fine. My parents love you." She wasn't totally sold on that, but she had to admit she and Naomi had made great strides in their relationship. To the point that Luke was complaining that they were ganging up on him and texting about him behind his back. Which was so silly. Talking about him behind his back would be so unproductive and a waste of time. So much easier to just address the issue with him directly. But she was grateful to Naomi for all the fun baby pictures and childhood stories she shared.

Who knew the cool, suave, popular ladies' man Luke Trudeau once trod the boards at Braddock High School as Professor Harold Hill sporting braces and awful acne?

Beyond adorable.

"But now it's both our parents. The combination could be catastrophic." Ever since the idea of this dinner had been broached, Rachel's palms had been sweating. It was one thing for Luke to make a good impression on her parents and for the Trudeaus to gradually come to accept her. It was the idea of both sets of parents that was worrying her.

"It won't be. I think your mom really likes me now. She asked me how many new clients I got last month and why it wasn't more." Luke's new firm was up and running and slowly but surely, he was building a steady, successful new practice. The work excited and energized him, and nothing made her happier than seeing him loving and embracing his job.

With a grimace, Rachel patted his arm. "Sorry, unfortunately that's how Asian parents show their love. Nagging and sky-high expectations that can never be met."

"Come on, the sooner we go in, the sooner we can get it over with and we can go back home."

She couldn't help but pout slightly. "I really wanted to stay in my pajamas this weekend. Is that so much to ask?"

"I don't know why you bother—it's not like you end up wearing them for long." He gave an innocent look, and she blushed furiously.

"Stop it," she hissed.

"What can I say? I enjoy taking advantage of the fact that the All Clothes Must Stay On mandate has been repealed."

"You're impossible," she muttered. But Rachel took a

breath and they walked into the restaurant.

As the hostess led them to their table, she saw something that stopped her in her tracks.

"This isn't good," she murmured. And for once, Luke agreed.

"Our mothers are chatting. Likely plotting. No good can come from this." Indeed, Rose and Naomi were deep in conversation, heads together, laughing like old friends. The fathers meanwhile were studiously poring over their menus.

Naomi looked up and saw them. "There you are," she said, standing up gracefully to embrace them both.

"Good to see you, Mama."

"Hi, Naomi," Rachel said, relieved at the warm welcome. As she sat down she saw her mother's raised brow.

"She told me to call her that," Rachel insisted, defending herself.

"I did," Naomi confirmed. At that, Rose gave a small nod. Crisis averted.

Their waiter Kenji came by to drop off water for everyone at the table and take their order.

Clinton put his menu down and gave Rachel a look. "I should be making you pay for dinner, with the way you scalped me last night," he muttered, only half joking.

Rachel shrugged. "You're the one who insisted on playing five-card draw. It's not my fault you got unlucky." She couldn't quite hide her grin. That had been a fun night, though the only person who'd enjoyed her win more than her was Luke, who hadn't bothered hiding his glee at seeing his father lose his shirt.

"Unlucky?" Clinton sputtered. "I had trip sixes and you bluffed me by going all in with a measly pair of twos!"

"The odds were in my favor. And you won a few hands too," she pointed out. Part of Rachel was still salty that her queens and sevens lost out to his full house. At least she'd only lost a hundred dollars on that hand, which she made back. But still. She'd get her revenge next time.

Ray sighed and rolled his eyes. "What did we say about you taking people's money like that, Rachel?"

Clinton turned to Ray, flabbergasted. "Are you saying she's always been like this?"

Her father shrugged. "We stopped letting her play mahjong and poker with us when she was fourteen."

With his jaw clenched, Clinton turned his ire to his son. "And the reason why you didn't tell me that your girlfriend is a card shark…?"

"Sometimes, like Edmund Burke says, Dad, people only learn by touching the hot stove. I heard that quote from a friend recently and it seemed applicable." Luke's grin was unrepentant. "Besides, she fleeced me too, so it's only fair you get the same experience." At that Clinton shook his head ruefully.

"Is that all you do these days?" Rose asked her daughter. "Go to work and play poker? You need to get some exercise and fresh air. You look pale and tired."

"Don't worry about it, Mrs. Bai. I'm making sure Rachel gets plenty of exercise." Luke's tone was so innocent, but when Rachel looked at him, his eyes were anything but.

She nearly spat out the water she was drinking as her face went tomato red. She took a quick look around. The fathers were oblivious, but Naomi's eyebrow had disappeared into her hairline.

After a thoughtful pause, Rose said with an approving nod, "Good for you, Luke. I appreciate you looking after my girl."

"The honor is all mine," he assured her, pious as a schoolboy.

Her mother took a sip of her saké. "I assume you are also exercising and looking after your own health." She gave Luke a once-over.

"Yes, ma'am. I go to the gym at least two or three times a week."

"You mean you two don't exercise together?" Rose queried, her tone pleasant and mild. "I'd assume you of all people would know and appreciate the benefits of a couple exercising together. I thought that's what you were referring to earlier."

Now Rachel had to suppress a laugh as it was Luke's turn to flush beet red and be rendered speechless.

Rose finally took pity on him after a few seconds and stopped letting him dangle. "And that's what you get for trying to be cute and making sex jokes. You should know better," she lectured.

"Yes, ma'am" Luke mumbled, suitably chastened.

Naomi shook her head. "I apologize, Rose. I promise you, his father and I did try to teach him better, but you know, kids these days." She gave a delicate, helpless shrug.

Rose nodded her head in commiseration. "We all do the best we can. Look at me and my husband. We did the best we could with our girls, and they still make us worry and act silly and foolish. And do things like move away to the other side of the country."

Rachel's shoulders hunched up defensively, and she was about to protest that it was her job, and she was happy here, but then her mother patted her hand. And her shoulders relaxed.

"She just misses you, is all," Luke whispered.

"She could just say that," Rachel muttered back, but there was definitely someone cutting onions nearby. And she reminded herself, Asian parents were not necessarily known for being the most touchy-feely. Especially her parents.

That being said, it was nice to hear, now that she understood.

"I miss you too, Ma," she said. "And I promise I'll fly back and visit soon, okay?"

Rose's eyes brightened, but still maintaining her dignity and poise, she answered back, "We'll see. Who knows when you'll be able to visit? This promotion is keeping you so busy."

"Your mother and I are lucky if we hear from you once a month," Ray grumbled.

Rachel looked at Luke who just shrugged. She suppressed a sigh. She'd tried her best. But she knew this communication thing would be a lifelong process. For her and her family. They were trying, and that's what mattered.

"Well, Luke calls once a week but, but half the time I have to remind him," Naomi put in.

"The time zone difference can be hard to navigate sometimes. Especially around daylight savings time."

"That's no excuse, son."

"Maybe we should all move to Arizona, where they don't change the clock at all," Rachel suggested.

"They do have good golf courses there," Clinton mused.

"I've always wanted to see the Grand Canyon," Ray said with an air of excitement.

"Hold on now," Naomi said. "No one's moving anywhere just yet. Rose was telling me she and Ray have never been to Texas and I told them they were invited for Thanksgiving."

"That's a great idea. I do a mean deep fried turkey—it's my specialty," Clinton said. "Y'all are more than welcome."

Rose had a polite smile on her face, but Rachel could tell her mother truly appreciated the invitation and the welcome gesture.

But Thanksgiving? Turkey?

Lips twitching, Rachel's eyes met her mother's.

With a slight brow raise, Rose gave her daughter the patented Mother Death Stare. *Don't you do it. Don't you say a word. I mean it.*

"It's true," Luke said, oblivious to the subtext flowing. "Dad still won't let me or Ben near the turkey."

"When the time is right, son, I will pass on the tongs. Until then, I'm in charge of that operation, you understand me?"

"Yes, sir."

Kenji reappeared at the table and discreetly served everyone their food. There were a few moments of silence when everyone focused on eating until the conversation thread was picked up again.

"Having a traditional meal sounds like fun. We'll be looking forward to it," Rose said smoothly. "It'll be a new experience for us."

At the Trudeaus' confused look, Rachel explained, "In our family, we never did the traditional Thanksgiving meal. We always had hot pot instead." In fact it wasn't until she'd gone to grad school that Rachel got to experience her first traditional Thanksgiving meal.

"Oh what's that?" Clinton asked, interested.

Ray blinked. "You've never had hot pot?" he asked as if Clinton had just announced to the table that he kicked puppies for a hobby.

"No, but it sounds interesting."

"It's one of my favorite holiday traditions," Rachel explained, warming to the subject. "We get a ton of seafood, noodles, tofu, meat, veggies, and cook it up in a flavorful broth or stock. It's great because it's done family-style. And Ba makes the best dipping sauce." She gave her father a look and then turned to Luke. "He won't tell me how to make the sauce either."

"You wouldn't know how to do it right anyway," Ray mumbled.

Clinton nodded in vigorous agreement. "That makes

total sense to me."

Ray turned to look at him.

Was she mistaken or did the dads just have a bonding moment?

Naomi spoke next. "A hot pot sounds delightful. How's this for an idea? We can do our turkey meal on Thanksgiving, but what I'd love to do is have a hot pot dinner Friday. What do you say?"

There were nods all around.

"It'd be a good break from the usual Thanksgiving leftovers," Clinton agreed. He then turned his attention back to his meal.

"Rose, dear, there is an Asian market about twenty minutes away from the house. If you give me a list, I'm more than happy to pick up any special ingredients we need." Naomi turned toward Rose to get her take.

Her mother pursed her lips and shook her head. "No, I'll go with you—that way I can show you which brands are the best and help pick the freshest ingredients."

"Excellent." The two mothers smiled at each other in perfect accord.

Rachel turned to Luke. "Are you sure your siblings will be okay with it?" The parental units had moved on to other topics and were ignoring them. And eating.

Luke shrugged. "Doesn't matter. Mama's decided and that's the final word. They either get with the program or they leave. No one is stupid enough to risk her wrath. Besides, nothing wrong with starting new traditions, right?" He popped the last bit of a hand roll in his mouth.

The thought of that warmed her heart. The two families were blending traditions and she couldn't think of anything lovelier.

"Rachel?"

She turned to her mother. "Yes, Ma?"

"Can you find a nice place for us to stay when we're in Texas?" Rachel nodded, making a mental note to go Google options as she finished her miso soup.

Naomi looked scandalized. "Absolutely not. You are staying with us. We have plenty of room. Wasting money on a hotel? I won't hear of it." She put her napkin down next to her chicken teriyaki.

"But separate bedrooms for you two," Clinton warned Rachel and Luke. "Y'all aren't married yet."

Rachel took it in stride. It seemed to her like shutting the barn door after the horse had already bolted but their house, their rules, she supposed. She could live with it.

Look at her using a horse metaphor. Luke definitely was rubbing off on her in more ways than one.

Luke heaved a sigh. "Fine. I'll sleep on the couch."

Her father looked ready to argue, but Clinton just shook his head. "You aren't going to win this one, Ray. Trust me. You're staying with us."

Ray gave a look. "Sounds like our wives have a lot in common."

"I'm sure I don't know what you mean," Naomi sniffed.

Rose just shot her husband a look. *Don't you embarrass me in front of our daughter's boyfriend's parents and possible future in-laws.*

Luke leaned over. "I'm actually terrified right now. If our mothers join forces, there is no telling what they'll do. They may end up planning our wedding for us whether or not we even want to get married. And decide how many grandkids they want."

Just the thought was enough to send shivers down Rachel's spine. Not just the wedding and grandkids bit, but the idea of Rose and Naomi taking over the world through sheer force of will was terrifying. There would be no stopping them.

Luckily the rest of the meal went off without incident. That is, until it came time to pay the bill. The minute the check hit the table, all hell broke loose.

Clinton made a move and Rose practically slapped it out of his hands, to Rachel's horror and chagrin.

"Our treat, we insist. Especially after your generous offer to host us for Thanksgiving."

Luke's father made another grab for the check and Rose's smile turned practically feral.

"Really. I insist. You can pay next time," her mother offered, her tone sweet as syrup. Translated in Asian that meant the Trudeaus would pay for a meal when hell froze over.

"I already said this would be our treat," Clinton said.

Rose just shook her head and gave the check to her husband.

"I should have just paid when I went to the bathroom earlier." Ray sighed.

"Would it solve things if I paid instead?" Luke offered. Rachel shook her head. Poor deluded innocent Luke.

"No," was the resounding reply from all four parents.

As Ray got out his wallet, Clinton tried to make one last play for the check. But Rose grabbed it away again in the nick of time.

"At least let me cover the tip," he insisted.

At that point Rachel decided enough was enough. "You need to let this one go," she said to Clinton. "You're not going to win. They've been doing this for almost forty years—we're all rank amateurs by comparison."

"Rachel, how many times have I told you it's rude to discuss someone's age?" Rose said without ire, her feathers no longer ruffled since she had emerged victorious in the Battle of the Check.

"You'll get it next time, dear," Naomi said, giving her husband a comforting pat.

Rose just gave a serene and unsettling smile.

Rachel closed her eyes and gave a little sigh as she turned to Luke. "Please don't hold this against me," she murmured. "It's in the Asian DNA—we can't help it."

"Never," he assured her, giving her a quick kiss on the cheek. Which resulted in a disapproving look from both mothers for the unauthorized display of PDA.

"Just know that my parents will have their revenge. Somewhere, somehow, some way. Their honor has been impugned and this insult cannot stand," he continued, his lips twitching.

Rachel's eyes widened in horror. "This could get ugly,

couldn't it?"

"Absolutely. But it's fine. It's nothing we can't handle together."

As the six of them made their way out of the restaurant, the word *together* kept pinging in Rachel's brain. For as long as she could remember, she'd always been a loner, for better or worse. The idea of her finding such wild happiness with someone who loved her—because of not despite her eccentricities and quirks—was unfathomable. But here she was. She'd gotten the promotion she'd always wanted, she didn't have to go to Omaha, and her relationship with her team was getting better all the time. She had a drop-dead gorgeous, funny, charming, sexy guy who loved her just as she was, and friends—real actual friends—in Cecily and Adrienne. Maybe she'd always be an awkward turtle, but that was fine. She was who she was and that was good enough. The people in her life were more than proof of that. She never had to be alone again.

Together. What a beautiful word.

The End

Don't miss the next book in the From Sunset Park, With Love series, *Bethany Meets Her Match*!

Join Tule Publishing's newsletter for more great reads and weekly deals!

Acknowledgments

It truly takes a village for a writer to write a book, and I am beyond fortunate with my village.

I am so lucky to have Sinclair Sawhney as my editor. You had me dig deep and level up with this book and I appreciate it. It was hard to hear that I needed to correct course and rewrite the book, but I am grateful you had faith in me and believed I had what it took to deliver a better book. It made all the difference. Thank you for helping me make Rachel's story the best it can be and one I could be proud of.

Thank you to the entire team at Tule—Jane, Cyndi, Meghan and Nikki. Thank you for giving me this amazing opportunity to share these stories. Working with you all has been great!

Thank you to my amazing and supportive agent Courtney Miller-Callihan who always has my back. You believed in me from the start and that means the world to me. Here's to many, many more years together.

Lizzie and Liana—what can I say? I wrote the first version of Rachel during the height of the pandemic and would have never finished if not for you both. You guys refused to let me quit, and listened to me vent and rant without judging. Well maybe a little. ;) Thank you for being there. Liana, thank you for all the sprints that allowed me to finish version 2.0 of this book.

Tessa Dare and Courtney Milan are the best Romancelandia big sisters anyone could ask for. I am unbelievably lucky you both took me under your wings way back in 2012. God knows I would not be where I am without you two. Thank you for always cheering me on, supporting me, and believing in me—for that I am forever grateful to you two beyond measure. I can only hope to pay forward 1/100,000 of what you both have done for me and mean to me. Love you both!

Susannah Erwin—I love you because you tell me I don't suck even when I don't believe you and send you suckage. Thank you for helping me get the subtle details about San Francisco right. As always, all mistakes are my own.

Sally Kilpatrick, Southern sensitivity/authenticity reader extraordinaire, blesser of hearts, and disser of heffas, who was kind enough to give me an amazing blurb for my debut. You're the best. But my deepest thanks for being such a lovely and amazing friend, for reading an early version of this book, and not hating it. Lurves you muchly!

Adele Buck and Jayce Ellis—thank you for never allowing me to beat myself up and refusing to let me engage in negative self-talk. The only people who are allowed to beat me up are you two. HA! Xo.

Thank you to Alexis Daria who reminds me why I'm doing this, who I'm doing this for, and why it matters. Our stories ARE important and deserve to be told and shared.

Felicia and Stacey—you two are the sweetest and I am so lucky to know you both and call you friends. Your friendship and support mean so much to me!

Thank you to the ladies of the Tule group chat Mia, Stacey, Kelly, Denise, Heather, Janine, Rebecca, Fortune—I have been so lucky to learn from all of you!

Thank you to Halidon Music and their Best of Mozart YouTube video. I played it too many times to count while drafting this book.

Thank you to my mother and sister who continue to do their best to be as supportive as possible. Special thanks to my sister for the hard work she did on #thesummerofcecily. She was the real MVP. I really do appreciate it and the both of you!

If you enjoyed *The Rachel Experiment*,
you'll love the next book in the…

From Sunset Park, With Love series

Book 1: *The Year of Cecily*

Book 2: *The Rachel Experiment*

Book 3: *Bethany Meets Her Match*
Coming in October 2023

Reader Discussion Questions for *The Rachel Experiment*

1. The book begins with Rachel getting a great job opportunity but her perceived lack of social skills is a drawback. What did you think of how she decided to tackle the problem and improve said social skills? What would your strategy have been if you were her?
2. Characters from *The Year of Cecily* make an appearance in this book. Do you like books where previous characters from the series make cameos? Do you like catching up with them and seeing how they're doing, or do you prefer to solely focus on the main couple of each book?
3. Rachel and Luke meet as a result of a one-night stand. Did it seem out of character for Rachel and Luke based on what you've read of them so far, or did it make sense? Is this a trope you enjoy reading? Why or why not?
4. On the surface, Luke and Rachel seem to be polar opposites and don't have much in common. How significant do you think these differences are? Is it a problem if two people in the relationship are too different or too similar? Do you think a relationship where people are so different can work, or does there

need to be common ground in terms of values, belief systems, etc?

5. In the book, Rachel sees herself in a certain way, but we get a glimpse of how her family sees her, Luke, Cecily, Naomi, and others. Which view is the "real Rachel?" Do you think we always have the most accurate perception of ourselves? Why or why not? Do you agree with Rachel that our family's view of us is probably the most accurate because they know us longer and best? Or do you think that closeness and longevity bring their own biases and blind spots?
6. Rachel's sister's wedding combines Eastern and Western traditions. Do you like weddings? What are your favorite unique wedding traditions that have been passed down in your family?
7. We meet Rachel in *The Year of Cecily*, where she and Cecily began to form a friendship. What were your impressions of her in Book 1 and how have they changed after reading her story?
8. What did you think of Luke's teaching methods and how he helped Rachel get comfortable interacting with people? If someone came to you for help like Rachel did, what would you do to help them? Do you think socializing/networking is an innate skill, or something that everyone needs to learn?
9. Rachel thinks of herself as someone who doesn't make friends easily. What did you think of the development of her friendship with Cecily and Adrienne? Why do you think the author included it as such a big element

of the story and how does it impact Rachel's growth as a character throughout the book?

10. What were your feelings about Rachel's family at the beginning of the book, and how did they change by the end? For Rachel, her perception of her mother undergoes a shift over the course of the book, and she makes peace with her relationship with her sister Claudia. Do you think that would have been possible if she'd stayed the same person she was at the beginning of the book?
11. In the book, Luke and Rachel are both poker aficionados. Why do you think the author made that choice? Discuss how their approaches to the game are similar and different and what it says about Luke and Rachel as characters.
12. Discuss Luke's motivations for starting his own law firm and how it shifts by the end. What do you think Luke learns about himself and why do you think he made those changes? Compare that to Rachel's approach to her career and how she tackles goals and objectives. Are you more a Rachel or a Luke in that regard and why?

About the Author

Lisa has been an avid romance reader and fan since she read her first Nora Roberts novel at the age of 13 after wandering the aisles of her local bookstore. Lisa loves that romance has the power to inspire, and believes that HEAs are for everyone.

Lisa writes light contemporary romantic comedies with a liberal dash of snark and banter. She enjoys delving into the complexity of Asian and immigrant family experiences, and celebrates female friendships in her trademark dry, witty style. As an Asian-American author writing own voices Asian American stories, Lisa hopes that her books will show the diversity of the Asian-American experience, and the importance of every reader being able to see themselves represented on the page.

Having grown up in Pennsylvania and helping out at her parents' restaurant, Lisa has never bothered to learn to cook. She has two liberal arts undergraduate degrees and a J.D, and in her former life she was an intern, then Legislative Assistant for a PA State Representative. She also worked as a paralegal at a boutique law firm. Lisa is a politics junkie (don't get her started on the wonder that is The West Wing!), indulges in naps whenever possible, and believes Netflixing in her pajamas and ordering take out qualifies as the perfect weekend.

Thank you for reading

The Rachel Experiment

If you enjoyed this book, you can find more from all our great authors at TulePublishing.com, or from your favorite online retailer.

CPSIA information can be obtained
at www.ICGtesting.com
Printed in the USA
LVHW052014100523
746641LV00002B/164